Returned to the Land

Gail Fisher

DEDICATION

To Jason and Suzanne

and to Alex, Lily, Barrett, Haley, and Jasmine

My muses

For, behold, days are coming, declares the Lord, when I will restore the fortunes of my people, Israel and Judah, says the Lord, and I will return them to the land that I gave their ancestors, and they shall possess it.
- Jeremiah 30:3

Chapter 1

The application form was blinking insistently on Rachel's screen, but she was no longer seeing it. Her chin cupped in her hand, she was gazing out her window at the weather that mirrored her mood all too well. It rained yesterday, it had rained the day before, it was raining now; it seemed like it was going to rain forever. But then, nobody could hope for better weather in Anatolia in the autumn. Rachel felt mildew growing on her very soul. She looked out the window. The weather dampened her spirits as surely as it drenched the trees climbing the mountain behind their house. She closed her coffee-colored eyes for a moment.

Then she glanced over at her twin sister, sitting at her desk in front of her own window. "I know it's what you really want," Rachel said to Leah.

"Please say you'll think about it," Leah said. She looked back at Rachel beseechingly.

Rachel smiled wistfully at her sister. "I really don't know, Leah," she said. "This senior seminar in Mycenae is exactly what my university studies have been leading up to. When will I get another chance to participate in an archaeological workshop in Greece?"

"But this is a perfect opportunity for us!" Leah pleaded. "Ima and Abba can't go this time, and neither can Jesse. Every single festival when we've gone on pilgrimage to Jerusalem, we've been with our family. This could be our last chance to go by ourselves."

Rachel rubbed her ear. "I'm so torn! I wish the timing were better. These two things are so big, so important, and cost so much. What about Shavuot instead of Pesach? Maybe we could still get permission to go alone then."

Leah wrapped the end of her dark braid around her finger. "I'm trying to arrange my final apprenticeship to start then. And after we graduate, we're out of here!"

Rachel looked away from her sister's persuasive eyes. "Being in Jerusalem with all the excitement at the Temple and all those crowds is amazing. The thought of going just with you is special beyond words. But I just don't know ..." She pulled her necklace out from under her linen frock and clutched the smoky quartz disk, warming it in her fist.

Leah leaned forward, resting her forearms on her knees, swiveling her chair so that she could face Rachel fully. She widened her amber eyes. "The two of us there at the Temple. Just imagine!"

Rachel thumped one hand on her desk, looking down at her lap. The curls that had escaped her own dark braid cascaded around her face. "It would be such an adventure!" She paused for a second, reflecting. *For the first time in my life, I really believe that I'm capable of going somewhere without my parents. Or at least as long as Leah is there with me.* Then she continued, "I'll tell you what. There's no guarantee that they'll admit me to the senior seminar in the first place. What if I apply and we see what happens? We can decide then."

"I guess so." Leah took a breath. "You know, you've never really explained to me how this senior seminar is so special in the archaeology program. How does it differ from the Twelfth Month II study that you'll be doing anyway?"

Rachel cocked her head, fingering her necklace, before she answered. "Well, it's limited to twelve seniors from all over Anatolia, not just from Trabzon. We'll have some of the greatest scholars in the world meeting us at the archaeological sites, and the group leader is my thesis advisor, so I already know him. The Twelfth Month II program for archaeology is just for our university. It's a week in the field, classes before and after, and a research paper at the end. Probably a lot like your Twelfth Month II program in cultural art."

"Oh, I see. Higher level and more exclusive," Leah said.

"And after dreaming of a career in archaeology my entire life, this would be a giant step in that direction!"

"I know, I know," laughed Leah. "You won't rest until you have made a major discovery that completely revolutionizes what we know about precivilizations! But what's the worst thing that can happen if you aren't accepted?"

"For one thing," Rachel said slowly, "I'm hoping to do graduate study in archaeology. That's the profession I want to follow. But the best programs are highly competitive – not just in Anatolia, but anywhere else I might go, like Greece or Judea. They look at everything on your record, a whole lot more than just your grades. The senior seminar would almost guarantee that I could go anywhere I chose after graduation."

Leah shook her head, bemused. "You always have it all figured out, always a step ahead of me."

"At least one thing is working out okay for us," Rachel observed. "Twelfth Month II didn't have to fall during our senior year. But it does! Since I can count on that program for sure, I can live without getting into the senior seminar if it turned out that way. But what a credential it would be on my graduate school applications! That could make the whole difference in my future – a top-rated school or just a mediocre one."

"I'm hoping my program will lead to a job after we graduate," Leah said. "I've been looking into opportunities to work at an art center in one of the Eleusinian villages south of here. I'd love to help with sculpture or maybe with charcoal drawing. Having done an internship at Kayra Han would be a great credential when I am ready to find a real job."

Rachel focused more intently on her twin sister. "I had no idea you were thinking about that! I don't think you've ever mentioned it."

"Actually," Leah said slowly, "I have brought it up a few times. But you're so involved with your own concerns that I'm not sure you've even really noticed it before."

Rachel found that she was unable to meet her sister's challenging gaze. She looked downward at her desk. She was going to have to take time to process this realization of the toll her self-absorption took on those she cared about, but not with her sister right in front of her. "I'm so sorry," she said, biting her lower lip. "I do tend to get all wrapped up in myself and I miss things that are going on in other people's lives. But I never thought of myself doing something like that to YOU!"

3

Leah shrugged and replied lightly, "It isn't the first time. But I understand what makes you tick."

Rachel glanced around their room, searching for a new direction to their conversation. There were the two desks, each under its own window. Two dressers along the side wall. Two beds on the inner wall, separated by the doorway into the hall. Everything came in twos, just like they did. "I forgot why you said Sarah's family isn't going for Pesach this year."

Leah said, "They went for all three festivals last year. And this year, they're doing all those renovations to their house. I really don't have anybody else to go with. For Ima and Abba, it's either my twin sister or my best friend. Nobody else is worth considering. Period!"

Rachel looked back down at the letter that lay on her keyboard. It seemed to glow with an inner radiance, her name right at the top of the page, one of the group of seniors studying archaeology who was being invited to apply for this special seminar. In her mind, the four-week program had grown in magnitude until she now saw it as the capstone of her entire academic career. "Okay," she said. "Let me apply for it at least – no commitment! – and they say that they will announce their decision in three weeks. Can we hang on until then to make reservations? Can you wait that long to know?"

"Of course, since there's still plenty of time," Leah replied. "We have a good six months until Pesach. But I got so excited when Abba and Ima offered to let us go to Jerusalem on our own! I suppose Sukkot last week made them think of it. You're not talking about waiting too long, and maybe you won't even be accepted."

"Thanks for your confidence in me!" Rachel forced a laugh. She glanced out at the interminable rain once more. The little rise in front of their house blocked her view of the Hospitable Sea, but she knew that the rain must be pounding on that as well. Gray sky, gray water; dreary day. Her clothes, her chair, her skin: Everything felt damp. Then, with renewed resolution, she looked back down at the letter. "But nothing will happen at all if I don't start working on that application." She pulled up the application package on the university's website and started reading the instructions for the hundredth time. Her fear of rejection had held her back long enough. The deadline was fast approaching.

Chapter 2

Jesse came bursting out of the house and ran right up to where the twins were reclining on lounges on their patio, enjoying a sunny afternoon after a long string of rainy days. They smiled indulgently at their younger brother. He danced excitedly in front of them. "Guess what, guess what?" he asked.

"What, Jesse?" Rachel smiled at him obligingly.

"Abba just said that we are going to that resort, I forgot what it's called, and we'll be there for three whole days, Fifth Day through Shabbat. He said we can rent a boat to take out on the Hospitable Sea!"

"Do you know where the resort is?" Leah asked.

"Yes, it's in Hopa, but I can't remember what it's called."

Rachel's eyes widened. "Oh, it must be Sunset Hills! Everybody raves about that! Ima and Abba went there back before any of us were born, and I've always been so jealous! The beach is supposed to be just amazing."

"Yes, that's the name," Jesse said.

"Sarah went there a few years ago and had a fabulous time! She said the food was the best she'd ever had, and there were activities from morning to night," Leah said. She bounced a little bit on her lounge. "But Abba would never let us take a boat out on the Hospitable Sea. We've been begging him for years, right here in Trabzon. He always says it's too risky because the wind is so unpredictable. Why would he suddenly change his mind just because we're in Hopa?"

Jesse slapped his hands onto his hips. "Well, we're going on Fifth Day and you'll just see! He really did say we could take a boat out there."

The twins glanced at each other. "Which Fifth Day?" Leah asked him, remembering that Rachel was expecting to hear about the senior seminar by Sixth Day of the following week.

"This week! This very week! Just two days from now!"

"Don't you have another of those kickball games you have to play then?" asked Rachel idly.

"Not this week! We are off! Our team is really great this year, and I bet we're going to go to the tournament!" He plucked a leaf off the tree that hung over his head and began stripping the veins from its back. "Aren't you excited? We've never been there, and we've never rented our own boat!"

"We ARE excited! We were just talking about how there's nothing to do this week. Everybody is studying for midterm exams and there are no parties." Leah smiled at his enthusiasm. "But we're so terribly grown-up that we can't let ourselves act as excited as you are."

"Just so terribly sophisticated," Rachel added. She tilted her nose up in the air and put on a haughty expression. "Do you know what got Abba to think of this?"

"There's a conference in the resort center that he wants to go to," Jesse replied. "Some huge Torah scholar is going to be speaking, and he's never heard him in person before. But it's just in the afternoons and evenings, so he can take us out in a boat every morning!" His message delivered, Jesse turned around and dashed back into the house.

"Youthful energy!" sighed Leah from her lofty vantage point of being four years older.

Rachel pulled up the website for Sunset Hills on her phone, shading it with her hand. "It is just gorgeous! There's a little indentation of the Hospitable Sea there, like a protected cove. The beach is much wider than it is here and doesn't seem to be as rocky." She switched to a different view. "And the mountains are farther back and stand in a ring around the whole resort area."

Leah said, "I found the website, too, and I'm trying to read what activities are there. But it's too sunny out here."

Rachel mused, "You have that one take-home exam, which you could do from anywhere. We both have our papers almost ready to turn in. So really, we're free."

Leah said, "Your mind would go first to school! I can't believe you sometimes." She got up and started back toward the house.

"Where are you going?" Rachel asked her.

"I'm going to call Sarah to talk to her about this. Can't deal with the sunshine any more. And we do have to decide on what to pack to bring with us."

Rachel rose from her lounge and followed her sister into their house. "I'll call Deborah, too," she said. She started to key in the telephone number of her best friend. "Maybe Abba will even let us bring friends along if they can get away."

"Not a chance!" laughed their mother, Gveret Dina, who had overheard them as they walked through the kitchen on their way to their bedroom. She was busily starting to prepare their evening meal. "It's just going to be the five of us. Family bonding experience!"

The girls looked at each other, shrugged, and continued into their room to call their friends. Each climbed onto her bed and nestled among the many pillows they had accumulated. Rachel picked up her phone and called Deborah. "Guess what?" she began, as soon as Deborah had greeted her.

"You already heard from the committee?" asked Deborah, breathlessly.

Rachel pulled her head a little away from her phone at Deborah's squeal. "No, I wish. I keep checking their website, but there's still the notice 'Successful candidates will be contacted by Sixth Day of next week'. I'm impatient, but at least I don't have to make any decisions yet."

Deborah answered, "Oh, I know, Rachel. This has really been eating you up. I have to admit that I'm a tiny bit jealous that you might even have this choice to make. We don't get to go for every festival, either. Sometimes I feel so left out when it seems like everybody else is going on pilgrimage and I'm stuck at home in Trabzon. But it would be worse to think that I had the opportunity to do two things that I want to do so badly and could only choose one of them."

"Thank you. I know how you feel, having to miss another festival. But you never did guess why I'm calling. Ima and Abba are taking us to Sunset Hills this week!"

"That fabulous resort in Hopa?" gasped Deborah. "We've never been there!"

"We haven't, either. I know a bunch of people from the university will be going the following week, during the midterm break, but Abba has a conference this week and Leah and I don't have midterms to worry about."

"And you called to invite me to come with you?" Deborah asked. She giggled.

"I wish!" laughed Rachel. "But it's just the family."

"That's okay. I have three midterms. You're so lucky that your classes are structured differently and you aren't facing any tests."

"Yes, but there is much more pressure with the final exams then. It's almost our entire grade!" Rachel wriggled against her nest of pillows to get situated more comfortably. She glanced across at Leah's bed, where her sister was lying with her back to her and talking on her own phone. "And you know it's always raining in Hopa, even more than Trabzon, so it might not even be that great."

A few minutes later, the girls heard, "Rachel! Leah! I need your help setting the table."

"Coming, Ima," they chorused, and they both ended their conversations and ran lightly down the stairs to the kitchen.

As Rachel was carrying the water glasses out to the table, the back door slammed and her father, Adon Shimson, walked in. "Hi, Abba. Thank you for having that conference!"

He laughed and pulled her braid. "Yes, it's all up to me, and I arranged it just for you. But seriously, Ima and I haven't been to Sunset Hills in years, and I don't think any of you have ever been."

"No, we haven't, and it's very exciting. And I admit that it will be good to have a distraction while I'm waiting to hear back from the committee about the senior seminar."

"I'm sure you'll be at the top of the list," her father said, reassuringly. "And by the way, girls, I'll be giving you a little extra spending money for the trip. You never know what you might find there to do or buy."

"Thank you, Abba!" said Rachel. "You're always so generous to us!"

"Ima and I decided back when you started at the university that your education is your job," Adon Shimson said. "We've never wanted you to feel forced to work to earn money. We wanted your focus to be on your studies.

So I'm happy to hand you a little cash when you might be able to use it." He continued on his way out of the room, and Rachel turned back to placing cups on the table.

"I *am* grateful that I can focus on archaeology," Rachel called after him.

Leah walked into the room with a handful of silverware. "All you think about is excavations and the dusty past! I wish you liked live things as much as dead things," she remarked, setting the silverware out at each place. "I'm much more interested in people and their cultures than in piles of rocks."

"But I'm interested in people and their cultures, too, Leah. It just happens to be people from 5,000 years ago. And since they didn't leave recordings, the only way to find out about them is to dig down through the layers of rocks," said Rachel.

Leah laughed. "You're so defensive about this! You know I'm teasing you."

Rachel grinned. "Of course I do. I'm just so passionate about it, I guess. And what about you? There's nothing you would rather spend an afternoon with than a rock. I just know that!"

Leah elbowed her sister sharply in the ribs and went back into the kitchen to start helping bring in the food. Rachel joined her, picking up a dish of fruits and cheeses to carry in. Gveret Dina followed them with a platter of baked fish. Jesse soon came into the dining room, sniffing exaggeratedly, as he joined the rest of his family taking their seats around the table. "I wonder if we'll be able to do any fishing while we're there?" he mused, helping himself to some vegetables.

"I think so," his father replied. "There is an area for swimming and one for boating, and then beyond that, you can go out into the middle of the lake or into little coves and fish. We can rent all of that equipment if we have time to try it out."

Gveret Dina, handing the fish to her husband, remarked, "We do only have a few days there, and only the mornings as a family. But —"as Jesse's face fell — "I think they have an activities director who plans various programs for people of all ages, even high school age like you. Maybe there will be a fishing expedition that you can join."

Jesse smiled at his mother before shoveling some cheese into his mouth. The others soon turned their own attention to their evening meal.

Chapter 3

A few days later, the twins were over at Deborah's house, relaxing with their friends. Deborah's mother, Gveret Esther, waddled out the back door and onto the patio, bearing a tray loaded with a pitcher of lemonade and a stack of empty cups. She set it down on a table in the midst of the young people gathered there. Deborah leaped up from her chair, with a quick, "Thank you, Ima!" and a kiss in the direction of her mother's cheek. She headed into the house quickly, returning a moment later with a second tray bearing bowls of snack foods.

The group lounging on the patio stopped chatting and started helping themselves to the food and drink, thanking Gveret Esther as she went back into her house. It was most of the usual gang – Deborah and her brother Aaron, Rachel's boyfriend Samuel, her sister Leah, Leah's best friend Sarah, and Simon and Judith, who lived across the street from Deborah. Rachel looked around at them, noticing that Aaron's best friend was missing. She idly asked Aaron, "Where's Jacob?"

"He had to work tonight. He switched with somebody else so he could be off for his Greek midterm," Aaron replied.

"I'm so glad we don't have midterms to worry about!" Judith said.

Deborah laughed. "Well, Simon has already graduated, and you go to that haughty school where you have oral exams in front of a whole committee instead of written tests. I think I prefer our way!"

Judith shuddered somewhat dramatically. "I do hate walking into a room and finding three teachers sitting behind a table waiting to make a fool out of me. You never really get used to that."

Samuel, stretched out on a chair next to Rachel's, gave her a sidelong glance. "Some people think they can go out of town partying and pretend there's no such thing as midterms!"

Aaron looked over at him. "Who could that be?"

"Rachel bat Shimson, for one." Samuel replied.

"AND Leah bat Shimson, don't forget," Sarah added.

"Do I detect a little bitterness that you weren't invited?" Leah asked her, sticking out her tongue.

"You know I couldn't go anyway. I'm stuck with that huge Hebrew poetry exam, and I'm so weak in languages." Sarah pulled on her earlobe.

"But Hebrew is so much like Aramaic!" Deborah protested.

"For the rest of you, maybe. For me, there are so many differences and that's what I am stumbling over all the time. You should see the flashcards I had to make."

General laughter broke out on the patio. "Oh, Sarah, you make flashcards for every single class you take!" teased Leah.

Sarah finished her lemonade and refilled her cup before answering. "Well, maybe, but it works for me, and the grades are what matter in the end."

Just then, Rachel's phone rang. "Who could that be?" inquired Samuel. "I'm right here."

"And you of course are the only person who might ever call her!" giggled Leah.

Rachel glanced at her screen. "It's Ima. Do you suppose ..." She looked up at her twin sister nervously. "What if the decision has already been made about the trip to Greece? Nobody said that they were absolutely going to take until the final day to decide." She put her hand on her chest, feeling her necklace beneath the thin material of her summer frock.

Leah shrugged. "Well, we could speculate forever, or you could answer the phone."

Rachel excused herself and walked off the patio and into the surrounding garden as she started speaking to her mother softly. There was a little gazebo down the path, and she wandered into that and sank onto a bench while they spoke. Her friends looked her way for a second before resuming their chatter. She soon returned and quietly sat back down in her chair.

"Well?" demanded Deborah.

"Ima was looking in our closets to see what we might want to bring to Sunset Hills, since Leah and I haven't started packing yet. She found my best beach frock torn right up the side seam. I'm going to have to repair that if I want to bring it along. And I do; such a delicious shade of blue."

"Do you have to go home and sew it up right now?" asked Samuel.

"No, she just wanted me to know so I could plan time for it."

"So I wonder why she had to call you?" mused Aaron. "She could have waited until you got back home."

The twins exchanged a glance. "Because she's a mother!" chortled Leah. She reached out for another handful of trail mix. "It's in the job description."

"I hope we are never like that when we are mothers," said Judith.

"Oh, you probably will be," teased her brother. "When you have your first baby, they hand you the Mother Book and you start saying all those things you promised yourself you would never say!"

"Simon's right," nodded Aaron. "You girls are doomed!"

Just as the sun set, the wind picked up and a light rain started to fall. Rachel shook her head in disgust, then stood up and grasped her sweater from the back of her chair.

"I guess we all might as well go home now," Sarah said, as she too stood up. "And then you can sew your frock, because that absolutely has to be the most important thing on your mind right now!" Then she giggled.

Rachel looked at Leah. "I wish. I still don't know if I'm going to be accepted to senior seminar. And if I am, I have a huge decision to make."

"I can't imagine you girls wandering all around the Temple Mount on your own," Simon said.

Judith asked, "Why wouldn't your whole family be going to Jerusalem, anyway?"

Rachel said, "Abba has a reunion for his college class then. They're deliberately doing it over Pesach so they can spend the festival together. And of course Ima will go with him. Our brother Jesse is very active in sports and there's usually a tournament at that time of year. So them suggesting that we could go by ourselves for the first time is a big deal."

"You'd be far better off on a trip with adult supervision," drawled Aaron.

"Yes, because we're only 22," retorted Leah. "We might wander off and end up in Hebron or something if we don't have a grownup with us."

Samuel looked at her thoughtfully, and then over at Rachel. He started to say something, but there began a general move to get up and go back through the house to their cars parked out on the street, and he joined in the goodbyes instead.

Driving home, Rachel remarked to Leah, "That was really fun. We have the best group of friends!"

"We really do," Leah agreed. "I don't know Simon and Judith as well. I only just met them a month or so ago at Deborah's house, but they're as nice as the rest of our friends. I hope we can all make our careers in Trabzon or at least nearby and be friends always." She parked the car in front of their house.

Rachel got out of the car without answering her sister, deep in thought, as the girls went inside to get ready for bed. *I wonder what was on Samuel's mind at the end?* she thought, followed by, *Is there any way I would stay in Trabzon for my career? I absolutely cannot imagine that. But that's not something I should bring up with Leah right now.*

Chapter 4

Fifth Day had arrived at last. Rachel had packed her newly-mended beach frock, a pretty dress for an occasion such as a family outing, and a white dress for Shabbat. She was wearing her everyday sandals and checked for the third time to make sure that her beach sandals were indeed packed. Then she sat down on her desk chair so that Leah could braid her hair. She ran her fingers through her curls to give them some semblance of order. "I feel like we have everything, right?"

"If we don't, I'm sure that they have shops in Hopa and we can buy anything we forgot," Leah said around the ribbon she was holding in her mouth.

"It's a resort town, though. Probably would cost a whole lot more than it would around here."

Leah tied on the dark green ribbon with a flourish and gave Rachel's braid a little tug. "My turn!"

They switched places so that Rachel could braid Leah's hair. "What do people do who don't have a sister right in their bedroom?" Rachel wondered aloud.

"They learn to braid their own hair!" Leah laughed.

"At least yours is easier to do," Rachel said wistfully.

"Why, because it's so straight? You know I've always wanted lovely curls like yours!"

That conversation was on well-trodden territory and was not going to accomplish anything new.

"I really wish we could bring friends," Rachel said slowly. "Abba will be tied up all afternoon and tonight with his conference. We'll probably do things in the morning but be stuck hanging around the hotel all afternoon.

You have your take-home exam to work on, but I'm going to get tired of just sitting around reading." She grimaced.

"Bring your sketchpad." her sister suggested. "You've been wanting to learn to draw in charcoal ever since I got started myself. This would be a perfect time to practice. Just think of all the scenery!"

"What a great idea, Leah," Rachel enthused. "I'll never become as good as you, though. You got all the artistic genes! But it would be a lot of fun."

"I don't know that I'm particularly good with charcoal yet," Leah replied. "But I think I will hold my own by the time of that internship."

"Look how creatively you think! We've lived just down the road from the village of Kayra Han our whole lives, and nobody else at the university thought of assisting with their arts program for their internship until you did."

"Oh, come on, Rachel! There have been several internships in Kayra Han already."

"But they're all tutoring in math or reading with the younger grades. You're the first one who thought about volunteering at their community center to work with classes there."

Leah smiled. "And I'm already not the only one. Abigail bat Judah will be helping to teach their folk dancing classes. She's really fascinated by their cultural dances."

Rachel tweaked Leah's braid. "All done! And yes, you've mentioned that about Abigail before. See, I do listen to you sometimes!"

Leah stood up and laughed, but Rachel remained sitting on her bed and picked up her phone. "What are you doing?" Leah demanded. "It's time to leave!"

"Just texting Samuel a quick good-bye. I'm promising to send him photos so he can see what he's missing."

Leah snorted. "You and Samuel! I think you can handle being apart for a few days."

Rachel looked up dreamily. "Maybe. But it doesn't mean I won't be missing him!"

The girls took a last look around their room, grabbed their bags, and started downstairs, still talking. In the kitchen, they found the rest of their family gathered around Gveret Dina. "We have plenty of snacks, Ima, right?" Leah inquired anxiously. Everybody chuckled.

Jesse said, "Leah, it's always you who worries about food!"

"Oh, yes, dear," Gveret Dina said, in answer to Leah's question. "And water to drink along the way. Are you both ready?"

"Yes, Ima!" they chorused. Then they smiled at each other. As twins, they so often seemed to be saying the same thing at the same time.

The drive to Hopa passed with talking, dozing, and singing; there was only a little bit of snapping at one another. At long last, they were in their family's suite at the resort. Rachel looked around with shining eyes. There was a very pronounced beach theme going on: Seashells hung from all the lampshades and were glued around the mirrors in the foyer and bathroom. And then she noticed that there were even seashells glued around the top of each wastebasket. The bedspreads and curtains were all in swirls of sage green and cream, probably to represent seaweed. She noticed approvingly that there were three bedrooms in the suite and two bathrooms. Her parents would most likely take the bedroom and its associated bathroom on the right side of the foyer, and then the two bedrooms on the left side of the foyer would go to the three of them, with the second bathroom to be shared. The foyer itself opened into a fairly large sitting area, with a sofa, loveseat, and two armchairs decorated in the same seaweed-like pattern.

Rachel and Leah immediately laid claim to the second bathroom and changed into their beach attire. Their parents went into their room and closed the door, presumably to do the same. Jesse, almost hopping with excitement, had worn his swimsuit under his clothes and was waiting impatiently in the sitting area for the rest of his family to join him. Adon Shimson led the way to the boat rental piers, since the first event of his conference was not until evening, when he would go to an opening banquet. He cast a sharp eye over his three children and his wife, making sure that everybody was fastening a life preserver sufficiently snugly. Then he grasped firmly the bow of the boat they had been assigned, while the resort agent assisted each person on it.

The sun shone brilliantly and a soft breeze blew, as their father took the oars and rowed them out onto the Hospitable Sea. The mountains ringed the resort in the distance. Their mother threw her head back so that she was facing the azure sky and closed her eyes. Rachel quickly followed suit. There was something quite peaceful about being out on the water, especially after the long and noisy trip on the crowded highway. She thought wistfully of all the times they could have had this experience before, but did not do so because of their father's concerns. She wondered languorously what had happened to change his mind, but she was too lazy to ask. About an hour into their trip, Adon Shimson looked over at Jesse and said, "I'm getting tired, and we need to be going back in now. Want to trade places with me?"

"Sure!" Jesse answered eagerly, and he followed his father's lead in stooping down low and keeping as close to the center of the boat as he could while they switched positions. His first few strokes splashed everybody, and he stuck out his tongue at their shrieks of surprise. Rachel, who had just been taking a photo to send to Samuel, gave an extra squeal as she grabbed hold of her phone more firmly so as not to lose it overboard. Soon enough, he fell into a strong, smooth rhythm and brought them back to the pier. When Adon Shimson gestured for them to change places again, he shook his head smilingly and brought them in slowly and carefully, with only one or two bumps of the boat against the pier. "I'm a natural!" he decreed proudly.

As they walked back up the beach toward their hotel, they passed a couple trailed by a young man who appeared to be about the age of the twins. "Hello, Hannah," their mother said to the woman.

"Dina! How lovely to see you here. I didn't realize that you were going to be here the same time we were."

"Shimson is here for the Boker Torah conference, so we all came along with him."

"Oh, that's why we're here, too!" the other woman exclaimed. "Asher also wanted to be here for that."

While the men were introducing themselves, Leah walked past them to the boy straggling behind them and said, "Hello, Joseph!" He mumbled a greeting back at her. Then his family continued on their way to the pier.

Rachel's head swiveled, as she first looked back at the other family and then stared at her mother and sister. "Who is that?" Rachel hissed as soon as they were far enough up the path back to the hotel that she was sure the others were out of earshot. "I was surprised enough that Ima knew them, but then you know Joseph. Who is he?"

"Oh, they're the new family who moved across the street from us, where Yael used to live," answered Leah.

Rachel persisted, "But how do you even know them? Why don't I?"

Leah smiled. "Ima brought a cake over to welcome them last week, and I went with her. You were over at Deborah's house."

"He's really cute!"

"Yes, he is."

"Does he go to the university?"

Leah furrowed her brow, trying to remember. "No, I think he's helping out in his father's business. He's a little older than we are, and I think that he graduated last year."

"Well, if we see them again, introduce me," Rachel said, elbowing her sister in the ribs. "It's the polite thing to do, after all."

"Yes, of course. I know that Samuel would think so, too."

Rachel elbowed Leah more sharply. "I didn't say I was going to go after him, silly! I just think I should know somebody who lives on our block, especially if you've already met him."

"Ha ha, you walked right past the elevator!" Jesse called out in a mocking tone. The girls stopped and looked back. There were their parents and younger brother clustered halfway down the hall in front of an elevator. They hurried back and reached it just as the door opened.

"It was nice to see Hannah and Asher here," their mother was saying as they got on the elevator. "I didn't realize they were coming here, too."

"And the son – Jacob, is it?" asked their father.

"No, it's Joseph. They only have the one child at home. There's an older sister I haven't met who's married and lives maybe 100 kilometers away."

"When do you think you'll be done with the banquet, Abba?" asked Rachel.

"By 20:30. So it's not going to be a very late evening."

20

"Is there anything else going on here tonight?" asked Leah. "Maybe something Rachel and I could do instead of just sitting in the hotel room?"

"First of all, it's a very nice suite! But I do believe there is a club room of some kind," their mother answered. "It might be a good place for young adults to gather."

"Could I go, too?" Jesse asked eagerly.

"I wouldn't think so. You still have that paper to write," their mother answered. "You stay in the suite with me. It's a great opportunity to get some of your work done."

Jesse made a face but said nothing further, dragging his feet to follow the rest of his family as they reached their suite. Their father unlocked the door with his keycard and waved them all inside. He stepped into the bathroom and changed into business attire. Then he came out, hugged each of his family members, and went back out down the hallway again. Their mother suggested briskly, "Let's go down to the restaurant for dinner in a few minutes, and then Jesse and I can come back upstairs while you ladies look into the social situation in the club room."

"Sounds good!" the girls chorused, then giggled, as they each changed into a dress and prepared for the evening.

It all transpired just as their mother had planned. After dinner, she took Jesse back to their suite, leaving Rachel and Leah in the lobby. The girls headed down a corridor that they had not investigated yet. They passed a few meeting rooms, and then they started hearing music and laughter. "I think we found it!" Rachel said, just as they arrived at a room filled with young people eating, drinking, dancing, talking - everything they imagined they might find.

Edging hesitantly farther into the room while looking around, Leah whispered to Rachel, "I don't see Joseph ben Asher in here."

"Let's just stay a few minutes and we can always leave if we're not really comfortable," Rachel whispered back at her.

They found space at the unoccupied end of one of the longer tables, after determining that the chairs at those spaces were not already claimed by anybody else. Rachel sat down and continued looking around while Leah went over to the bar to get two beers.

"Hi, I'm Shira, and this is my brother Eli," said the girl nearest to Rachel, smiling at her.

"I'm Rachel." And then, as Leah walked up gripping a glass of beer in either hand, she added, "And this is my sister, Leah."

"Would you like some hazelnuts?" asked Shira.

"Sure, thank you," said Leah with a smile, taking her own seat. She leaned a bit toward Rachel, who whispered the names of their two tablemates to her, and then looked back at them. "Where are you from?"

"Esenkiyi, just a little northeast of here. I just finished all my midterms and Eli was able to get some time off from work, so our parents brought us to enjoy a family vacation."

"Oh, we're here for a conference with some Torah scholar. Our father signed up and then brought the rest of our family so we could have a vacation, too. It's the two of us and our little brother, Jesse," Rachel said.

Eli looked up from his phone. "Did you get to go to Jerusalem for Sukkot?" he asked.

"No, we weren't able to go. But our parents offered to let us go on our own for Pesach," Leah said. She took a sip of her beer.

"We weren't there for Sukkot, either. I was in the middle of a big project. But my family might go for Pesach, so maybe we can try to connect with you if we all go," Shira said.

Leah swallowed some more beer and then took another handful of hazelnuts. "It isn't for sure yet. Rachel has a chance to do a senior seminar and might do that instead, if she's accepted."

Eli looked startled. "I can't believe they would plan anything to conflict with one of the festivals!"

Rachel put down her own beer. "Oh, no, it doesn't. We'd be back a few days before Pesach," she assured him. "But neither time nor money will stretch to cover both in our family."

"Which are you hoping for?" asked Shira, curiously.

The twins exchanged glances. "I can't honestly tell you," confessed Rachel. "I'm almost glad that I haven't been faced with a decision yet, though, because they're both tempting. The senior seminar might determine the whole course of my professional life, so I'm leaning that way.

But then Leah is leaning on ME to go with her, and that could be an amazing experience."

"And when do you find out?" Shira continued.

"In another week. I'm climbing the walls waiting! I thought this would be a good break and help put it out of my mind, but it isn't working that way. I do love being at the Temple. The thrill of being on pilgrimage with all those crowds is like nothing else."

"We try to get to the Temple for every festival," Eli told them. "Our father is a Kohen. He and I both enjoy helping out whenever there's an opportunity."

"Oh, my boyfriend is a Kohen!" Rachel exclaimed. "And his family definitely goes a lot more often than we do. I'm just left back home getting his texts and photos."

"Yeah, we haven't been there nearly that much," Leah said. She flashed a brief scowl at Rachel.

Shira smiled at her sympathetically. "Don't worry; most people can't go as often. It's different when you're a Kohen. But you mentioned a senior seminar. Are you seniors at your university?"

"Yes, at the University of Trabzon," said Rachel. "What about you?"

"I'm only a junior at Esenkiyi College, but Eli graduated last year and he's working in medical research right now."

"You must be on a different schedule than we are," Rachel commented. "We have midterms this week."

"You're right. Our midterms were last week. That's why we were able to get away this week. How could you do it, if you are supposed to be having your midterms now?"

Leah chuckled. "Great planning on our part, although entirely accidental! I have only one midterm, and it's a take-home. Otherwise both of us only had papers to turn in."

A loud crack of thunder outside interrupted the conversation, causing everybody to look out the window. "I guess it's too much to ask that we have fair weather for one whole day," Leah said wryly.

"Not at this time of year!" Eli agreed.

The lights flickered, and they all pulled themselves out of their chairs, deciding it might be time to get back to their suites. They exchanged contact information and separated for the evening.

The next morning, Jesse found the activities director and learned that there was a fishing trip scheduled for high school-aged guests. He was overjoyed to sign up for it. Gveret Dina wanted to sit out on the balcony with a book for a lazy morning. Rachel and Leah found a group of young singles that was going to take a hike along the lakefront and signed up for that. The cost included a picnic lunch, and they agreed that it sounded like a lot of fun. They each tucked a sketchpad into their backpacks, hoping there would be some time to try to capture the scenery around them. When they went to join the others in the lobby, they noticed Eli, Shira, and Joseph among the dozen or so young people waiting for the hike.

"Let's go!" came the leader's voice, above the chatter of people getting to know one another while tucking the box lunches and water bottles that were provided into their backpacks. Rachel fell in step with Shira. Looking around for Leah, she noticed her walking along with Joseph a little bit behind her.

"Where did Eli go?" she asked Shira.

Shira nodded toward the front. "He's right up there with Saul. He always needs to know exactly what's going on."

"Who's Saul?" asked Rachel idly. She straightened her hat a little more on her head, trying to get more shade.

"Saul ben Gershom, the guy from the resort. He's leading the hike. You got here just a few minutes after he'd already introduced himself. He's pretty cute, if you like that type."

"I'm not interested anyway," Rachel said. "Remember, I have a boyfriend back home. We're pretty committed. What about you? Do you have a boyfriend back home? Or maybe you have your eyes on Saul?"

"Nope, completely single and looking to stay that way!" laughed Shira. "But your sister isn't wasting any time with that cute guy back there."

"That's Joseph ben Asher. He just moved in across the street from us back home. Leah already met him last week, but I haven't met him yet. She's definitely very outgoing when it comes to men."

24

"Tell me about your boyfriend," said Shira.

So Rachel told her a few stories about her experiences with Samuel as they walked side-by-side along the lakefront, the rocky path being wide enough for two. They were both soon laughing with tears streaming down their faces, as she regaled Shira with the story of how she and Samuel had first met. "We were both ten and it was lunchtime at school. I remember that he was ahead of me in line. There was one cupcake left on the dessert counter, and we started arguing about it. The polite thing for him to do, of course, was to let me have it. Or at least, he could have offered to cut it in half and split it with me. But no, he grabbed it and shoved it into his mouth while I just stared at him. And then he started choking on it. I laughed until I just about wet my pants. He was really embarrassed. After that, he kept calling me 'Cupcake Girl,' until I finally had to say, 'My name is Rachel. At least call me by my right name!' His hair was always messy, but he had these gorgeous hazel eyes even back then. They were so warm; they just melted me every time he looked at me."

"And they still do?" inquired Shira, fascinated.

Rachel blushed and nodded her head in answer.

They emerged from the path in the forest into a charming little park that extended all the way to the lakefront. There was a grassy meadow to their right, spotted with clumps of flowers and several bushes. The mountains in the distance, dappled in various shades of green from all the trees climbing up their flanks, encircled the meadow. To their left was the Hospitable Sea, little waves dancing on its surface, glinting in the sun. The deep blue autumnal sky stretched over the entire vista. The park proffered rustic wooden tables and benches, and everybody started moving toward them. Rachel kept watching for Leah, who finally straggled in with Joseph several minutes after everybody else had already found places around the tables. Leah winked at Rachel and went to sit with Joseph at an open spot at a table nearby.

Rachel pulled her lunch out of her backpack and began to examine its contents. "This looks really good!" she commented, stuffing cheese and tomato slices into her pita.

"And I'm famished from all that walking," Shira agreed as she popped an olive into her mouth. "What a beautiful spot!"

Rachel spotted a few colorful butterflies in the meadow. "This whole area is so beautiful. We don't live far from the lake ourselves, but the area where we live is different from around here. Not as much flat area by the lake. The mountains are much closer. I'm really glad we came!" she exclaimed. She pulled out her phone to take a few pictures to send back to Samuel.

"I am, too. It's been a lot of fun to get to know you. Let's make sure we stay in touch after we go back home."

Rachel smiled at Shira and agreed, taking another bite of her pita. She closed her eyes briefly, enjoying the warmth of the sun on her head and shoulders. She stretched out her right leg to loosen a tight muscle. All too soon, they would be on the move again. But in the meantime … She reached into her backpack and pulled out her sketchpad. Shira stared at her, clearly intrigued. "You draw?!"

Rachel shook her head, smiling. "Not really. Leah's the artistic one. But I would love to get better, and where is there a more beautiful spot to model for me?" She pulled out her charcoal pencil and gazed around the picnic table. *The sea, the mountains, the meadow? Water would be difficult.* She started roughing in the lines of the mountains on the horizon with the meadow in the foreground.

Shira watched her intently. "Maybe you can put this table in front and draw us!"

Rachel grimaced without looking up from her sketchpad. "I can't really do people. And I'm afraid that I can't do *anything* if you are watching me! I told you, I'm really just a beginner."

Shira shrugged, picked up her backpack, and went over to find her brother. Rachel, oblivious, continued trying to capture the various shapes she saw before her. She jumped when somebody shook her shoulder. Looking up, she saw Leah towering above her. Leah glanced at her sketchpad and smiled. "That's a really good effort, Rachel! I can see what you're doing here. But you need to pack it up now, because we're getting ready to go back to the main lodge."

Rachel shook her head. "I know you're trying to encourage me, but it's just terrible."

Leah laughed. "Okay, you got me. It's pretty bad!"

Rachel giggled and then stood up, stretching. She shoved everything back into her backpack and went to join the group clustered around Saul. Time to see what they would do next!

Chapter 5

Shabbat dawned sunny and a bit cooler than the previous days had been during their stay. The girls showered and put on their white frocks to spend a contemplative day with their family.

There was a buffet breakfast set up outside by the pool for the guests. One of the meeting rooms had been turned into a chapel, and a Kohen who had come to the conference was leading some prayers and songs for those who wished to join him. Rachel, Leah, and Gveret Dina decided to stroll around the landscaped grounds of the resort instead, enjoying their beauty. It was possible that none of them would have the opportunity to return to this resort.

The day passed quietly, first at the pool and then, later on, they took a picnic lunch to the lakefront and sat there reading, relishing the breeze blowing in off the lake. In the evening, Jesse and their parents went to a marshmallow roast, while Rachel joined Shira and Eli at the pool with a few of the other young adult guests. Leah stayed back in their room, nursing a headache from the sun. She also hoped to finish and submit her midterm exam.

As Leah was combing the kinks out of her hair, the ribbon from her braid carelessly dropped on the floor, Rachel bolted into their room and sat down on her bed with a thump. "That was fun, but I'm so tired! Maybe I should have stayed back in the room, too." Yawning widely, she checked her phone to confirm that her papers had both made it on time and were accepted for grading. She sent one final text to Samuel, smiling dreamily over his immediate response. Then she joined Leah in getting ready for bed.

The next morning, the family drove home. It was rather silent in the car, as each of them savored memories of the vacation or dozed off briefly. The sudden cessation of noise from the engine awakened Rachel, who stretched and exclaimed, "Home at last. What a long drive!"

The twins sauntered into the house. Rachel removed her backpack and slung it to her bed, just as Leah dropped her own backpack onto the floor of their room. They were both tired from the trip but still glowing from the wonderful time they had.

"I rather thought we were getting past the age of family vacations," Rachel remarked, as she started pulling clothing out of her backpack and sorting it into piles to be dealt with later. "But this was actually quite pleasant!"

"It helps that it was a fabulous resort with a whole lot to do!" Leah answered her, kicking off her sandals and flinging herself onto her bed.

Rachel glanced slyly at her sister. "You sure seemed to have a good time with Joseph."

"Well, he's been great company, and it was worth getting to know him since he lives so close. And yes, since you're probably about to ask: I just might want to spend some time with him," Leah answered.

"He definitely is nice," Rachel agreed. "I think he'd be fun to hang out with." She opened up her laptop and started checking her email. "Oh, dear," she said with a rising inflection. Leah sat up while Rachel scrolled farther down the page. "They say that they're missing one of my three letters of reference for the senior seminar. Looks like it's my Classics professor. I'll have to call him." She pulled out her necklace and held it tightly in her left hand, absently rubbing her thumb over the quartz as she reread the email.

"Will that hurt you since it's past the application deadline?" Leah asked, concerned.

"No, because it's not within the candidates' control for the letters to be sent in." Rachel called her professor, nodding politely while she spoke with him, and then afterwards announced to her sister, "He says he sent it in a few days ago. I'm going to call the committee to follow up." She called the number that was given on the application form. Her face relaxed into a smile as she looked over at Leah. "They have the letter! The email was sent out automatically based on the status at the time, but the letter did come in and my file is complete." She picked at her cuticle. "They were genuinely nice to me, at least. They must know we're all anxious over this!"

"It's a really big deal, Rachel!" said Leah. "A credential that most of your competition won't be able to brag about. A path to the career of your dreams."

"Not to mention all there is that I can learn!" She dropped her phone on the bed beside her. Just then, it rang. She recognized Samuel's ringtone and smiled as she picked it up and answered it.

"You're home now, right?" Samuel asked.

"Yes, we just got back a little while ago. I'm still unpacking – very slowly!"

"There's something I've really been wanting to talk to you about, and it's been hard not to say anything, but I had to clear it with my parents first."

Rachel said, thoughtfully, "Yes, I could tell you had something on your mind. I'm glad you're ready to share it with me."

Samuel continued, "My mom is going to talk to your mom about you and Leah coming to Jerusalem with us for Pesach! She doesn't feel right about the two of you going all on your own and thinks you'll be better off with my parents looking after you. AND me, of course."

"That's a great idea!" Rachel exclaimed. Leah looked up and noticed that Rachel's brow was furrowed and the expression in her eyes did not match her tone of voice. She held up a finger in Leah's direction. "I'd love being with your family, and I know Leah would, too."

"You know that they've exposed more of Herod's Temple, right? 1500 years older than the complex we have now! We HAVE to see those excavations," Samuel said.

Rachel said, "I didn't realize that King Herod's construction was still being uncovered under the present Temple. Very cool!" She dug her fingernails into her blanket and threw an impenetrable look at her sister. She and Samuel chatted for another few minutes before she quietly put down the phone and then gave a long, shuddering sigh. Her right hand remained on the phone for a long moment.

"What is it, what is it?" demanded Leah when Rachel had hung up. "Are they going to Jerusalem the same time that we are?"

"Yes, and they've invited us to come along with them so we aren't wandering all over Jerusalem lost and alone and maybe get mistaken for Temple prostitutes!"

Leah laughed, and even Rachel managed a weak smile, since they had been to Jerusalem at least a dozen times since infancy. Granted, it was always with their parents in the past.

"Well, that would certainly make Ima and Abba a little more relaxed," Leah said, "and you could spend all the time you want with Samuel because you'll have the best chaperones there are. But oh, Rachel, this must make it so much harder for you!"

Rachel picked at her cuticle until it bled. "I know. A tiny part of me hopes I don't get accepted to the senior seminar so I won't be forced to choose. It would be lovely to be with Samuel day after day, and for you and me – we'd still be in Jerusalem without our parents but having parent-types around to help make arrangements. But oh, I want to go to Greece!"

"I have to admit that I was a little bit nervous at the thought of getting around all by ourselves with all the crowds," confessed Leah, looking down shyly. "If we do get to go, it would be helpful to have parents along, especially since they aren't ours. But what are you going to do?"

"I just don't know, Leah." Rachel looked away and Leah could see her trembling a bit. Leah moved over to Rachel's bed and put her arms around her. Rachel started crying softly, clutching her necklace in her right fist.

"Let's just do what you've been saying all along," Leah soothed. "We won't borrow any trouble from the future. We'll wait until Sixth Day and see what you find out. And we'll face it then when we have to. But now I really want to go more than ever, so it's going to be hard not to beg you to decide that way." She gently eased the necklace out of Rachel's hand and dropped it back down inside her frock.

"I know," mumbled Rachel, still looking down at her phone. "I want to go more than ever, too. I really don't know what to think."

"Then don't think for now! We still have a few days." Leah glanced quickly at her sister's bent head, then looked away and tried to keep an even tone as she asked, "Remind me why Deborah isn't going."

31

"She's working on her major project for Greek classics. She has to translate some ancient source from Greek and then write a commentary about it." Rachel looked up with a watery smile. "And I know what you're doing. You're looking for every possible temptation to get me to decide to go to Jerusalem!"

"I admit it! That paper sounds like a lot of work, though," Leah shuddered. "I wonder why she even signed up for that elective."

"She's interested in the period when Judea was under Roman rule," Rachel explained. "So many documents of those times are in Greek because of the dispersion after the First Temple was destroyed. A lot of Jews didn't even speak Aramaic or read Hebrew who were scattered around the Roman Empire."

"So much was going on back then," Leah agreed. "All those different factions. I wonder what happened to them all. Where are the Essenes today, or the Nazarenes?"

"I think their genetic descendants are still around after 2000 years, but their beliefs and practices made more sense in those stressful times. They faded away into the more mainstream practices once Rome fell."

"Interesting that there are still Romans around," commented Leah. "I guess you never know what will make it through the centuries and what will not."

"Still Romans, yes." Rachel gave her sister a long, level look. "And still Greeks, too. Or at least those people are all the descendants of the ancient people, but just like us, a lot has happened to their culture in a few thousand years."

"Okay, okay, Rachel, we are NOT talking about the Greeks right now! It isn't helping."

"I just wish there was an obvious choice," Rachel moaned. Leah gave her an extra hug and then stood up.

"But hey," Leah said, "do you suppose Shira and Eli will be going?"

"LEAH!"

Leah grinned guiltily. "Meanwhile, we do have to unpack and wash some of these clothes. Let's make a point of keeping very busy so we don't have to think about it until Sixth Day comes."

"I don't think that's going to work for me," Rachel said. "I haven't been able to put it out of my mind since I first heard about it in my archaeology class! But yes, we'll pass time the best we can – fill it right up – and I'll try not to think about it more than I have to till then."

Rachel stood up as well. She shook out her empty backpack over their wastebasket to remove any last vestiges of sand and then hung it up to air out. She started sorting her laundry while Leah glanced at her own backpack. "Let's get some laundry going," she said.

Leah watched Rachel take an armload of laundry and start to walk out of the room before remarking, "You have been very industrious. I have my own pile of laundry that I've been neglecting!"

Rachel giggled and headed down the hallway. In her wake, Leah heard a soft moan. This was not going to be easy for Rachel.

Chapter 6

Rachel promised herself that she would make full use of the few days she had left before hearing from the committee. No more wallowing; time to take a more active role. She would pick everybody's brain that she could think of. There was no point in putting off any longer pondering her decision, since she would be expected to accept or reject the offer on the spot. She spent several hours talking to Leah and to her parents. She was on the phone with Deborah several times each day. She sat out on the chair swing alone with her thoughts. Samuel met her for coffee each day and came over for two of the evenings to talk. Finally, she scheduled an appointment to meet with Adon Yehuda, her thesis advisor who was also the head instructor of the senior seminar.

Seated across his desk from him just before lunch on Fourth Day, Rachel toyed with the end of her braid. "How candid can I be with you?" she asked.

"You can tell me anything you want in complete confidence." Then one eyebrow went up. "Why are you asking?"

"I don't want to prejudice our relationship either for the senior seminar or for you as my thesis advisor."

He smiled reassuringly. "I have known you for four years, Rachel. I've already made up my mind about you, academically and also professionally. You aren't likely to tell me anything that would affect my opinion of you."

"Thank you for that," she said.

"When you called to schedule this appointment, you mentioned that you have some difficult decisions to make."

"Yes. My boyfriend's family invited my sister and me to go to Jerusalem with them for Pesach this spring. This would be the first time we would be going without our parents. But because it would be during the same month as the senior seminar, my parents have said that it is not financially possible for me to do both."

"I think you also said something about how long you'd have to be away from home if you were to try to do both."

"That's correct," she said, her hand moving toward her necklace before she caught herself.

"I absolutely will respect whatever decision you make and will not try to force you," he continued, "but I am obliged to remind you that you can go to Jerusalem for any festival at any time in the future, with or without your parents. This is literally a once-in-a-lifetime opportunity and only a tiny fraction of those who are interested are able to go."

"I do know that," she agreed. "You need to understand how drawn I am to be going to Jerusalem with my sister and my boyfriend both. Our family is not in a position to go very often, and in fact we've only been there a few times in my lifetime."

"I understand that, too. But you are getting older, and once you're done with the university, you will be supporting yourself. You'll possibly be living in an entirely different situation. How can you forecast how many more times in the future you will be able to go to the Temple for one of the festivals? Without your parents, with your sister, with your boyfriend – the possibilities are endless. But you will never have this precise opportunity again, this senior seminar that you spent a lot of time applying for. That could be the guarantee that you get into the graduate school of your choice and launch your career from a better position. You know that the best jobs are offered to people who've come from the strongest programs." He cleared his throat and then continued. "I'm going to be candid with you, too. Not trying to hurt your feelings, just help support you in seeing things clearly. It strikes me that your dilemma is grounded in somewhat – immature thinking. The whole future you've been working so hard toward vs one festival in Jerusalem with your sister out of many possible?"

"You're right, I know that. A career move should make any other choice irrelevant. Frivolous, really, to be deciding between these two things. But there are some other issues," she said softly.

35

"I think we might be able to find a stipend to cover most of your expenses. It would be a shame for you to miss out."

"It's not just the money. There's more," she whispered.

Adon Yehuda folded his hands on his desk and leaned forward inquiringly.

Rachel's eyes darted around the room for a few seconds before fixing on his face once again. "I have never spent the night away from Leah before," she blurted out.

Adon Yehuda smothered a smile, but not so quickly that she didn't notice it. "Well, it seems to me there will have to be a first time at some point. And at 22, I think you'll do okay."

"I just can't seem to face the thought."

He looked at her steadily. "This seems deeper than just a twin thing. Is there a story behind this?"

"When we were ten, there was a camping trip in the mountains that we had both been planning on," she said. "Leah was sick, but our parents convinced me to go anyway. That very first morning, there was a monsoon, and our leaders – they were the mothers of some of the girls - made us pack and load up the bus to go back home." She swallowed and looked down. He continued waiting patiently. She looked back up at him and said, "I've never told this story to anybody outside my family before, not even my best friend or my boyfriend."

He continued to wait in silence, not wanting to press her in this fragile moment.

"I had wandered off to collect stones," she said. He chuckled briefly and she smiled. "Yes, I know, you can see the future archaeologist in the child already. Something about rocks has always intrigued me. Were they arranged as they were by nature alone? Anyway, we had just come back from a rock climb when the storm hit. I had taken off my necklace" – she pulled it out from inside her dress and showed it to him – "because I didn't want it to get damaged by the rocks if I scraped it or something else happened to it. It was lying on my sleeping bag. So when they were gathering all the girls, they found my necklace but couldn't find me."

She paused for so long that he prodded her gently, "Go on."

"The bus went back with all the other girls. One leader had come earlier in her own car to get a few things set up, and she stayed behind to look for me. The wind and the rain were terrible. I was lost in the woods and couldn't find my way back to the clearing. A tree fell down just to my right – it didn't touch me, but I could feel the whoosh! as it came down almost on my foot. I thought I was going to die out there." She paused, swallowed, looked away for a second, and then continued. "Well, it turned out that I was only a few trees away from the clearing, and when I saw the shelter in a flash of lightning, I went back. It can't have been more than half an hour, but it felt like I was lost forever. I saw my sleeping bag with the necklace on top of it when I got back inside, but nobody else was in sight. The bus was gone. As far as I knew, I was abandoned there and nobody would ever know where I was. I sat right down on the ground and cried."

She gulped and he nodded sympathetically. "The leader must have been looking for you in the woods and wasn't there when you found the clearing," he suggested.

She gave him a small smile. "That's right, but of course I didn't know that. The more I cried, the more I panicked, until I just plain started screaming. Time dragged on and on. Finally, the leader who'd stayed behind came rushing out of the woods and grabbed me and hugged me and said I could probably be heard all the way back in Trabzon. Adon Yehuda, it felt like forever to me."

"So you were traumatized."

She nodded. "And more than that. I was absolutely convinced it had only happened because Leah wasn't there. Leah would never have let me be left on my own for a single moment. I was only away from home for half a day, but it seemed like – well, that day split time into Before and After. Do you know what I mean?"

"I do," he said. "But I also know that you are now 22. You would be with other professionals and me and also eleven other young men and women. It might be good for you to TRY to be apart from Leah, because you will never be able to do it if you continue giving into your fears. And maybe talking about it to me made you realize that it isn't a fear worth holding onto any more?" As she shrugged, he smiled at her and said, "Let's do this:

I will still find out about financing. It's very possible you'll be able to do both trips, and I will let you know at once when I find out. If that isn't by Sixth Day, I'm sure they would hold your place a few more days while I search for funding. In the meantime, you will have to consider whether you'll be okay without your sister. Can you agree to face this challenge?"

She caressed the smoky quartz oval briefly, before slipping the necklace back under her dress. "I think I can do that. Go ahead, because doing both would be amazing, and I'll try to evaluate as honestly as I can how I could do without Leah for a whole week."

"That's already a good sign, Rachel, that you're even able to consider it!" He stood up and offered her his hand, which she shook gravely. "I'm honored that you trusted me with your private feelings. I will do the best I can to make this trip work for you, but nobody will force you to come if it's beyond your capacity emotionally."

"Thank you so very much, Adon Yehuda," she said earnestly. "It does sound like a childish fear now that I hear myself saying the words. I will do my best." She cleared her throat and looked away from him.

Adon Yehuda noticed her hesitation and asked gently, "Is there something more?"

She blushed and looked back at him. Resuming her seat, she swallowed, then exhaled audibly, before her words rushed out. "I've been feeling a bit unsure of myself. Sometimes I don't think I could live up to the others if I was selected to be part of the group. Like I was a fraud somehow. Maybe I just wrote a good application, or maybe —" Rachel paused, then looked down — "you had some influence over the committee."

Adon Yehuda waited a beat before he answered. "I really do hope that these are just superficial feelings and don't relate to your actual understanding of yourself. If you are accepted into the program, it will be on your own merits. The applications will be judged by a committee for whom I only serve as an advisor. I have no influence over their decisions. You need to be taking an objective assessment of yourself and your own abilities. You and Batya have been taking turns leading the class in performance throughout your university career. You are as strong a candidate as I can imagine."

Rachel whispered, "Thank you," under her breath, as she rose once again.

"Rachel?" he called out to her, as she started to leave his office. She turned around and looked up at him inquiringly. "I've never noticed that necklace before. I suppose because you mostly keep it inside your dress. It must have special meaning for you."

She pulled it back out and showed it to him. "My grandmother left it to me. My father's mother. I was really so close to her. Once my sister and brother had scarlet fever, and I stayed with her for a few weeks. After that, I spent a lot of time with her. I miss her a lot, and the necklace makes me feel braver. It's like her love is with me."

"The engraving is very faint. What does it say?"

"It's her Hebrew name, and then it's surrounded by olive branches. They were already alarmed about me being missing. And then they found the necklace but not me. I think that scared them even more, because I almost never take it off."

He nodded at Rachel sympathetically. She turned once more and walked out of his office with a lighter step than she had walked in with. It had never occurred to her that there might be a way that she could do both things. It still, however, seemed very remote that she could be away from Leah. Or that she was good enough to be chosen. *But how supportive he was! I feel like I can tell him anything and he would really hear me!* She strolled toward the Student Union and her friends, suddenly looking forward to a good lunch.

Chapter 7

Rachel dragged herself down the hallway to breakfast. Her typical morning enthusiasm had been replaced by a profound weariness in the past few days. Now it was only Fifth Day; time had moved too fast and also too slowly. Tomorrow was the day she would find out whether she had been selected. An endless tape loop was playing in her head, as she revisited her meeting the previous day with her thesis advisor. Could he actually obtain financing for her? Would that make it all the harder to turn down the opportunity to join the senior seminar if she just could not conceive of being away from Leah for an entire week? Leah, who at that very moment was sitting at the table smiling at her. Leah, whether laughing, talking, or just breathing, who was always there. Would turning down the seminar even be an option for her, realistically? She sank into her chair and thought back to her return home after that meeting the previous afternoon.

Her mother had greeted them at the door and then took Rachel aside. "How did your meeting with Adon Yehuda go?" she asked.

Rachel sidestepped out of the foyer and into the den, and her mother followed her. "It went fine. He gave me some hope that I could do both programs. There might be some kind of stipend he can get for me."

"That would be wonderful! It would certainly ease all of our minds financially."

Rachel nodded. "He has been so supportive."

"That's good," her mother said. She took a breath and then continued, "How much did you tell him?"

Rachel lifted her eyes to her mother's, basking in the love that shone from them. "I told him the whole reason, Ima. I've never done that before."

"And how did he react?"

"He seems to think it's something from childhood that I can put behind me now if I think about it from a more mature perspective."

Gveret Dina rubbed her right ear. "I don't know, Rachel. It was the most traumatic memory I have since having children; maybe the hardest time of my life."

Remembering now, Rachel thought back to what her mother had told her over the years about that day. Ima and Abba had gone to the school to pick Rachel up when they were supposed to, but only Rachel's best friend Deborah was there, and she was crying. Deborah's mother, Gveret Esther, was standing there with her daughter. One of the mothers who had been a leader on the trip told their parents that they could not find Rachel and had to bring the rest of the girls home, leaving one mother behind to search for her. Gveret Esther, her arm around the sobbing Deborah, said, "Deborah refuses to leave until they find Rachel and bring her back home. She seems to think it's her fault that Rachel got lost."

"Oh, no, Deborah," Gveret Dina had told her. "You can't blame yourself. Go home with your mother now, and Adon Shimson and I will wait here for Rachel. We promise to call as soon as they find Rachel."

Deborah followed her mother reluctantly, still crying, and then she stopped and looked back at Rachel's parents. "All they found was her necklace!" Her mother tugged on her hand and she turned once again to leave.

" How could that be?" Rachel's mother had demanded yet again the day before. "You never take off that necklace! That leader was distraught. Were you kidnapped? Eaten by wild animals? Lost in that monsoon? She assured me right away that the mother they had left behind to look for you was not leaving until she found you. But we didn't know what to think."

"I do take the necklace off sometimes, Ima," Rachel said. "I was trying to protect it from the rocks and left it with my sleeping bag. And I take it off every day when I shower. It's just that nobody sees me when I'm not wearing it." She had pulled it out from inside her dress and clutched it in a damp fist. Then her face had crumpled. She had sought the comfort of her mother's arms, crying, holding her necklace up high above them both like a torch. "I miss Savta so much! She loved us unconditionally. I always rushed home

41

from school to tell her all about my day. And now she is gone forever and all I have left of her is this necklace!"

Gveret Dina held her sobbing daughter tightly in her arms, a faraway look in her eyes. *"We kept waiting for information. It was more than an hour before we finally received a phone call. You had turned up and you were going to be brought directly home. I aged ten years in that hour."*

"And," Rachel concluded, *"this would never have happened if Leah had been with me. I could never have been alone and separated from the group."*

"But of course you could have!" her mother exclaimed. *"You could have wandered into the woods together and both been lost temporarily in the monsoon. Leah is not magical protection for you!"*

Looking back now, Rachel remembered that there had been a long, thoughtful pause. "You know, I never saw it that way before, Ima!" She had impulsively hugged her mother. "The fact that I've never traveled without my sister doesn't mean that I never could. I'm not ten any more!"

"You surely are not!" her mother had laughed, looking up at her daughter. "You've been towering over me for five years now! Nobody could mistake you for a child." Then she had paused, scratching the back of her neck, before continuing more softly, "Adon Yehuda did have a good point, though. Putting this senior seminar on an equal footing with a trip to Jerusalem is a bit childish. It's exciting to think that you and Leah can go for the first time by yourselves, of course, but it's hardly the last time in your whole life that you'll have that opportunity. In my mind, there isn't any real decision to be made." At Rachel's sharp intake of breath, she added, even more gently, "And yes, I do understand the aspects of the seminar that make it threatening for you. The emotional side of things. But I ask you to consider only the seminar in your thinking rather than offsetting it against the trip to Jerusalem, because I don't see them as comparable in the least."

"I understand you, Ima. Listening to you, I'm becoming aware that maybe I'm using the trip with Leah as a foil. Something else to latch onto for my poor anxious brain, so that I don't focus on my sense of disappointment in myself if I am accepted to the seminar and feel compelled to turn it down." Rachel had hugged her mother and then walked outside, feeling the need to be alone with her thoughts for a while.

42

Thinking about it now, Rachel was torn between embarrassment and heartbreak. Her reverie was broken when her mother walked into the room with a platter of scrambled eggs and steamed greens. *Breakfast, class, lunch, class, dinner, study, sleep. I can get through this one more day. And then I'll hear from the committee, and at least the waiting time is over. No more uncertainty. I'm tired of being stuck without having any action I can take.*

Leah put down her fork and turned to Rachel. "I really love you, and I believe in you," she said.

Rachel got up out of her chair and hugged her sister impulsively. Whether it was some kind of mindreading because they were twins or just that she was such a caring sister, Leah seemed perfect in her eyes and she had never loved her more.

Chapter 8

Rachel was inclined to blame the loud clap of thunder for waking her, but she admitted to herself that she would be lying. She wasn't even sure that she had ever actually been asleep. She was convinced that she had seen every hour as the night dragged by at a most painful pace. She glanced over at Leah's bed across the room, but she saw only a cylindrical roll of body and blankets out of which arose an indistinct grumble as lightning flared in their windows. Leah was clearly not going to wake up and keep her company, but Rachel might as well give up on trying to get any more sleep. The illumined dial of her phone showed her that it was 3:20 on Sixth Day. And not just any Sixth Day, but the day on which the committee had promised they would be releasing the names of the twelve lucky seniors who would be attending senior seminar in Mycenae. What time might that happen? Would it be by phone call, email, or text? *How do I not already know this?*

She slipped out of bed, leaning down to pick up her sandals, and left their room as noiselessly as she could. Walking through the kitchen on her way to the back door, she verified that it was indeed only 3:20 – well, now it was 3:23. Sliding her feet into her sandals, she opened the sliding glass door to the patio in back of their house as quietly as she could. It was absolutely pouring outside, but the thunder seemed to have moved farther off, so she grabbed a hooded jacket off the hook beside the door and pulled it on, tiptoeing outside as she did so.

The overhang at one end of the patio offered a little shelter, so she stood there for a moment indecisively before stepping off the patio. The grass made little sucking noises as she hurried over to the lean-to shed in the middle of the yard. There hung the chair swing that had been her refuge for as long as she could remember. She slid onto the swing seat and pulled out her phone. There was nothing on the seminar's website to indicate that this day differed from any of the others that had dragged on so interminably before it. She hesitated over her phone before tucking it back under her jacket; it was an impossible hour to think of calling Deborah or Samuel. There was one other girl in her class who had applied for the seminar, Batya bat Somebody, and possibly she was awake, but Rachel didn't have her contact information and would not take the chance of calling at this outrageous hour anyway. She sighed and leaned her head against the wooden back wall of the lean-to, closing her eyes and forcing herself to take slow, deep breaths.

Time was not passing any more quickly out here than it had in her bed, and she WAS getting wet despite all of her efforts. So she went back into the house, leaving the sandals inside the door and the jacket on its hook, and stumbled into the kitchen. She opened the refrigerator and took out a slice of cheese. There was a container of crackers on the counter, and she pulled out two of those and broke the cheese onto them. As she was taking her first bite, she heard light footsteps outside the room. Glancing in the direction of the sound, she saw her mother, yawning and pulling a wrap more tightly around herself.

"Ima!" whispered Rachel, a bit guiltily. "I was trying so hard not to disturb anybody."

"I don't think I really heard you so much as felt you," Gveret Dina assured her. "You couldn't sleep?"

Rachel shook her head. "I don't think I've slept for more than ten minutes all night long."

"Do you have any notion of what might happen? How or when you will find out?"

Rachel shook her head again, more miserably than before. "If it were just at the university, I'd have a better idea. I've always been in the top five students in my program. But this is nationwide. I have no idea how many seniors are competing for twelve spaces. I only know one other person who's applied, so I don't know what their standings or credentials are, either.

Her mother glanced down, where drops of water were still falling from Rachel's toes to the floor. She opened a nearby drawer and took out two towels, then knelt down and wrapped each of Rachel's feet in one.

"But these are kitchen towels, Ima!" Rachel protested.

"Shhh! It's okay. I can easily throw them into the wash. I don't want you to get sick."

"I don't even know how I'm going to find out the news or when! It could be dinnertime for all I know!" She tugged at the chain of her necklace distractedly.

"The clock will keep moving along and the day will pass, and you'll find out at the right time. I do hope you will be able to focus in school today." Her mother reached across and gently removed Rachel's hand from the chain. "You don't want to break this."

With those remarks, which Rachel found less than reassuring, her mother stood up and got some cups out of the cabinet. She took a bottle of milk out of the refrigerator and poured a cup for each of them. Rachel received hers gratefully and started to sip it. Meanwhile, her mother inquired, "Do you think what you're most likely going to end up doing is working in Greece for your whole career? Or might you be one of those itinerant archaeologists who hops from dig to dig?"

Rachel's eyes looked timidly above the rim of her cup as she continued drinking. Then she set it down on the table behind her and said, "I wish I could tell you that I'd be happy staying in Trabzon, or at least at a Hittite site close by in Anatolia. But here on the coast, where the Greeks conquered us long ago, what they're finding is just a pale imitation of what is turning up in Greece itself. This seminar is my first step toward building a career, but I'm afraid it's going to have to be in another country. Maybe not Greece, but probably not Anatolia either."

"I did wonder," her mother replied softly.

"It's pretty recent for me," Rachel confided. "It would tie together all the different components of my life experience and my education, and so this seminar would really be a perfect credential. It positions me for getting into pretty much any graduate school program I end up choosing."

46

"That's really well thought out," her mother answered. "And certainly something you can make happen whatever you find out about this senior seminar today."

Rachel stood up and put both of their cups in the sink, dropping a kiss on the top of her mother's head as she did so. She glanced at her phone once again and saw that it was almost five o'clock. "Oh, well, it's just about time to get up and get ready anyway. I love you, Ima."

"I love you, too, Rachel, so much," her mother smiled, hugging her as she rose from her own chair. "And I'm cheering for you!"

Rachel shrugged her shoulders slightly. "I wish that could make a difference," she said, as she turned to leave the kitchen and go back into her own room.

Leah was already stirring as she walked in. "Where were you?" she asked, rubbing her eyes and stretching a little.

"I couldn't sleep," Rachel confessed. "I was in the kitchen and then Ima came in and I was talking to her."

"You're all tied up in knots!"

"I know, I keep trying to relax and put it out of my mind, but that just doesn't work. Oh, well, by this time tomorrow, I'll know one way or the other …"

The girls showered, dressed, and packed the things they would need for the day into their backpacks. Leah grabbed a protein bar and a banana, but Rachel just shook her head. There was no space in her stomach for food alongside all the lumps she could feel. As they left the house, their mother gave them each a hug and wished them a good day.

Rachel was arranging her space on the counter in her Archaeology Laboratory Methods class when another young woman came up to her. "You're Rachel, right?" she asked.

"Yes," said Rachel. "And I think you're Batya?"

"I am," she said, then impulsively reached out a cold hand and squeezed Rachel's equally cold hand. "I heard that you also applied to the senior seminar. Good luck to us both today!"

"Thank you. I just wish I knew when we would find out."

"They're supposed to be calling the successful candidates right around noon and then they'll call everybody else during the afternoon," Batya replied. "I guess that gives the successful candidates a chance to turn them down so that they can offer the spot to the next person on the list."

"How do you know all that?" Rachel demanded. "I've been wondering for days!"

"Abba called and talked to the chair of the committee," Batya replied.

"I would have been afraid they would reject me if I did something like that."

"Abba's afraid of nothing. I was driving him crazy wondering."

"Well, thank you, Batya," Rachel said. "I guess that means we can relax for our morning classes at least."

"Do you want to meet at the end of the day to compare notes?" Batya asked.

Rachel hesitated. "No, I might be too nervous to see you. Give me your number and we can text, though."

"Too bad this is Sixth Day, or we could meet up in our Metals class," Batya commented, referring to their class on Copper, Bronze, and Iron Ages that they all nicknamed Metals. "We could just nod yes or no and not have to say anything."

"Good luck!" said Rachel, as Batya returned to her own lab table. *It's funny that we've been in all these classes together but have never really talked before.*

The class dragged on forever, and the next class, which was Prehistoric Cultures, usually her favorite, seemed to do the same. Finally, it was noon. Rachel's custom was to meet Leah, Samuel, Deborah, and Sarah for lunch, but she just did not feel up to it this day. She sat on a bench under a tree in the central square of the campus and tried to meditate in order to relax. After half an hour, her phone buzzed with a text from Leah: "We're all wondering where you are."

"Not feeling like being with anybody today," she texted back.

"Oh, come on, you should be with people who love you!" came back at her.

She closed out her messages and sat for another few minutes, trying to get up the energy to go meet her friends. Finally, with a deep sigh, she pushed herself off the bench and trudged very slowly toward the cafeteria in the student union building, where they usually met. As she was turning the final corner, her phone rang. She stopped dead in her tracks. For a second, she could not catch her breath, but stared at it and tried not to faint. It rang again and she gradually realized that she was going to have to answer it.

"This is Persephone at the University of Athens," she heard. "Am I speaking to Rachel bat Shimson?"

"This is she," Rachel gasped out between frozen lips. She fumbled with her frock until her hand found her necklace lying moistly against her skin.

"We have selected you for our waiting list for the senior seminar in Mycenae this spring. Your position on that list is #2. What that means is, if one of our successful candidates turns down our offer for any reason, you will be the second person on the waiting list to join us in Mycenae this spring. Those chosen for the twelve spots have until 17:00 Ankara time to accept or reject their nomination, so you will be contacted again no later than 20:00 Ankara time should we be in a position to offer you that spot. A letter will follow confirming this conversation. I hope that you realize that this is truly a great honor. More than 800 applicants from all over Anatolia applied for the spots, and you are in the top twenty. Do you have any questions?"

During the course of this conversation, phone jammed hard against her ear, eyes closed, Rachel found herself sinking to her knees on the wet grass. She tried to control her breathing and her voice. Finally, she was able to rasp out, "N-n-no! Thank you for letting me know."

Persephone continued, "All of my contact information will be in the letter, should you have any questions in the future. Please recognize how highly the committee regards your application."

Without saying anything further, Rachel terminated the call. Then she called her parents, grateful for once to get voicemail. She left a very brief message for them, just laying out the bald facts and telling them that they could talk more when she got home. She pressed the phone to her heart before slipping it back into her backpack. She rested her elbows on her knees and dropped her head into her hands, taking deeper breaths, trying not to cry. For the first time, she admitted to herself how certain she had been of her acceptance. *I just can't face my friends now. Maybe I should get Leah alone.* She texted her sister – "Meet me outside the Student Union! Don't say anything to anybody else!" Then she turned the final corner and walked up the sidewalk to the building, passing the entrance. She looked into the window where the dining hall was and spotted her sister, who was just standing up. Leah caught sight of her standing outside and widened her eyes, obviously realizing what must have happened.

Rachel moved away from the window and pressed her back against the wall of the building. She stared straight ahead without seeing anything. Then she turned her head slightly as she heard steps running toward her.

Leah swung around the corner without slowing down and read her face instantly. She ran right up and embraced her sister. Rachel pulled back slightly and met Leah's eyes with a stricken look, but by silent agreement, they continued to hold one another wordlessly for another few moments.

Rachel cleared her throat and choked out, "Ever since I can remember! It's all I've ever wanted to do!"

Leah heard the crunching of branches. She looked over at the corner of the building and saw Samuel and Deborah just emerging. She shook her head to warn them away. Then she stroked the back of Rachel's head lovingly until the worst of the sobbing had ended.

Rachel pulled back from her sister and looked at her with bloodshot coffee-colored eyes. She inhaled slowly, her breath hitching several times, and then tried to smile. "I guess that sounds melodramatic, but it's how I feel right now. I had a career path all mapped out, and the senior seminar was going to launch it. I don't know what to do instead."

"Were they kind at least?"

"Oh, yes. It was a woman named Persephone at the University of Athens, the host institution. She tried to make it sound good. There were 800 applicants and they selected twelve, and then they set up a waiting list in case any of the people they chose couldn't participate for some reason. I was #2 on the waiting list. That's supposed to be a good thing – in the top fourteen out of 800 people."

"Not a good enough thing, though, is it?" Leah murmured, reaching out and squeezing Rachel's hand.

"What did they all say at lunch when you left?"

"Well, I didn't officially know anything at that time, so I just said I saw you outside and was going to talk to you." Leah deliberately failed to add that the others had clearly caught on, since Samuel and Deborah had come out seeking Rachel as well.

"Leah, I'm not an idiot. I'm not going to sit around waiting for them to call me off the waiting list for one of the spots. This is really it."

Leah bit her lip. So many thoughts went through her head, but she forced herself to suppress them all, or at least not speak them aloud. Time for that later. She asked only, "What about Ima and Abba? Do you want me to run interference for you?"

Another shaky intake of breath. "No, I already called them. I didn't want to come home and find a congratulatory banner strung across the whole living room."

"You still have another class this afternoon, don't you?"

"Yes, and Batya is in it." Long gaze into Leah's eyes. "I'm afraid to face her."

"Should we just go home?"

"No, I'll go to class." Rachel pulled out her phone and looked at the time. "There's fifteen minutes until it begins. I'll meet you afterwards."

"You'll be okay?" At Rachel's nod, Leah gave her another hug and said, "Okay, I'll meet you at the car after class. Text me if you just can't stand it, and I'll take you home earlier. I'm done for the day."

Rachel trudged across the courtyard in the middle of the university complex for a while, then sank down onto a bench under a sheltering tree. Its branches swayed very slowly above her head. She could feel the breeze ruffling her hair. The bench was just slightly damp, but at least it wasn't raining that afternoon.

Eyes closed, focusing on breathing slowly, suspended in timeless space, she instinctively stroked her necklace where it lay under her frock.

She started slightly when her phone buzzed with Samuel's ringtone. She wiggled a little to come back to the world as she looked down at the screen. "Coffee after class?" it read.

She considered briefly. "Maybe not today. But I promise we'll talk tonight." She squared her shoulders, resolving to go to class and face her fellow archaeology students no matter what. Slipping the phone back into her backpack, she headed off to class. What if Batya had made it while she had not? She had to know, but at the same time, she dreaded sharing her own information.

As she settled into her seat, Batya came in, incandescent. No need for subtlety here! Batya virtually danced over to Rachel's seat, exclaiming, "I made it! How about you?"

An exceptionally long pause, while Rachel cast about for the right words. "I got waitlisted."

Batya widened her eyes. "But you and I are the top students in the program! How could I have made it and not you?"

Rachel was spared from answering because the instructor rushed into the classroom just then, taking his place at the front of the room. Batya squeezed Rachel's shoulder sympathetically and then walked over to her own seat.

Class seemed to drag. It took even longer than the previous two, before that fatal phone call. Rachel somehow kept her focus on the lesson, but whenever she investigated her emotional state, she was dismayed to notice that it was fluctuating between heartbreak and anxiety.

Rachel packed up while the instructor was delivering his final words and escaped from the classroom before anybody else could approach her. She had no strength for making small talk right now, and certainly no desire to answer questions from anybody who might be aware that today was decision day. As she made a beeline for the parking lot, she saw Samuel waiting for her beside a tree.

"I just had to see you," he said. "Waiting until later on to talk isn't enough for me. But you don't have to say anything you don't feel up to."

"You are so good to me. I really appreciate you just being here. You and Leah both."

"That's what it means for people to care about each other," he said. "You must be wondering how this could have happened. I know that your grades were top-notch, and I am absolutely confident that you submitted a really strong application. Your references had to be great. And you read me your essay, and I thought it was super."

She touched her head wryly. "This poor head is spinning too much to think those things through! I do want to talk to you, but I can't just now. I have to start processing all this first."

He nodded. "Of course. Whenever you're ready. You know we're all here for you. Even Adon Yehuda might be a good person to talk to."

Rachel put her right hand over her eyes. "I feel like such a failure in front of him. Like I let him down. My best wasn't good enough. I don't know if I'll be able to talk to him."

"Not now." Samuel nodded understandingly. Then he glanced over at the path and said, "Oh, there's Leah. Go home and take a nice hot bubble bath and then go right to bed. Call me only if you're up for it, but I'll understand if you can't this soon."

She met his eyes. "I hope that means you understand if I just can't come to your house for Shabbat tonight and be surrounded by all those people."

"Of course. I'll be thinking about you and sending you strength."

Rachel smiled at him tremulously and turned to go meet Leah in the parking lot.

When the twins arrived home, Rachel lagged behind Leah, walking very slowly up the sidewalk, eyes on the ground. Her mother burst out of the house and ran down the stairs. She wrapped her arms around Rachel and held her very tightly. "No need to say anything," she whispered into Rachel's ear, smoothing a wayward curl aside. "Just come in and have some dinner."

With her mother's arm around her, Rachel walked into the house. Her father and brother were talking with Leah in the living room but fell silent as she approached. She closed her eyes as her father gathered her into his own arms. "Rachel, I know it's hard to see right now, but Ima and I are really proud of you. Your application was better than almost everybody else's."

Rachel sneered. "'Almost' didn't quite cut it here, Abba." She slammed her backpack onto the floor and then burst out with, "I was so sure of myself! I was really counting on this! Now my world has all fallen apart and I don't know how to put it back together." She stamped her foot and then rushed out of the room.

Leah followed her into their bedroom. Rachel lifted an embarrassed face to her. "I can't believe I did that. Ima and Abba were being so loving, and I'm such a brat."

"Home is the place where it's safe to act out," Leah said, practical as always. "Let's just have a quiet family dinner and you can talk about whatever you feel ready for."

Rachel nodded and followed Leah to the dining room. Jesse, already seated at the table, piped up, "Now you can go to Jerusalem!"

Rachel looked stricken. Gveret Dina glared at him. "Hush! This isn't the time for that." Then, as Rachel made a move to get up and leave the table, she shook her head. "Sit down, sweetie. Have a meal with the family. I made all of your favorite things."

I'm surrounded by people who love me. That's a big thing. Rachel nodded and picked up her fork.

After dinner, the twins went outside and sat on the front porch, not talking. Rachel's phone buzzed with Samuel's ringtone, and she read his text quickly. "If you're not going to bed and you're up for it, I'd rather come over and be with you than just talk on the phone."

Rachel looked up and found Leah watching her. "Samuel might be a comfort to you," she said. "But only if you feel up to it."

Rachel nodded and texted back to Samuel, "Come on over, but don't be prepared for very much fun."

"I only have an hour," came the return text. "I have to help Abba with Shabbat after that. But I really want to see you."

"Do you want me to stay?" Leah asked.

"No, I think I'm ready to face Samuel alone. You're the best sister there is!"

"Just text me if you need me." And with that, Leah went back into the house.

Samuel's car pulled up shortly, and he was soon sitting beside her on the porch. His warm hazel eyes looked into hers. "How are you doing now?"

"Not much better. It's all tumbled down around me. But I still have some kind of future ahead of me and I'll figure something out. Just not yet."

Samuel smiled at her gently. "I have confidence in you. You are stronger than you think."

"Do you know what Jesse said? He told me that I can go to Jerusalem now! Not very supportive, was it?"

Samuel turned his head away, but not so fast that she failed to see a flash of joy in his eyes. "That's not something you have to think about now. But of course, the offer still stands if that's what you decide."

"Not tonight."

"No," he agreed.

"Tonight I think about what I'll do and where I'll go if I'm not going to work in Greece."

He shrugged, not unkindly. "You could still work in Greece, of course. Or anywhere else in this world. There are ruins everywhere. Something else you don't have to decide tonight."

Rachel opened her eyes wide in wonder. "You're so right! I keep thinking this is the end of the world. But not going to senior seminar, maybe not even getting into whatever graduate school program I think is the best — there's still possibilities for me!"

Samuel smiled at her tenderly. "Yes, you can reconstruct your life in whatever direction it takes you. There was never only one path. And I'll be there to talk it all through."

They were silent for a few more minutes, and then Rachel said, "You know, I really would enjoy being in Jerusalem with you and your parents. I'm not up for it now, but it's a long way off. I'd get to know them better and spend time with you away from home. And of course, Leah really wants to go and wouldn't go without me."

"You've never been apart before, have you?" His hazel eyes were very perceptive.

"Not even for a single night. I was a little anxious about that with the senior seminar, in fact. If I had gotten to go, Leah would be in one place and

I would be in another, and –" looking at him beseechingly – "I'm not sure I could even do that." Rachel's hand slid toward her chest.

Samuel noticed and said, "That necklace is really an amulet for you, isn't it?"

"I'm not sure I would think of it like that. It was my grandmother's, you know. It makes me feel – safe? Loved? Not alone? You know, like everything is going to be okay."

"And it will," Samuel nodded, eyes warmly intent on hers. "You will find some path forward and then you will live with it. No looking back, no regrets. I know you, Rachel!"

They chatted for a few more minutes, deliberately keeping it light and inconsequential. Then Samuel glanced at his phone and said, "I better get going. Abba will be waiting for me."

"Thank you again for being who you are! I promise I'll stay as calm as possible and we will work this all out," she said. She could hear the tremor in her voice.

He smiled and nodded, then stood up and headed down the stairs, turning to wave at her before getting into his car. She also stood up and went back inside. Her family was sitting in the living room, sipping cups of juice. Gveret Dina rose quickly. "I'll get you one, if you like."

"How was Samuel?" asked Adon Shimson.

"So good, so caring. No grilling. You've all been wonderful."

"I wonder who the people were who they accepted. Do you happen to know any of the others?" asked her father.

"No, I haven't seen the list, but I know that Batya from my class got in."

Jesse looked up quickly from his phone. "Batya bat Reuven?" he asked.

"Maybe," said Rachel. "How in the world would you know her whole name when I don't?"

"Because her sister Noa bat Reuven is in my class. She is always bragging about how her sister Batya is the smartest person in the world, #1 student in the archaeology major, and sure to win a spot in some exclusive program over everybody else in Anatolia." He took another sip of juice. Then he met his father's cautioning eyes and realized that he had once again said exactly the wrong thing.

"And what do you say to her about Rachel?" Leah wondered.

"Nothing!" he said, smugly. "I'm not going to sound as ugly as she does!"

"Batya might be nicer than Noa," Rachel observed. "She brags a bit, but she's mostly been nice to me. She was definitely sympathetic this afternoon."

Their mother came back with Rachel's juice. "We still have enough time for a piece of pie before it's Shabbat. I'm assuming you'd be happier if we just stay home tonight."

"Yes, Ima," Rachel said gratefully.

"I hope it's blueberry!" Jesse said, grinning as their mother once again left the room.

Chapter 9

Another Shabbat at the beach. Rachel sat under a large umbrella with Leah, Deborah, Judith, and Sarah, chatting casually. They had rinsed off their sandals in the Hospitable Sea because the previous night's rain had turned the path from their neighborhood to the beach muddy. Through half-closed eyes, Rachel watched children playing in the water, shouting to one another. She was feeling grateful that her friends had closed a loving circle around her, giving her space when she needed it initially, and now granting her a day filled with companionship, a day as normal as they could make it.

"Nothing says you can't still work in Greece," Deborah said to her.

Rachel nodded. "That's what Samuel said last night, too. In Greece or anywhere else I find a decent job. But think of all that I would have learned from this seminar. Not to mention what a great credential it would be when I did apply to graduate school or for a job."

Leah pulled a brownie out of a bag and took a bite. She glanced over at her sister but said nothing. Rachel, feeling her gaze, turned and looked at her. "You're right — you all are. This isn't the end of the world. Samuel already made me realize that last night. But while I'm still picking up the pieces and rewriting my life plan entirely, it really feels like it."

Deborah shrugged. "At least you know what you want to do with your life. I haven't figured that out yet for myself. But you're going to work as an archaeologist, somewhere or another."

Judith added, "Yes, I don't even know Rachel as well as the rest of you, but I already know that nothing can ever stop her from being an archaeologist!"

Rachel stretched out on the reclining chair, looking up at the bright blue beach umbrella above their heads. Her mind drifted away from her friends' conversation and back into the whirlpool of her own thoughts. She surely did have to reconstruct her life. But not yet today. Lying there with her eyes closed, she was unaware that Deborah was rolling her eyes at Leah.

The next day, the twins and their best friends were in the Student Union between classes. As they were leaving, Deborah mused, "I wonder where Rosh Chodesh is going to be this month."

"Is it time for Rosh Chodesh again already?" asked Leah, looking at her phone.

"Yes, it starts at sundown tomorrow. Ninth Month already."

Sarah looked over at the bulletin board. "The signup sheet must already be posted over there. Let's go see. I don't want to miss it two months in a row."

They sauntered over to the bulletin board and found the list. "Oh, it's at Batya bat Reuven's house," Sarah said.

Leah poked Rachel in the ribs. "Your favorite person!"

"I hardly know her," Rachel protested. "It would be good to get to know her in a more everyday setting, not just in class. And she's really been sympathetic to me. She could be putting on all sorts of airs that she got in and I didn't, but she doesn't brag as much as I assumed."

"Shall I sign everybody up?" asked Sarah.

There was a general agreement, and Sarah signed them all up for the Rosh Chodesh observance.

The next evening, they all met at the park behind the university and drove over in Sarah's car. They felt more comfortable arriving as a group when they did not know the person whose house it was at. Batya greeted them at the door, wearing a bright pink silk dress with a matching ribbon in her hair. She was wearing more makeup than was commonly the case among their circle of friends, which enhanced her blue eyes dramatically. A bit more stunningly, her light brown hair was down, curling softly around her face and shoulders, not pulled back in a braid as girls and young women typically wore it out in public. Leah's eyes widened. "She's so pretty!" she whispered to Rachel.

"And even you wouldn't wear a dress that bright!" Rachel whispered back. "It makes her look like a princess."

59

They entered the living room, nodding at people they knew and introducing themselves to those they had not yet met. A younger girl walked into the room, and Batya said to the group in general, "This is my sister, Noa. She'd like to join us tonight." With a sideways glance at Noa, she added, "Even though she's still only in high school and not used to hanging out with adults!"

Noa grimaced and shoved her sister a little, muttering something under her breath that Rachel couldn't hear.

"Of course!" called out a young woman who had introduced herself as Batya's first cousin. "She's a woman herself, after all, even if you feel the need to tease her!"

Noa blushed and joined the others. Rachel glanced around the room before they started, noticing that the house was bigger and more elegantly furnished than her own. The group went through a brief ceremony, involving readings and singing and a few minutes of silent meditation. Then Batya's mother came into the room bearing a platter of pastries, and people got up and started toward the table, talking.

A little time had passed when Rachel overheard Batya saying to two other girls, "Oh, no, he's no challenge! I can get any guy I want!"

"Like you have some kind of magical power over all the boys," was the scoffing answer.

Batya preened. "Name me any boy in our university and I will get him to take me to Solstice Ball!"

Somebody threw out, "Judah! The president of our class!"

Batya stood up, jutted out her hip, thrust forward her chest. "Consider it done."

Rachel made a disgusted face and then caught Leah's eye. She had had enough of this. "Are you ready to go home now?" she asked.

"Sure, let's find the others."

Rachel and Leah quickly rounded up Deborah and Sarah. They expressed their thanks and made their farewells and were soon back out in the night. "So she's the smartest person in Anatolia and also the most desirable?" asked Deborah.

"I think we've seen all we need to know about Batya ben Reuben!" Sarah laughed.

Rachel shivered. "Let's just put it behind us and go home. I'm really glad we got to Rosh Chodesh anyway. I love being in a group of just young women doing things that women have done for hundreds or maybe even thousands of years."

Deborah threw back her head and laughed. "Next you'll be reminding us about the days when everybody was Eleusinian and the goddesses ruled the earth!"

Still laughing, the foursome got into the car and headed home.

Chapter 10

Early in the morning on Fourth Day, Rachel sat up suddenly in her bed. She looked around the room, a bit disoriented, unable to capture the dream that had been so clear just moments before. Somehow, though, a feeling of serenity lingered with her, and she hugged herself. *That has to be a good sign. Whatever it was, it brought me a sense of peacefulness. I think I'm beginning to heal.* As she started doing some morning stretches, her phone rang. Leah, who was sitting at her desk, glanced at her over her shoulder. "Wonder who THAT is?" she said, voice husky from disuse, then cleared her throat.

Rachel, turning her hands palms up, answered her phone. "Hello, this is Adon Yehuda," she heard. "I wanted to let you know that we have a guest scholar from Judea coming to the department. Because it is a woman and she has made a dramatic discovery at a site that's been excavated for years, I thought of you. She's speaking mainly to faculty and graduate-level students, but I believe this would be perfect for you to attend. And I do hope you will! You would be such an asset to the group, and you would benefit immeasurably from the experience."

"Thank you for thinking of me, Adon Yehuda." The serenity left behind by the dream permitted her to see other opportunities in her life, doors that might keep opening for her if she was mindful of them. A wave of gratitude for his call and this realization washed over her.

There was a long silence. Then his gentle voice came over the line again. "I really hope you'll take advantage of this. There are so many opportunities out there for a student as gifted as you."

His warm words enfolded her like a loving parent holding her in his arms. She brushed away a tear with the back of her hand. With a tremor in her voice, she asked, "When will it be?"

"She'll be here the evening of Third Day, all day on Fourth Day, and then at a dinner we'll have in her honor that evening. It's broken up into one- or two-hour segments, so you might be able to attend a number of them even during the day, between classes. If you're interested, I will send you the schedule."

Rachel lay back down on her pillow and stared at the ceiling. "Yes, I'm interested. Please send me the schedule. And thank you so much for thinking of me. I do feel honored."

As soon as Rachel had said her goodbyes and ended the call, Leah swiveled her head in her direction, followed by her entire chair. Rachel looked at her sister. "There's a scholar coming here in a few days for a special program. A successful archaeologist from Judea. It's mainly for faculty and graduate students, but he thought of me and invited me to join them."

"And it sounds like you will, right?"

Rachel tried to smile, hearing both optimism and timidity in her sister's voice. "Yes, I will! I have to build a future. Not the one I thought it might be, but that wasn't the only option."

"Baby steps," Leah whispered into her hand, but Rachel heard her.

"I guess I've been a brat. It's not like the whole world even fell apart, or even my life."

In a very small voice, Leah said, "I was actually afraid you might turn down the senior seminar, and only because of me. Even though I really want to go to Jerusalem with you!" She picked up the end of her braid and slipped it into her mouth. "I didn't feel right bringing this up before, but you're — well, you're a bit too dependent on me sometimes."

"You don't have to sugarcoat it. I had all sorts of nightmares about being away from you. But that's ridiculous. It's going to happen sooner or later. Sooner, in fact, since we're about to graduate."

"I wouldn't have wanted to be the reason you didn't go."

Rachel sat up in her bed again, cleared her throat, and then met her sister's dark eyes openly. "I've spent a lot of time searching my soul since this all came up. I really think that I could have gone, and I would have done okay, if I had been selected. And carrying your love and belief in me is a lot of what helped me get there."

"I'm glad to hear that, because I was worried! You did this once before!" Leah cried out, pointing a long finger at her sister. "You did it when we were fifteen! There was that trip to Hattousa that our class took. You were fascinated by it – Hattians, Hittites – all the documents and statues and pottery shards that have been found there! A legal code that predates ours and which we can trace to ours! But I had no interest in going. Sarah and I had just had that big fight when we ended up not talking to each other for almost a year, so I was also pretty grumpy then. And you decided not to go only because I was not going!"

Rachel looked down and smoothed the edge of her nightgown over her knee. "That's the biggest regret of my whole life."

"And let it remain that way! Please, no new biggest regret! You're good enough for anything you want to do, and you're strong enough to do it all – even be away from me." A giggle, then, in a lighter tone, she added, "I'd be just fine if I were going to be apart from you!"

Another weak grin. "Nobody can pull me out of my own navel like you can! And you know, ultimately, I probably won't be working in Greece. Maybe I'll actually have my career in Judea."

"I was wrong. I won't be just fine away from you. I don't want to think of you being in a whole different country from me."

Rachel lifted up her head. Tears still glistened in her coffee-colored eyes as she met her sister's amber eyes. "If it did come to that, I think I'd be okay. Talking to everybody, especially Ima and Adon Yehuda, has made me trust in that. And like I said, your love and support."

"YOU would be okay, but what about me?"

Rachel pulled on her braid. "We're both going to start our careers and we wouldn't live in the same place anyway. And of course we can talk and visit all we want once we're making money."

Leah ran over and pulled her sister up out of her bed by both her hands. Then she hugged her. "Of course, forever! We're twins, after all! But now we need to get ready to go to class."

"One more thing." Rachel's voice was low and her mouth was set resolutely. No point in holding off any longer.

"What?"

Rachel tried to suppress a grin as she made her announcement. "I've decided to go to Jerusalem with you. And with Samuel and his parents."

Leah's whoop of glee made it all seem worthwhile.

Chapter 11

Rachel and Samuel were sitting on the front porch of her house. The sun was getting low in the sky and there were long shadows of trees falling on them. "Yes, it was just wonderful!" Rachel gushed. "And such an honor to be the only undergraduate student there. I'm going to buy the book she wrote about her huge discovery in the Galilee."

Samuel leaned back a little and grinned at her enthusiasm. "I love seeing you so excited! And I hope you realize what a tribute to you it is that Adon Yehuda included you in the group. Everybody else who was there is already a professional – that says a lot about his opinion of you."

"And I got a dinner out of it!" They both laughed. She was thrilled to see the deep admiration in Samuel's eyes.

"Well, after all this high living with fancy people in your field, I'm honored that you'll still associate with me," he teased her.

Rachel's face softened as she met his eyes. "Always. In fact, I made it a point to be taken home before everybody else had even left, just because I knew you were coming over."

Samuel crossed his right ankle over his left knee. He cleared his throat and scratched above his left ear. Rachel watched his clear quandary but waited for him to speak. Finally, he asked her, "So did you learning with this scholar affect your thoughts about your future?"

Now it was her turn for discomfort. She did a quick intake of breath before answering, "Yes, I'm leaning more and more toward Judea."

"I suspected that." Pause. "First Greece, and then Judea. You're coming to all these decisions. And I have no say in it?"

"It's my decision about my own career, Samuel."

"It seems to me that, when people are in a relationship, any life-changing decision one of them might make would affect them both. I'm probably in

Trabzon for the rest of my life. You were going to live in Greece and now you might be living in Judea. Seems like we aren't going to be able to stay together either way. And my thoughts weren't worth considering?"

Rachel rubbed her eyes and then touched her necklace where it lay under the thin linen of her light blue dress. "I'm thinking about my future, Samuel. That's what people do during their senior year."

"YOUR future. Not OUR future." His hazel eyes turned stormy.

They both looked up at the sound of a door slamming across the street. Rachel felt relieved by the reprieve. They watched as Joseph came out of his house, sauntered toward them, and mumbled a greeting as he walked past them to knock on the front door. Rachel's eyebrows went up as she looked at Samuel. Leah opened the front door and greeted Joseph in a relaxed tone, as if this were not an unusual occurrence. The two disappeared inside the house.

"How long has Leah been hanging out with Joseph?" asked Samuel.

"This is the first time I've actually noticed them together," Rachel confessed. "She did seem comfortable with him when we were at Sunset Hills, but I didn't know they were seeing each other back here at home." There was a long pause while Rachel stared at her feet, uncertain what to say or do to break the suddenly uncomfortable atmosphere.

"I used to think your passion was part of your charm," Samuel said. Rachel didn't answer, so he continued, "With all you've been going through these past few weeks, it's a wonder you even notice me when I'm right in front of you."

Rachel was framing an answer when a car drove up and stopped in front of her house.

"Your house seems to be the center of all the activity in Trabzon tonight," Samuel commented.

The passenger door opened and a teenaged girl stepped out. "Oh, that's Noa bat Reuven," Rachel said, recognizing her from Rosh Chodesh. "I wonder what she's doing here?"

They watched as the girl walked up the sidewalk and ran lightly up the stairs. She stopped on the porch as she reached Rachel and Samuel, looking at them uncertainly. "Is this where Jesse ben Shimson lives?" she asked. "We're supposed to work on a project together for school."

"Yes, he's my brother," Rachel said. "He should be inside."

"He's your brother? Has he ever mentioned me?"

Rachel was saved from having to tell Noa exactly what Jesse had said about her the one time she did hear him mention her by the door opening, and Jesse himself stood there. "Come in, Noa," he said, not looking at Rachel or Samuel, and they both went into the house.

Meanwhile, the sound of the idling engine of the car that had dropped off Noa cut off abruptly. The door opened and out stepped Batya, her yellow silk dress shimmering in the sunlight, looking very overdressed for running an errand. "Why, hello, Rachel!" she simpered. "I'm so glad to run into you."

Rachel suppressed her quick retort and said instead, "Come on up and sit down with us for a few minutes. We were just talking about going to the Temple for Pesach."

"Oh, are you? I'll be there, too. My family hasn't missed a single festival at the Temple in years and years."

Rachel looked over at Samuel to share a sardonic reaction with him, only to see him staring at Batya. Oh, yes, she was pretty indeed. Rachel was beginning to feel invisible, a sensation she didn't especially cherish, especially where Samuel was concerned. And who knew what might be going on in his mind, given the tense feeling between them. She cleared her throat and said, "Batya bat Reuven, this is Samuel ben Jonathan HaKohen."

"Oooh, a Kohen, really?" asked Batya, batting her eyes at him as he continued to stare at her in fascination.

Samuel cleared his throat. "I don't remember seeing you around the university."

She smiled, dimples appearing in her cheeks. "That's because I have a part-time job in the bookstore. My parents think it's important to learn the meaning of responsibility from an early age."

"I couldn't agree more!" Samuel said, fervently.

Rachel was now entirely invisible. She put her hands behind her back and surreptitiously pinched her right arm to make sure she was still there. She had to reclaim some attention. She cast about frantically for something to say, then fell back into a hostessing role. "Why don't you sit down, Batya?" she said, pointing to the bench on the other side of the front door. "Would you like some lemonade? I was just about to get some for Samuel and me."

"That would be lovely. Thank you," said Batya, sitting down, silk slithering across her legs as she did so. She crossed her ankles demurely, calling Samuel's attention to them.

Rachel was reluctant to leave this scene and go into the house, but now she had no choice. She mentally kicked herself for leaving Samuel alone with Batya, but it was difficult for her to sit there with him and pretend in front of Batya that everything between them was okay. She walked through the living room, where Jesse and Noa had books and laptops spread around them on the two sofas, and into the kitchen, where she found Leah and Joseph talking to each other in soft tones. Their conversation cut off abruptly as they became aware of Rachel's presence. She smiled at them tentatively and said, "Just getting some lemonade."

Leah's attention sharpened as she watched Rachel take down three cups. "Who else is here?" she asked.

"Batya ben Reuven," Rachel answered. Leah rolled her eyes, and Rachel continued, "She was dropping Noa off to study with Jesse and then HAD to come out and talk to us once she noticed Samuel on the porch with me."

"Oh, good luck!" Leah said sympathetically. "She really is a boy magnet."

Rachel swallowed. "And Samuel and I have been going through some … stuff. The timing is terrible. He's upset with me because I'm figuring out all by myself where I want to have my career. I'm supposed to be consulting him or something."

Leah looked at her sister with more steel than usual in her eyes. "Don't make me take sides on this one, Rachel. You won't like what you hear."

Rachel did a doubletake and stared at her sister intently. Then she sent a look of helpless entreaty at Joseph. He caught the hint and raised his eyebrows. "Hmmm, let me come back out with you and you can introduce me. Check out those magic powers and all."

Leah glared at him, but Rachel said, "You could help me with this, actually. I'm not sure I can carry three cups of lemonade and open the door."

69

Joseph took a cup from her as she filled it and walked back to the front door with her, opening it to let her go out first. "Hi, Samuel," he said. "And you must be Batya bat Reuven! Nice to meet you. I'm Joseph ben Asher. I live across the street. I've been dating Leah."

Rachel was stunned. She had just become aware that Leah and Joseph were spending time together and now was learning that they were dating. *Too wrapped up in my own head*, she chided herself.

Batya accepted a cup of lemonade from Joseph, while Rachel gave the second cup she was carrying to Samuel. "It's lovely to meet you, Joseph," she said, turning the full charm of her smile on him. "I'll probably see more of you, since Rachel and I are becoming such friends."

Once again, Rachel tried to make eye contact with Samuel to show her amused reaction to this assertion, but he was looking down at his cup. The charged energy coming out of him made it clear that he was not the least bit mollified.

Joseph smiled and nodded. "It's nice that you dropped by. I'm sure that Rachel and Samuel are glad to have the company." He put a hand on Rachel's shoulder before he turned to go back into the house.

Batya pulled out her phone as he left and said, "Oh, my goodness, I need to get to work!"

"Are you coming back to pick up Noa?" asked Rachel.

"This is only supposed to be a four-hour shift, so yes, I was planning on it."

"If she and Jesse are done with their project early, we can drive her home so you don't have to come back here."

"Oh, it's no trouble at all," said Batya, looking at Samuel from beneath her eyelashes. With a pretty little wave, she turned and glided back to her car. Samuel exhaled and then looked up at Rachel.

"This is the person who's so competitive with you in school?" he asked. "She's just lovely! Probably just that she's ambitious. You want to be the best, too!"

Rachel's head was spinning. She shuddered to see that there was no warmth in his eyes. Was Samuel entirely aware of what had just happened? Could he not understand how she must feel about having to compete with

Batya? Better not call negative attention to herself, if he was inclined to compare them, especially while he was in this inexplicable mood. So she shrugged and said lightly, "She showed us her good side today. She can be nice."

"You know, I should go, too," he said. "I have to finish that paper that I've been putting off."

"Okay, Samuel," she said. She stood up, shaking out her dress so it would hang straight. He stood up as well and she walked him down to his car. "I'll see you tomorrow."

"Great," he replied. "Tell Leah goodbye."

She watched him drive away, feeling a bit troubled, rerunning the conversation in her mind for a few minutes. Where did it get derailed? And then how much worse were things after Batya arrived? She went into the house, where she found Leah and Joseph still in the kitchen. Once again, all conversation ceased as she walked in. Was she going to be the one left out this entire day? "So what did you think of the famous Batya?" she asked Joseph, putting the cups in the sink.

He looked over at her and shrugged. "She's very pretty, but not really my type. I like friendly girls more than flirtatious girls." He smiled at Leah.

"Let's hope Samuel feels the same way," Rachel muttered under her breath.

"Oh, Rachel, you're not worried about Samuel, are you? You've been together forever! He's just really nice to everybody." Leah frowned a bit at her sister. "Everybody who's nice to *him*, of course."

"I hope 'nice' is all that was going on," Rachel said, "but he definitely couldn't take his eyes off her."

"You can admire a work of art without it meaning anything," Leah said.

Rachel became aware that she was interfering with their budding relationship and withdrew from the room, saying, "You're probably right. It's wonderful to see you again, Joseph."

Almost an hour later, Leah joined Rachel in their room, where Rachel had been alternately sulking and cursing all men. "Are you really worried about Samuel?"

"I shouldn't be. But there's nothing that says we have to be together forever, and for all I know, I'm just a habit to him."

"He doesn't act that way."

Rachel flushed and looked away miserably. "I didn't really help things much, either. He's really upset with me over my thinking of working in Judea. What's wrong with being ambitious, with having dreams?"

Leah said, slowly, "Nothing would be wrong with them if you lived all alone in a cave."

Rachel couldn't stand the thought of fighting with her sister on top of everything else, so she changed the subject. "So how long have you been seeing Joseph?"

"Oh, just since we got back from Sunset Hills. That's when we really noticed each other. I didn't want to bother you with it because you were so wrapped up in your decisions."

Rachel got up off her bed and took Leah's hands impulsively. "You mean my drama! I don't want to be that way. And I don't want you tiptoeing around me any more. You and Samuel have both made me realize that sometimes I can be self-absorbed to the point of being indifferent to the people I care about most. I care about what is going on in your life and what matters to you!"

"You say that," replied Leah. "And you probably really believe that. I've always told myself that you're just a lot more intense than I am and I should understand. And gosh, when I think of all you've been going through! But, Rachel -"

"You're a better friend than I am! I want to try to be more like you, more attentive to what is going on with the people around me."

"It's never too late to change. Being aware of how people are you are feeling is a good first step." Then, smiling impishly, Leah added, "Maybe you want to take flirting lessons from Batya?"

Rachel's answering smile faded quickly. "She does have it all," she said. "She's so bright – don't forget, she got accepted to senior seminar, too. And yes, she DOES lead our class some trimesters – it hasn't always been me. And she's prettier than anybody else I know and she really does know how to get noticed. And – I have to admit it – she's nice, too. I feel like a big clod next to her." She sank back down on her bed and confessed, in a lower tone, "Leah, I'm really terrified that Samuel is – noticing her."

Leah sat down next to her sister. "I'm sure you have nothing to worry about. He's just friendly. And just maybe trying to get back at you a little for how you're making him feel."

"You didn't see the kind of 'friendly' he was being," said Rachel, who had focused only on the first part of Leah's words. "He couldn't take his eyes off her. I don't even know how to compete with her, even to dress like her!"

Leah glanced at the simple cotton dress that Rachel had changed into after getting home from school. "Yes, you are a real loser, not wearing fancy silk dresses to run around the neighborhood!"

Rachel punched Leah lightly in the ribs and they both started giggling. Jesse appeared in their doorway, smiling. "What's going on in here?"

"Are we interrupting your study session with Noa?" asked Leah.

"No, in fact we're done. We were wondering if one of you could drive her back home, since Batya won't get off work for another few hours to pick her up."

"Of course," said Rachel, picking up her keys from her dresser. "So how are you getting along with her? Is she still being a nuisance?"

"She's actually pretty nice," he said. "She is just a little insecure and puts on an attitude to keep people away from her. I'm glad we're working on this project together, because I'm getting to know her and I'm seeing her differently now. Not like my first impression."

Rachel raised her eyebrows at Leah. Jesse had never really dated, let alone had a girlfriend, and they made a quick silent pact not to tease him in what might be the fragile beginnings of a new relationship. *But why couldn't it be somebody else, anybody other than Batya's sister?* "Let's go," was all she said, and she walked behind him to the living room to get Noa.

73

Chapter 12

Adon Shimson shepherded his family down the sidewalk toward the house of Samuel's family. "A lot of people here this evening," he commented.

Gveret Dina agreed. "We had to park way down the block." It seemed like a bigger crowd than usual was gathering for Adon Jonathan to lead them in Shabbat services.

They trooped down the flagstone path around the house and into the back yard. In single file, they crossed over the brook on the little wooden bridge that Adon Jonathan had built and into the clearing in the woods behind his house, where he had constructed a large wooden shelter, supported by beams but open at all sides, and had installed some rustic wooden benches. Adon Shimson chose the third row from the front and sidled along the bench until there were spots for his whole family. Many of the other benches were already occupied, and the family nodded at various people they knew as they waited for the service to begin.

Adon Jonathan stepped up to the front and faced the crowd. He started singing some psalms and everybody joined in. Suddenly, Jesse turned around and waved at some latecomers taking a back bench. Rachel and Leah followed his gaze and then looked at each other and rolled their eyes. Batya, Noa, and presumably their parents were just filing into that row. "You don't see them at services very often," whispered Leah to Rachel.

"I think they go to that Kohen who lives on the other side of the university," Rachel whispered back. "I've heard her mention him in class." *Jesse has to like the one girl that I would rather never have to think about!*

Adon Jonathan cleared his throat to draw attention to himself in front of the group. He started reciting some of the commandments from the Torah concerning Shabbat, and the girls turned around and focused on the service.

At the end, the crowd filed out past a long table to one side of the shelter, where they helped themselves from platters heaped with two kinds of hot pancakes made with olive oil, some with wheat flour and others with barley flour, and cups of wine. Rachel inhaled appreciatively. She loved the sweet smell of the incense that was burning on stands on the far side of the tables.

They mingled with the crowd for a few minutes, greeting their friends. Then Gveret Dina said, "We need to get home, because dinner will be ready to take out of the oven." So they walked over to where Adon Jonathan was standing with his wife, Gveret Ruth, and their son Samuel, wished them a peaceful Shabbat and thanked them for another meaningful service. Samuel motioned Rachel aside and whispered to her that he would see her the next day, and she smiled at him happily. Then she joined her parents heading to their car. Jesse was straggling a bit behind, and when Adon Shimson turned around to motion him to catch up, they all noticed that he was deep in conversation with Noa. The girls turned indulgent smiles on him and then winked at each other.

Jesse hurried to catch up with his family. Noa, waving goodbye to him and at the same time twisting around to look for her own family, tripped over a tree root and fell down with a thud. The sound attracted everybody who was still outside, and they all turned to see what had happened. By the time they got back to where the crowd was gathering, they saw Noa, sitting up, holding her ankle, and trying awfully hard not to cry.

Batya emerged from the crowd that was still leaving the prayer shelter (Adon Jonathan called it a "Tabernacle," but that formal name never caught on with the community) and sank down on the ground next to her sister. With visibly gentle fingertips, she touched the skin all around Noa's ankle and foot. Then she looked up and organized the people closest to her with great authority. One was soon seeking Adon Isaac, who was a physician, a second was going into the house to get a glass of water for Noa, and a third was reassuring the girls' parents that it was really only a minor accident. Batya's obvious love and concern for her sister made a deep impression on Rachel. Watching, Rachel saw how Batya stayed by Noa's side until Adon Isaac had bandaged the now-swollen ankle. At which point, Batya solicited more aid in getting Noa to her car without forcing her to put any weight on that foot.

Samuel, attracted by the commotion, came out the front door of his house just in time to catch the end of these events. Rachel swallowed hard, looking at him. Things were still a little rocky between them, and it didn't help that once again he couldn't seem to take his eyes off Batya.

Jesse hovered nearby as well, until he was satisfied that Noa had been cared for as much as possible and that she was not seriously injured. Then he got up and joined his sisters and their parents, and they turned once more to their car, comparing their differing perspectives on what each had seen.

Just before they got into their car, Jesse dropped a napkin-wrapped parcel into a nearby trash receptacle and remarked, "I can't ever stand those pancakes! They reek of olive oil! At least we have the wine to drown out the flavor and that greasy feeling."

"This is how we share in the sacrifices that are made in the Temple on Shabbat," their father answered, patient although it was seemingly the thousandth time he had told them this.

"Just think," Leah began, making a disgusted face at him. "If this were 500 years ago, we would still be sacrificing animals in the Temple instead of just oily pancakes and incense!"

Rachel shuddered. "Ugh, it's really revolting to think about that. I'm glad the Kohenim decided that we have moved beyond that; there are more modern ways to worship God. I wouldn't want to show up at the Temple and watch them cutting some poor little lamb's throat."

"Well, of course, we women wouldn't actually be able to see that," their mother said, practical as always. "And even Abba and Jesse would be standing out in a courtyard and probably wouldn't see it."

"But Samuel could!" said Jesse, making a slicing motion with his hand. "He could even be the one cutting the little lamb's throat!"

The girls put their hands over their faces, trying not to visualize gentle Samuel in this archaic role. Gveret Dina changed the subject. "I noticed you back there talking to Noa. She's really a lovely girl, isn't she?"

76

Jesse blushed and looked out the window, pretending not to hear his mother.

"When are you going to take her out for a proper meal?" Leah joined in the teasing.

"Okay, if you need to know, that's what we were talking about. We have a date after Havdalah. I can give you every detail if you really need to know!"

Adon Shimson, eyes on the road ahead, said, "You know we're only teasing you out of love. It's wonderful to see you take an interest in a girl."

"And one from such a fine family," Gveret Dina continued. "She's lovely and so bright."

"And of course, they're quite wealthy, which isn't a bad thing," Adon Shimson added.

"AND she has the most perfect of sisters," Leah whispered to Rachel, who did not join in her giggling.

"I keep forgetting that Samuel is a Kohen," Gveret Dina remarked, as they all went into their house. "He just acts like a regular young man. But seeing him standing there next to his father, so straight and tall, dressed so formally, makes me realize that he will be serving in that role himself some day."

Left floating in the air was her mother's clear expectation that Rachel would be by his side on that day. She had to make things right with him. She wasn't really sure who she might be with Samuel not firmly in the center of her life.

Meanwhile, they reached the kitchen and started bringing out platters of food from the oven, where they had been kept warm for the first Shabbat meal. Rachel dragged her feet as she joined her family at the table, still deep in thought.

Chapter 13

Leah's eyes were shining. "Joseph and I have hung out a lot already, but this is the first time he's asked me to go somewhere special with just him!" She twirled around to her closet, pulled out a dress and a frock quickly, and twirled back around to Rachel. "Which one?" she demanded.

Rachel was laughing softly. "Because going to the diner three streets over is somewhere special to take a date!" At Leah's glare, she relented. "The frock. This is just a casual afternoon after we get home from the university. And the emerald green is so good with your complexion."

Frowning, Leah hung the dress back up in the closet. Her fingers lingered on the hanger. Maybe they would go out to a nice place for dinner some evening and she could wear it then. "So do I wear it to school or come home and change?"

"Since Joseph is out of school already, it doesn't really matter. He won't see you in it during the day." One look at Leah's crestfallen face, and she quickly added, "But it will be fresher looking if you change into it when you get home. We can make a point of being home at least half an hour before he comes over to get you, so that you can primp all you want."

"Will Samuel be coming over today, do you think?" asked Leah casually.

Rachel rubbed her nose. "I haven't really heard much from him for a few days. I suppose he's busy with his paper. But it's safe to leave me home alone, you know. I have plenty of work to do." She thought grimly, *This is not the time to bring Leah down. But I can't deal with Samuel's continued coolness.*

Leah smiled and hung the frock on the hook in the back of their bedroom door. The twins finished getting ready to go to school. Rachel was already focused on her first class.

At last, the day was over and the girls were back in their bedroom. Rachel plopped onto her bed and watched as Leah changed into the green frock. She readily sat up and rebraided Leah's hair when asked. She enjoyed the feeling of the soft locks in her fingers, so vastly different from the coarser texture of her own curly hair. Then she watched as Leah freshened her makeup. "I'm so happy for you!" she said impulsively. "Joseph really seems like a nice guy."

"That he is!" laughed Leah, giving a final tweak to her green hair ribbon. She hugged her sister and danced out of their room.

Just as she was crossing into the living room, she heard a knock at the front door. "Your gentlemen caller," teased her mother.

"Be nice, Ima!" Leah replied, and flung open the door to reveal Joseph, dressed much more nicely than she usually saw him around the neighborhood. They greeted each other. Leah shrugged into a sweater, and the two of them set off down the front steps and along the sidewalk to the diner. Rachel watched them through the front window, smiling indulgently. It was so heartwarming to watch a new relationship developing, particularly since Leah had never had a real boyfriend. She giggled to herself. *I'm acting like her mother, not somebody who's only a few minutes older!*

Her phone buzzed and she looked down at it. A text from Shira! She had not heard from her since texting about her failure to be selected to participate in the senior seminar. She smiled as she read, "I do hope you'll decide to go to Jerusalem now. I feel badly about not being able to go myself and not seeing you there, if you go. But we have to make plans to get together before much longer."

Rachel wrote back, "I appreciate your validation. And yes, I did decide to go to Jerusalem! Anything new and exciting in your life?"

That line had been intended humorously, so she did a double take when she read, "YES!!! Call me!"

Rachel promptly pressed the icon and immediately heard, "I have a new boyfriend!"

"Whatever happened to 'single, want to stay that way, focusing on my schooling'?" Rachel teased her.

"Absolutely the right decision in theory! A mature way to go! But my life plan was not figuring on meeting Judah ..."

"Judah! Nice name. If he's anything like the Judah in my class, he's a real go-getter."

"He sure is!" Shira giggled.

Rachel snuggled back among her pillows, a smile on her face, as she asked for details. This was such a great distraction from her worries about Samuel; she decided not to say anything to Shira about what was going on with him.

The next morning, Rachel and Leah left early for their classes. Twelfth Month I and the trimester were both coming to an end. Everybody was studying hard for their final exams or drafting their final papers. Because Rachel had some time before her next class, she impulsively decided to drop in on Adon Yehuda. She walked down the hallway where the instructor offices were located and knocked on his door.

"Ah, Rachel!" he said, a look of genuine pleasure on his face, as he looked up and saw her in his doorway. "What can I do for you?"

"I wanted to thank you again for including me in that program with the scholar from Judea. I was the only undergraduate there, right? I appreciate the honor. And I learned so much!"

"You might have been the only student present, but you're already a senior and a few of the participants only graduated in the last few years. I think you fit in well," he answered. He gestured her to a seat and they started talking. Rachel told him that her thoughts had shifted more toward having her career in Judea, largely as a result of this program, and thanked him once again. She really savored his concern about her plans for her future, but also that he saw her as a full human being, not just as a student. The time went quickly, until he glanced at the clock on his desk and announced that he had to get ready to teach his next class. Rachel realized that she had to get to class herself and said her good-byes. How quickly the time had passed while she was talking to him!

In their archaeology program, she and Batya continued to trade off who was in first place. The class was extremely focused on their Twelfth Month

II project. This year, they were going to spend a week in Catalhoyuk and then work in teams on a research report to submit at the end of the month.

At one point, Rachel found herself working at the same table as Batya. Curiosity got the better of her, and she asked, "How are you going to be able to go to Catalhoyuk in Twelfth Month II, Mycenae at the beginning of First Month, and then Jerusalem in the middle of First Month?"

"Magic!" said Batya. Rachel found herself laughing with Batya, who continued, "It's only the first week of Twelfth Month II that we'll be in Catalhoyuk. We'll be here the rest of the month. Mycenae is the first week of First Month, then a week here again, and then Jerusalem. It will be hectic but physically possible, and these are all opportunities I would never want to forgo. My dream is to be a world-class archaeologist on a dig of historical importance."

"Mine, too," Rachel confided.

"I thought as much, since we both work so hard in this program. You know, having you here to compete against is so good for me. I think it spurs me on to work harder than I might have otherwise."

Rachel looked at her in surprise. "You know, I think I feel the same way." She was feeling an unexpected touch of warmth toward Batya, and she was on the verge of telling her about the flattering invitation to join the group learning from the Judean archaeologist, but that was spoiled a moment later when Batya's phone rang. She winked at Rachel and put a flirtatious look on her face, before simpering, "Hello?" Rachel murmured an apology and moved away. She did not need to hear Batya enticing yet another male into her dominion.

Chapter 14

Joseph was sitting on the twins' front porch waiting with them when Samuel's car finally pulled up. The three of them grabbed their towels and water bottles and ran down the stairs and out to his car. As they were piling in, Jesse appeared. "Are you going to the beach?" he asked.

Leah, still standing by the open door of the car waiting her turn to climb in, called back over her shoulder, "Yes, want a ride?"

"No, thank you. I'm supposed to meet Noa there in about an hour. Maybe we'll find you then."

"Sure!" said Leah, sliding in and pulling the door shut behind her.

Samuel shifted into gear and removed his foot from the brake. As he was pulling away from the curb, he said, "Can you believe finals are behind us once again?"

Joseph, who was sitting directly behind him, shook his head. "This was a tough one, at least for me. Two long papers and three exams!"

"But we only have one more final exam period ahead of us, probably the last one in our whole lives," Rachel said, craning her neck so she could see Joseph in the back seat. "I can't believe we'll be graduating in just one more trimester." She glanced over at Samuel. Things seemed to be back to normal between them now, although she was still a bit tentative in talking about their future beyond the university.

"We've been in school our entire lives," Leah agreed.

Once they were parked at the beach, they each took their things and trudged through the sand toward their favorite spot. Deborah was already there, as were her brother Aaron and their neighbors, Judith and Simon. Deborah shaded her eyes and waved at them. Her brother stood up and went to meet the foursome, shaking Joseph's hand as he reached them. "Haven't seen you for a long time," he commented.

"Yes, nice to see you again," Joseph said. "I don't see as much of anybody since I'm not in school any more. Well, except for Leah and Rachel!"

Just as they were settling in on the blanket that Samuel had produced from the trunk of his car, they heard Sarah's voice calling to them. "I guess we're all arriving at the same time!" she said, jogging over, a little out of breath.

"So is everybody packed for your trips next week?" asked Deborah, popping a grape into her mouth from the bowl nearby.

"Not yet," said Rachel. "I just had my last exam yesterday. It should be pretty warm in Catalhoyuk already."

"I'm lucky I have my train tickets!" laughed Sarah. "Packing would be an extra for me."

"Are all the trips for a full week?" asked Simon.

"They're not all exactly the same," answered Samuel. "Close, though. I think they range from 6 to 8 days long. Rachel gets home the latest, I believe."

She nodded. "I think it's actually Leah. But I'll likely be the dirtiest! We're looking at ruins of the Hatti and Hittite empires, of course, but there is an excavation that was just started recently, and we're going to finish with two days of digging."

"You'll love that!" said Leah. "I'm happy just to be working with some of the children drawing and painting. Charcoal is the worst thing I want on my hands!"

"What about you, Samuel?" asked Deborah. "I don't think I know what your program is."

Samuel was tossing a pebble from one hand to another. He looked up and said, "We'll be in Ankara, at one of the museums where they have a whole lot of Ancient Near East texts in their archives. We're going to have a chance to examine them and learn about some of the early law codes."

"Yes," Rachel nodded. "Samuel is fascinated by ancient law codes. Everything that might have been precursors to the laws in the Torah."

"Oh, that's really interesting!" Judith exclaimed. "I've always believed the that Torah didn't come out of thin air. There have to have been other societies governed by other laws that influenced our ancestors."

Samuel looked at her, an enthusiastic light in his eyes. "Exactly! Some of them were adapted into our Torah more or less and others got modified, but they all have a past."

Rachel smiled indulgently, so happy to see Samuel really into his work. *Makes it more likely he'll understand my own dedication.*

Joseph and Aaron went off to the shore and skipped pebbles on the water while they were chatting. Leah was talking to Sarah. It suddenly occurred to Rachel that she didn't sense a deep emotional bond between Leah and Joseph. Nor did Leah mention Joseph very often when they were alone in their room, although Rachel was sure that she peppered her conversation with Samuel's name. She shrugged mentally. Leah seemed happy enough, and not everybody needed an intense romance in their lives. She lay back and closed her eyes, feeling the breeze on her forehead and the sun warming her entire body. She listened to the others chatting around her. It became distinctly cooler and darker at the same time. She opened her eyes to see that the clouds overhead were no longer fluffy and white but were more threatening and had obscured the sun.

"I think it's going to rain," said Sarah, just as the first few drops splattered on their bodies and towels. Everybody got up and packed their things hurriedly. They had almost made it to the parking lot when the rain started falling much harder. Laughing, they called out their farewells.

"Almost just in time," Rachel said. "Too bad we're all in different programs. We'll have to get together and compare notes after we get back."

"We'll be spending a lot of time in our groups working on our research papers," Leah reminded her.

"Yes, I know, but I'm sure we'll find some time, maybe on Shabbat, to hang out again."

Samuel dropped everybody off at the twins' house. He had offered to turn around and drop Joseph off across the street at his own house, but Joseph insisted that he could cross the street in the rain and not be washed away.

Once inside, the girls changed into dry clothes and unbraided their hair so they could rub it dry. "Where's Jesse?" asked Rachel as Gveret Dina poked her head into their room.

"He went out to pick up Noa, just as the sky started to darken. He texted me that they're just going to stay over there and wait out the rain. Did you have fun?"

"Oh, yes! Even though it was cut short. There's nothing like having exams behind you instead of in front of you," Leah said.

"Rachel, I took your laundry out of the dryer since I had a few things to dry myself. I didn't know how long you would be, so I folded it for you."

"Thanks, Ima," Rachel said. "I guess we should start packing now."

Gveret Dina lingered in the doorway. "Why don't you come with me and get it now?"

Rachel wrinkled her nose and glanced over at Leah, but she obediently followed her mother down the hallway.

Once they were out of Leah's hearing, her mother said, "I know I'm probably just being an annoying mother, but I just want to make sure that you still think you're going to be okay spending a week on your own without Leah."

"Oh, yes, Ima, I think I really shook myself up a lot while I was still waiting to hear about the senior seminar," Rachel answered. "We're growing up and will be making our own way very soon. Graduation is only a few months away. I can't let myself be held back by those feelings."

"I'm proud of you for taking this stand, Rachel," her mother said. "And you know that I'm only a phone call away if you do run into any difficulties."

Impulsively, Rachel hugged her mother tightly. "A girl is never too old to need to be taken care of by her mother!"

Chapter 15

Rachel's class took the early morning train to Catalhoyuk. They arrived to discover that their lodging was in an old wooden dormitory building. It had two large rooms filled with cots; one room was designated for the men in the group and the other for the women. Once they chose their beds and dropped off their backpacks, they were supposed to assemble around a firepit nearby for lunch. She enjoyed the prospect of being in the mountains and living a bit more rustically. This first day was going to be an orientation, just a walk around the main archaeological dig and a few lectures on the various ruins they would be exploring for the first few days.

At the end of the day, after dinner, she strolled back to the women's room with the others, letting them chatter while she gave herself a mental pep talk. There was a flurry of activity as everybody washed and changed into their night clothes, but at last the lights were turned out. Rachel remained sitting on her cot in the darkness for a little while. She thought about being away from Leah for the first time and sent her a quick I'm-okay-good-night text. She reached for her necklace but then smiled in the darkness, realizing that she didn't really require that crutch. *I'm with interesting people and we're about to do interesting things. And I'm actually all right!* She slid under her blanket and was soon fast asleep.

The rest of the week passed in a blur, visiting the sites and then ending with the promised two days on the dig. She enjoyed every minute. She did take her pulse mentally now and again to make sure she was still doing fine, like worrying a loose tooth with her tongue, but she found every time she thought about it that she was happy, busy, and doing just fine. And then it was time for the group to go back to Trabzon.

Rachel's train arrived at 15:30. She stumbled down the stairs wearily, backpack slung over one shoulder, and straight into her mother's arms. Her smiling father and brother were visible right behind.

"Ima, it's so good to be home!" She strained to vocalize the words. "I'm afraid my voice is shot."

"You're so exhausted, Rachel!" her mother exclaimed, instinctively placing the palm of one hand on her daughter's damp forehead.

"Yes, it was a nonstop week for us. In the field all day long in the hot sunshine, and then up half the night either transcribing our notes so we'd be ready for the next day or else drinking wine and beer to try to unwind."

"Well, you're home now. How much time do you have off before you have to go back to class and work on your research paper?"

"Two days. Two short days! I will sleep the whole time!" She flung those words over her shoulder as she moved on to hug her father and then her brother. "When does Leah's train get in?"

"In only half an hour," her father replied. "So, if you don't mind, we'll just wait for her here."

"Maybe we can go get a drink at the snack bar inside," Jesse suggested.

Rachel giggled and punched him lightly in the shoulder. Jesse and Adon Shimson went on ahead, but Gveret Dina hung back with Rachel. She wrapped an arm around her daughter lovingly as she asked very softly, "How did you do there?"

"You mean, away from Leah?" At her mother's nod, she broke into a bright smile. "I did great. I had only the tiniest of qualms, and it really did go fine. I missed her – I missed ALL of you! – but I knew we'd be together again and I was enjoying myself with my class."

"Was it strange, though, not having contact with your own twin sister?" her mother asked curiously.

"Well, I have to admit that we did text at least once a day, just a quick message to be in touch. But I really didn't feel the need to have her there by my side. I didn't feel like I was any needier or lonelier than she was without me."

"I'm so proud of you! I knew you'd be fine!"

"It means a lot to me that you believe in me even when I have trouble doing it myself," Rachel confided, looking down at her mother as they entered the snack shop.

They were sitting around a small table inside, chattering and laughing, asking Rachel all sorts of questions about her week in Catalhoyuk, when Gveret Dina glanced at her phone. "We need to get back outside. Leah's train should be here in a few minutes. I just got the alert."

The family trooped back outside. As they approached the tracks, they saw Samuel coming toward them. The others, by unspoken mutual consent, continued on toward the platform where the train would stop, while Rachel froze in her position and stared at him. "Are you just getting back?" she asked. "I thought your trip was over yesterday." She blushed as she became aware that she had just let him know that she'd checked his schedule.

Samuel looked at her earnestly. "I knew you'd be here and I came here to find you. Rachel, I can't tell you how much I've missed you. Knowing we weren't even in the same city for an entire week made you seem way too far out of reach. I had to see you the instant you got back to Trabzon!"

"Oh, Samuel, I really missed you, too! I guess I've just come to expect that you'll always be around and I'm going to be seeing you off and on all day long. Without you there, even at the end of the day to tell you everything that was happening to me, I felt empty."

"Well, we're back now, and I'll be spending so much time with you that you'd wish I would go away again!"

Rachel looked into his eyes very seriously. "Never," she declared. "But I do want to catch up and hear all about your trip! They kept us busy day and night, so that I didn't even get much of a chance to text you, and it must have been the same for you."

"But you did get my good-night calls every day!"

Rachel blushed. "Oh, yes, every single night. That was the high part of my day!"

"We'll definitely get together and catch up during these next few days," he promised. "But not here and now, when your family is around. I just couldn't wait to see you and reconnect."

She pulled out her phone to check her calendar, but he, looking over her shoulder, said, "Here comes your whole family now. Leah is back."

Rachel turned toward the train platform and they walked over together, where he greeted her parents and brother warmly while she and Leah hugged each other tightly and squealed. Then he gave a little wave and walked back toward the parking lot. Rachel looked after him, but then she looked back at Leah and took her hand. "A whole week apart! We will have to sit up all night catching up."

Gveret Dina looked at her in surprise. "You're a whole different person, Rachel! I thought we would have to carry you back to the car when you first got off the train."

"Nothing a dose of Samuel couldn't cure!" laughed Leah.

"That's not all," Rachel protested, squeezing Leah's hand. "I'm back with my twin sister the way we were meant to be!"

"And I have so much to tell you! I'm on the short list for that internship I was telling you about once we've graduated in Sixth Month! I absolutely love working with children and art at the same time!" Leah gushed.

Rachel giggled. "Well, I love digging and sifting through dirt and brushing off dirt and rinsing off dirt!"

Leah shuddered. "Not exactly my taste, but it's so great to have it confirmed that we both made the right choices in our studies!"

Adon Shimson, overhearing them, laughed. "Yes, it would be a shame if you found out that you were both in the wrong fields one trimester before graduation!"

Laughing, they got into their car and headed back home.

Chapter 16

The late afternoon light filtered through the partially-closed blinds. Reddish gold pools highlighted a blue blanket, a dark curl, the red cover of a book opened upside-down on the navy rug. Shadows filled the corners of the room and touched the occupants here and there.

"I really wish you were going to Jerusalem for Pesach this year!" Rachel said, flopping over on Deborah's bed to look over at her. She shifted a pillow so that she could rest her arm on it more easily. "I resent that big project you have to do. We could have gone shopping together. Pesach dresses are so much prettier than Sukkot dresses."

"My mother and brother are going," Deborah reminded her, looking up from her cross-legged position on the rug, "but I probably won't get there until Sukkot. Maybe we'll do that shopping then."

"We're probably not going back for Sukkot, though," Rachel said. "No way we can go for every single festival. It would be different if we lived in Judea. Jerusalem would be just a few hours away, an easy drive by car."

"Why isn't the rest of your family going with you, again? I know you've told me before, but I was all wrapped up in my Twelfth Month II project."

"Jesse has some kind of sports tournament. And my parents are going to some kind of college reunion for my father's class." She examined her fingernails and then held up her hands, palms facing herself. "Do you like this new color? I ordered a bunch of them last week, but this is the first one I'm trying."

Deborah lifted herself onto her knees and peered over the edge of the bed. "Yes, I do. Are you thinking of these for Solstice Ball?"

"I am. I like this one the best, though, but I still want to try the rest of them. I just wish, instead of being so agreeable all the time, that Samuel would tell me which color he likes best on me!"

"And then what about your birthday the next day? Do you girls have any plans?"

"It's still too far off to be planning for," Rachel answered. "It's not such a big deal to be 23. So we haven't really thought about it much yet."

"Girls!" came a call from downstairs. "Dinner is ready. You're staying, Rachel, right?"

"I can't, Gveret Esther," Rachel shouted back in that direction. "Leah is picking me up in a few minutes to go to our new pottery class. The first one is tonight." Springing to her feet, she looked down at Deborah and said, "I wish you were taking that class, too. I'll let you know if it's any good and you can probably join it even if you miss the first one."

"Okay," replied Deborah, secretly doubting that she might ever have any interest in making pottery. "But you remember that I am taking sacred poetry this trimester." She too jumped up and gave her best friend a quick hug. "I'll see you at the Student Union tomorrow, okay?"

"Well, you know that I'm only taking it to please Leah," Rachel said. "She's the artistic one in our family. But sure, I'll see you tomorrow."

The girls pranced down the stairs, talking and laughing. Deborah broke off to wash her hands, while Rachel went into the kitchen to hug Gveret Esther around her ample waist and then out to wait for her sister on the front porch. Aaron and Jacob were coming up the sidewalk as she closed the door behind her. She moved to the side to make room for them.

"Rachel Bat Shimson!" said Aaron. "You're leaving just when it's time for dinner?"

Jacob added, "You'll notice that I have a better sense of timing. THIS is when I arrive!"

Rachel laughed. "Hi, Aaron. Hi, Jacob. It does smell awfully good. I really wish I could stay, but Leah is picking me up to go to our pottery class. Enjoy!"

The boys went inside just as Leah pulled up in her battered blue car.

"Hi, Rachel!" she shouted, popping open the passenger door. "I can't wait to see what our pottery class will be like."

"I think we're just making small bowls the first time," Rachel replied, settling herself in the front seat next to her twin sister. "I don't know any of the other girls who've signed up for it, but I did read that Gveret Judith is teaching it."

With that, the girls headed toward the pottery studio for their class. "Hey, Leah," Rachel asked casually, as they approached the building, "have you gotten around to asking Joseph to Solstice Ball yet? You can't put it off much longer."

"No, not yet." Leah focused on the road ahead for a few minutes, then continued, "It's been a bit strange between us lately, ever since I got back from the Twelfth Month II field trip. We get along fine, but …"

"It's more like friends than anything romantic," Rachel said, completing her sentence. She thought back to all the times Joseph was over at their house, when she watched the two of them eating cake together and chatting. Or sometimes they played games together. She never felt like she was interrupting anything significant when she came into the room. Nor could she tell the difference in Leah's demeanor when it was Sarah there rather than Joseph.

Leah took her eyes off the road and glanced over at her sister. "It's noticeable?"

Rachel shrugged. "Sure. You eat, you take walks, you play that dice game – you seem to be spending time together. But there's no special way you look at him. Nothing I pick up from you when you talk about him. No real glow."

"You know those tan-colored sandals of yours? The ones that you wore to death and now you can't wear them anywhere nice but you still wear them to the beach?"

"I can't throw them out!" Rachel mused. "Somehow they belong to me for always."

"That's how it is with Joseph and me, I'm beginning to realize."

"That's a good description of how it looks to me. The feeling I pick up between you doesn't seem anything like what I feel when I'm with Samuel."

"Well, anyway, I'm thinking it over. I don't want to give him the wrong message and I don't want to do something that doesn't feel special. After all, this is the Solstice Ball of our senior year!"

Rachel pursed her lips but said nothing more as they continued to the pottery class.

Chapter 17

Two days later, Samuel came by to visit, bringing a book that Rachel had wanted to borrow. He greeted her parents in a friendly way, and then the two of them sat down in the living room to talk for a while.

"Let's go over to Hamiskoy for lunch," he suggested after an hour or so. "I really could use some of their rice pudding."

"Oh, yes, there's nothing like it," said Rachel, pulling on a scarf. She stopped for a second to sniff it appreciatively – Ima bought such lovely scents for them to use on their laundry! "And we've been so busy for all these weeks that I'm afraid my Greek is getting rusty."

"We haven't been to Sunburst in a while – want to go there?"

"Uncle David told me that there's a new place that is already his favorite," Rachel replied. "He says it's right off the main square. I can't remember what it's called, something about willows."

"Sure, we can go find that." Samuel picked up Rachel's backpack and handed it to her. "Especially if they have roasted veggie wraps!"

Rachel stuck her tongue out at him and whirled around to head out, detouring first to the kitchen to tell her parents that they were leaving.

"Okay, kids, have fun," her mother said to them.

"And drive safely," her father added.

"Of course, Adon Shimson. Precious cargo!" Samuel gave a half-wave and a wink and followed Rachel out the front door. Then he looked back for a moment. "We'll see you tonight at services?"

"I wouldn't miss it, Samuel. Your father leads a uniquely beautiful service."

"Does Leah still want to volunteer in Hamiskoy after we graduate, Rachel?" Samuel asked a few minutes later, as he pulled his car away from the curb.

"Yes, she does. They're going to set up a new craft studio and she plans to help with that. Their crafts are so geometric, such bright colors, closer to nature. What about you? Have you decided yet?"

"I think I have decided to accept that fellowship in Ancient Near East texts at the university," Samuel answered. "That seems like a great move toward my future. I would rather research than teach. Be on the forefront of knowledge instead of passing along information that's a generation old. It wasn't easy, because I love to teach, but I love even more to learn new things as they are discovered."

Rachel's expression changed to one of admiration. "You're so ambitious, Samuel. You will really go far in life."

He sighed and looked out the window to his side for a second. "I don't have a lot of choice about that in the end. Abba really wants me to stay in Trabzon and take over his religious practice when he is no longer able to do it."

Rachel knew this all too well. "Maybe Adon Jonathan will let up on you when he sees all that you're capable of."

"No, Rachel, I'm afraid that Abba will just say all the more that I need to serve our people like he does. To bring them my gifts. He has even started talking about me going out to areas where there aren't as many Jewish people to help found a congregation from the ground up, like he always wanted to do but never had a chance at." He picked at a loose thread on the steering wheel and then added, staring at it, "I wonder what your father would think about you moving away to a remote place like that."

A shiver ran through Rachel, and she turned her head to look out her own window as she blushed intensely. This was the closest that Samuel had ever come to hinting that he had dreams of marrying her one day.

The two of them fell silent for a few minutes. Rachel had no idea what Samuel might be thinking, but she herself was casting about for something to say. While she was still thinking, Samuel pulled up to the first stoplight on the outskirts of Hamiskoy.

"You know, I think the important thing in life is to strike a balance between logic and emotion. That makes for a full, well-rounded person," Rachel mused.

"Where did THAT come from?" Samuel asked, raising his eyebrows while smiling at her indulgently.

"I was just thinking about how serious I have always been, how frivolous I think something is if it's only for recreation. But what makes a WHOLE person is somebody who is in touch with all sides of life. Left brain and right brain."

Samuel chuckled knowingly. It was only the week before that he had invited her to see a new comedy with him, but she had persuaded him to choose a different film because "comedies are so frivolous. What do you learn from them?"

They continued driving for a few more minutes, looking at the village around them.

"I've always liked that building," Rachel remarked as they turned onto the main road. "It's their library. I can definitely see the attraction that a quaint village like this has for Leah."

"But not for you." Samuel punctuated his assertion with a firm nod in her direction.

"And here's the city square. Should we park and just walk around looking for the restaurant your Uncle David likes?"

"There's a space over there – and oh look, Samuel, that must be the place right past it! WillowLawn. I hope it's good!"

The two got out of the car and strolled down the cobblestone walk to the restaurant. They paused to look in the window, which had a well-designed display of a variety of food and a sign that said, "Aramaic spoken here."

"Now remember," Rachel cautioned, "we're actually here for lunch. It isn't only about rice pudding!" Samuel, who was a little ahead of her and so was entering the restaurant first, made a gesture as if to let the door slam in her face. She giggled and stuck her tongue out at him.

Lunch was delicious. Rachel got her roasted veggie wrap, and then they both enjoyed warm dishes of creamy rice pudding, heavily scented with cinnamon and nutmeg. She shyly made a comment in Greek to the waitperson, who answered her in such a cascade of language that she could hardly pick out familiar words. Laughing, she reverted to Aramaic. Samuel told her in the car on the way home, "Don't be embarrassed. Rusty as it is, your Greek is still better than mine. You have an ear for languages that I've always admired."

"Thank you, Samuel," she replied. Then she added slowly, "I hope this doesn't make me sound like an idolator, but their religion really makes a lot of sense to me. Especially back thousands of years ago, when people didn't know anything about science, believing that one god is responsible for rain, another to make the crops grow, another to make your wife fertile, and they bicker and compete just like human beings. It seems logical."

"Because of all that, they do live a lot closer to the earth and feel so much more a part of nature," Samuel said after a brief pause. "I don't think appreciating somebody else's culture makes us idolators."

They continued in silence until they reached Rachel's home. Samuel walked her to the door but was not able to come in with her because he had promised his mother to run an errand on his way home. He cleared his throat as they reached her front porch and said, "I don't think I've told you how much it means to me that you are coming to Jerusalem with us. And my parents, too." She smiled at him as the world seemed to stop revolving for a minute. Then they said goodbye and Rachel went inside.

Chapter 18

It was the last weekend before the twins were to leave for Jerusalem. Deborah was over at their house, having come over to study with Rachel and then staying for dinner. Leah was not home; she had gone to the hotel where Sarah and her family were staying to avoid the latest dust and debris in their house. The renovations were well underway. The girls finished their schoolwork quickly and then started talking about their future plans.

"There's life after Greek classics," Deborah remarked to Rachel, throwing a baleful look at the book she had just closed. "Or at least I hope so!"

"Oh, there really is!" Rachel answered, excitedly. "There is so much more to learn and so much more of the world to see! I will definitely get to Greece some day, and other places as well. But increasingly, I'm beginning to want to spend time in Judea, finding out about our own homeland. There are archaeological sites everywhere a person might visit."

"So do you think going to Catalhoyuk last month and now Jerusalem will help you figure it out?"

Rachel looked away and then directly into Deborah's eyes. "More and more, I think I would like to be working in Judea. I love learning about all these precivilizations, but I think I would most want to pursue the history of our own people. We've been in that land for thousands of years, and of course there are countless lower layers for all the various peoples who were there before the Children of Israel even came into existence."

"So you're going to the right place. I wonder if you'll have any time for a little side trip in Judea, just to see what it might be like to be living there."

"I'll have to ask Samuel what he thinks tonight," Rachel answered. Then she giggled. "Believe it or not, he's texting me a dozen times a day about how he just can't wait until we're in Jerusalem together! So I will have plenty of chance to talk to him."

Deborah looked thoughtful. "You sound so much surer of yourself since that scholar in residence was here. How great that Adon Yehuda included you in that program!"

"Oh, yes." A brief pause, and then Rachel added, "He's really turned into a mentor for me. I find myself dropping into his office once a week or so. It's amazing how he helps me clarify my thinking. And that program was what pushed me over the edge in terms of thinking about working in Judea." She looked directly into her best friend's eyes and added, "Actually, I've felt a lot more confident since my experience with the Twelfth Month II project. How well I got along without Leah being by my side."

Deborah reached out and squeezed Rachel's hand. To dampen the emotion a bit, Rachel continued, "I guess the next thing is that we'll get married and have a family on top of our career and be busy for the rest of our lives."

"Well, you've just covered the rest of our lives in a single sentence!" laughed Deborah. "Although I really hope that we can keep learning and traveling and having adventures even with our husbands and children. I wouldn't want to marry anybody who wasn't interested in new experiences."

"You never talk about liking anybody," Rachel remarked. "I keep wondering about Jacob. You see him all the time."

"Rachel, he's Aaron's best friend! That's why he's always over."

"I know, but I wonder whether you like him?"

Deborah looked contemplative for a moment, then met Rachel's eyes. "I really don't think so. I think he's like another brother to me. But that's okay, there will be plenty of boys to meet."

Just then, Gveret Dina called up to the girls. "Come on down for dinner, girls. Jesse is already sitting at the table!"

The girls laughed. "Right away, Ima," Rachel called back to her, and they ran down the stairs to join the family.

The night before they were to leave, Samuel texted Rachel once more about how delighted he was that they were going to be in Jerusalem together. "I know I keep saying this, but it means the world to me that you will be there!" he wrote

She smiled and then texted back, "I've been looking forward to it so much! We never get to spend that much time together. Hour after hour!"

"It's great to think that you and my parents will be getting to know each other better, too," he replied.

She paused to think for a minute, then wrote back, "Yes, that means a lot to me. I can't believe that this time tomorrow, we will all be there together!" She smiled at the heart emoticon that he sent her, turned off her phone, and closed her eyes. She pulled her pillow more firmly under her head, aware that this was the last time she would be sleeping in her own bed until after the trip.

She woke up the next morning aware that there was no more anticipating; it was time to go to Jerusalem. Rachel reminisced about the previous few months. The twins had kept busy with their schoolwork, their pottery class, and their volunteer work, and meanwhile in the background, time had kept ticking by. They reassured their parents for the dozenth time that they had everything they needed, that they would not wander off on their own but would stay with Gveret Ruth, that they would regard Gveret Ruth and Adon Jonathan as substitute parents and listen to them, that Rachel wouldn't stick with Samuel and ignore Leah, and on and on, until Rachel wanted to burst out with, "Are we bringing along enough diapers? Because after all, we're only babies of 22! We could be having babies of our own at this age!"

Deborah and Sarah both came along to the airport with the girls' parents and their brother Jesse to say goodbye to their best friends, and after a flurry of hugs and kisses and last-minute admonishments, they were finally on the plane. Leah fastened her seatbelt and then leaned over and said softly to Rachel, "If we're going to have surrogate parents for this trip, I'm glad that at least we can fly down there on our own. There's SOME sense of being grown-up and independent!"

"Me too," Rachel replied. "I'm so glad we each already had our own tickets before they realized we were going by ourselves and invited us to join their family."

"So how is this working?"

"Samuel said that their plane lands only about 90 minutes before ours, so they'll stay at the airport and have something to eat while they wait for us. Then we'll take transport to the inn. No real reason to rent a car because we'll be on foot the whole time we're actually in the Old City anyway."

The time passed somehow, with books and talking and dozing and a few snacks, and eventually they were on the ground at the airport outside of Jerusalem. The twins hoisted their backpacks and walked off the airplane planning to go through the gate and then to the baggage claim, not knowing when Samuel's family would meet up with them. They each experienced a tiny twinge of relief, carefully not meeting one another's eyes to confess this, when they saw Gveret Ruth standing just outside the gate area, Adon Jonathan and Samuel right behind her.

"There you are, girls!" she exclaimed, giving each one a hug. "I'm glad the flight isn't that long. We've had the advantage of walking around and eating something already, but you must be so tired after all the fuss and flurry of getting off. Let's find your bags and get to the inn and you can rest a bit before dinner."

"The flight did seem to take forever, though," Rachel commented. "I think because we've been anticipating this trip for so many months."

"But you're finally here!" Samuel said. "I've been looking forward to being in Jerusalem with you ever since you agreed to come with us. We're going to have some great times here!" He had been holding his hands behind his back and now shyly brought them forward. He was clutching a bouquet of snapdragons in one hand and offered it to her.

Rachel, taking the flowers from Samuel, smiled into his eyes. "It's going to be wonderful. I think that seeing things with you will make it all seem fresh." She tucked the rose behind her ear and then teased him a bit. "I wonder how you were able to buy a flower for me if you've been in the airport since you got here." She nodded in the direction of a flower stand not twenty meters away from where they were standing.

Samuel threw back his head and laughed. "You caught me! But the thought is what counts."

"You're right. It's very sweet of you."

Rachel and Leah walked with Samuel and his parents slowly to the bus stop that serviced their desired route. Rachel looked around at the tawny sand in every direction, the Judean hills with the buildings of Jerusalem off to one side, and all the familiar signs that she was indeed back in Judea. The rainy season having ended around Purim, the sun as usual was shining and it just felt comforting and exciting at the same time to be in Jerusalem once again. Adon Jonathan consulted his phone, reserved the next route for the five of them, and paid for them. Their first bus arrived only minutes later, and he scanned the bar code proving that they had paid reservations and led everybody to seats near the back.

The landscape of the surroundings and then of the outskirts of Jerusalem flashed by. Leah was sitting by the window, intent on seeing everything they passed. Rachel tipped her head back against her seat and closed her eyes briefly. They were soon at their connecting bus stop, at which more of a crowd was gathered, all in a festive mood. "Pilgrims returning to Jerusalem for the holiday!" she whispered to Leah, as they climbed the stairs of the second bus. What was going to be an enjoyable vacation with Leah away from the rest of their family assumed a higher, more spiritual dimension in her mind.

It was only a little more than a kilometer from the bus stop to their inn outside the walls of the Old City. They strolled along slowly, weary but also enjoying the trees and flowers all around them, the crowds of people going in all different directions, and simply being able to move after having been cooped up on the airplane for so many hours. There was no escaping the heat of the sun on the route they were taking, and they were grateful to reach the inn at last. Samuel's parents checked them all in and helped them find their rooms. They smiled at the sight of a large orange on each of their pillows.

The evening passed in a bit of a daze, between the bustle of traveling and the emotions welling up in them. With a whispered, "I'll see you in the morning!", Rachel took her leave of Samuel. The girls gladly climbed into their beds and quickly went to sleep. Checking out the inn or even inspecting their room would have to wait until morning.

Chapter 19

The next morning was a bit lazy for all of them. They stopped at a place that Samuel's parents remembered from an earlier trip and had a lovely Judean lunch of falafel, salad, and stuffed grape leaves. Then the girls went into the nearby mikvah, while Samuel and his parents went to arrange for that evening's feast on the Temple grounds.

Rachel and Leah were just towel-drying their hair when Gveret Ruth came into the mikvah. "Oh, good, I was hoping you would still be in here," she said. "Adon Jonathan just got our passes, and we are scheduled for a 17:45 seating. I wanted to let you know that we have more time than we feared."

"I'm grateful we aren't going in at 16:30 like he was saying," Leah sighed. She shook out her new white frock and pulled it over her head. "After that huge lunch we had, I don't think I'd be ready for a heavy dinner quite that early."

"I hear you!" Gveret Ruth laughed. Her preparations completed, she turned and went through the doorway into the room where the pool was.

"Help me braid my hair, please," Rachel requested, turning her back to her sister. Leah gathered up the long dark coil of wet hair and began to braid it.

"What do you suppose people do who don't have sisters to braid their hair?" she asked, shaking her own wet hair that was waiting its turn. They both giggled at this refrain they commonly tossed at each other at such moments.

"I don't know," Rachel said now. "You CAN braid your own hair if you must, it just doesn't come out as evenly. Deborah always does her own, but Dinah still has her mother do hers."

Leah removed the white silk ribbon that she was holding between her lips and tied it deftly around the bottom of the thick braid. "Now you can do mine!"

That task completed, Rachel reached for her own white frock. "We haven't been in Jerusalem for Pesach in three years," she mused. "I love roast lamb and I definitely want to be able to enjoy it! But I also love falafel and salad and rice … I guess I love everything I've ever eaten here, whether or not it's been Pesach and we can eat it!"

Gveret Ruth, having concluded her immersions, came back into the room with a towel wrapped around her waist. "Well, we can enjoy it all while we're here!" she called over her shoulder, as she disappeared into one of the changing alcoves. "Let's meet just outside the Kiponus Gate at 17:15. See you later!"

"I do love roast lamb," Leah commented as the twins left the mikvah. "But I admit that I have to try really hard not to think about how things used to be done."

"I know," agreed Rachel with a shudder. "Slaughtering the lambs right in front of everybody and sprinkling the blood on the altar has to be one of the worst sights you could see in Jerusalem. I'm so grateful we don't live in the days of animal sacrifice any more! Somehow, burning incense and grains isn't as gross. I know they still slaughter them ritually, but at least it's done behind the scenes."

The girls wandered over to a shuk and began looking at some of the handicrafts. "We could buy a little something for Abba and Ima," suggested Leah, fingering a pretty necklace with topaz and Eilat stones. "Not that they need anything."

A sharp elbow in her back spun her around in painful surprise, and a hand reached out to take the necklace she had just been examining. An older woman wiggled her way in between Leah and the counter, clutching the necklace close to her chest like a prize she had won. "Let's get out of here," she urged Rachel. "It's just way too crowded with all these pilgrims!"

"Like us?" asked Rachel slyly, but she followed her sister out of the enclosure. They pushed their way through the crowds, Rachel trying not to lose sight of Leah, until they came to an open space under a carob tree. "I wonder what Jerusalem is like when it isn't time for one of the festivals. We've never been here otherwise. Never even to Judea at all for any other season. Too much commitment to the festivals, I guess."

"Well, it definitely costs way too much to come even three times a year," her sister agreed, "let alone other times, too. But there are places we've never seen – Sefad, Jericho, Hebron. So much history!"

Rachel looked down, quiet for a moment, and then met her sister's eyes very seriously. "I would like to make some time to see more of Judea while we're here. If we can work it out, I'd love to spend a day in the Galilee. Would you be willing to come with me?"

"We were going to come on this trip all on our own anyway. Sure, if it's okay with Samuel's parents, I would be happy to go with you. You've made me curious all these years about the archaeological sites that you love so much. Just so I don't have to get down in the dirt myself!" Leah answered.

"Oh, wait, while we still have time before we need to meet anybody, I need to stop at an exchange booth," Rachel said. "I don't have any half-shekel pieces."

"I have two of them if you have a shekel," Leah replied, placing her right hand protectively over her shirt, under which her money bag hung. "I can give them to you once we get a little bit more private."

As the girls stood under the tree and did their exchange, Samuel came up. His hair was still damp from his own immersion and Rachel thought he looked unusually handsome, easily the best-looking man of all those around them. "Oh, good, there you are!" he exclaimed. "I'm glad we can have a minute or two to chat before we're with my parents again."

"How were you able to find us?" Leah asked. "There are thousands of people close enough to hit with a stone. Even if I'm the one throwing it!"

"Friend tracking on my phone," he replied. After a brief pause, "You girls look really nice," he said admiringly, his eyes fastened on Rachel.

"You clean up okay yourself!" she replied.

"Do you know what time we're supposed to meet outside the Kiponus Gate?"

"At 17:15," Rachel answered. "Our reservation is for 17:45. That seems awfully far in advance, even with the crowds."

"The reservations are for time slots," Samuel explained. "We have to get in there and make sure we get five seats together at one of the tables. Plus, there's a bit of a bottleneck getting in, because we all have to pay our taxes."

"And what about Fourth Day?" asked Leah. "What happens with the Omer?"

"A lot of the action is out in the fields and small towns," Samuel replied. "The people all gather together with their offering of first barley and then they march here to the Temple. We'll get to see them coming in and hear their singing, but we don't really participate in the actual Omer ourselves here in the city."

"That is so exciting!" Rachel exclaimed. "I don't think we've ever done any of these things before."

"Oh, and my cousin Miriam will be coming to visit us on Fourth Day, too. She and her parents live in Mizpah, which is close enough to the Temple that they can go home every night during the festivals. She's a little more than two years younger than we are," Samuel continued.

"When's the last time you saw her? Is she nice?" Rachel asked.

"I haven't seen her for a few years. I do remember that she's a little reserved with strangers," Samuel answered. "Most of the times that we've come to Jerusalem, we've been able to see at least my Aunt Tirzah and my Uncle Joel. Miriam is sometimes away at a summer program or at her boarding school in the Galilee and doesn't come. But I think she's nice, just quieter."

Rachel and Leah exchanged glances. Then Rachel burst out, "Speaking of the Galilee, we've been talking about stealing a day on this trip and looking around there ourselves. Only if there aren't other plans and it's all right with your parents."

"Oh, gosh, Rachel, I completely forgot to mention this to my parents," Samuel said. "I don't know what all the plans are and I certainly don't know what they might say, but they're not very likely to stand in your way if the timing works out."

Rachel noticed something in his eyes that failed to match his words but decided not to pursue it just then. "That would be wonderful!" Then, mindful of her tendency to focus only on her own interests, she added, "Miriam sounds quieter, not like us at all. We'll need to try not to intimidate her."

Samuel paused and looked thoughtful for a moment. "I'm not sure that could happen. Aunt Tirzah is very strong-minded, and Miriam definitely comes out of her shell a little bit when she's away from her mother. And more so as she gets older. We'll see!"

The young people continued to chat until Samuel indicated that they should start moving toward the gate. They found his parents very quickly in that area, despite the crowds, and were soon standing in the Chel, the foyer, facing the Kiponus Gate. People were waiting all around them, relatively quietly and with little jostling, all facing the gate leading to the Court of Women, where the tables were set up for the Pesach feast. After just a few minutes of waiting, they heard three shofar blasts and the crowd started to press in through the narrow opening. Each family group was stopped by the Levites at the gate, had their names checked off a list, and paid their half shekel tax per adult.

"Do they really have a list of all the Jewish people in the whole world?" Rachel whispered to Samuel.

He laughed, then whispered back, "No, silly, that's a list of people who made reservations!"

Rachel blushed and looked down at her sandals as the line inched forward. "I knew that, of course," she said, mostly to herself.

As their little group was searching for a table, Rachel could hear a group of men's voices singing in harmony. "The Levites are singing Psalms of praise," Samuel whispered to her, noticing how her attention had been caught by the sound.

"And here's space for us," Adon Jonathan said, pointing a bit to their left. They quickly made their way to the table and took their places standing around it, nodding to the other occupants who were already positioned there.

Across the table from where Rachel was standing appeared to be a family with two parents and two very small children, who were trying extremely hard to stand still and be quiet but were clearly wriggling with suppressed excitement. "Is this your first time here at the Temple for a festival?" she asked the older of the children.

The little boy turned away and buried his face in his mother's long white frock. "We live in Sefad," she explained, "so we come to Jerusalem at least once a year. But this is the first time that Samuel is old enough to understand what's going on, because he learned about it at school."

"Oh, my name is Samuel, too!" Samuel had been listening to the little exchange and now leaned in from the other side of the children's father to look his little namesake in the eye.

"I'm Samuel ben Joab," the little boy announced proudly, half his face now out of his mother's skirt.

"Nice to meet you! I'm Samuel ben Jonathan HaKohen. So at least we won't get confused and go home with the wrong family."

The little boy giggled and emerged fully from his hiding place. "I know who my Abba and Ima are! I wouldn't go home with the wrong people!"

"And what is your sister's name?" asked Rachel.

"She's Deborah."

"Oh, Deborah, that's my best friend's name!"

"And my sister is my best friend, too," little Samuel announced solemnly.

"That's so sweet!" Rachel exclaimed, looking at their mother, who was smiling at the children rather proudly. "I'm Rachel bat Shimson," she continued.

"Nice to meet you," the mother said. "I'm Leah and this is my husband, Joab." Adon Joab nodded at them distractedly, his head buried in a book. Gveret Leah smiled at him fondly. "He isn't very comfortable in big crowds," she confided in them.

"And MY name is Leah!" Rachel's twin sister, sitting on her other side, chimed in. "So we're a whole big mixed-up table!"

"And you know what?" Rachel asked the children. "We live far away, in another country, so this is only our third Pesach here, even though we're 22 years old!"

The children's eyes grew very wide. They looked at Leah and she nodded in affirmation. Little Samuel blurted out, "That's so old! You should have children of your own!"

"We're still in school," laughed Leah, gratified not to be thought of as too young for anything. "So yes, we've been here a few times for the other festivals, but only our third Pesach."

The children next looked at Samuel, who said quickly, "These girls are my friends, not my sisters. I have been here a whole lot more than they have. SIX times at Pesach!" The children giggled because that still didn't sound like very many times to them.

"Well, I'm six," little Samuel announced, "and I've already been here four times for Pesach!"

"But we do live in Judea," Gveret Leah chimed in softly, leaning forward a bit. Adon Joab looked up for a minute and then immersed himself in his book once again.

"And if you live so far away, how are you able to be speaking Aramaic?" little Samuel asked.

"Jewish people all around the world speak Aramaic. That's our native language," answered Adon Jonathan.

"Are you a Kohen?" the little boy continued in his piercing tones. "Your name is like a Kohen. You are dressed like a Kohen. Why are you sitting out here with us?"

"Because if you're a Kohen from another country, you're still a guest. Although we do each have the honor of serving in the Temple at some point during our visit."

Gveret Ruth smiled warmly at the little boy. He reminded her so much of her own small Samuel. In a gentle voice, she asked him, "Do you know what a Kohen is?"

"Yes!" he cried out, clapping his hands together over his head. "Moses and Aaron were from the tribe of Levi. All of the boys who are born in the line of Aaron are Kohenim, and their job is to do all the service in the Temple. All the other boys from their tribe are Levites, and they help the Kohenim, mainly by leading songs and prayers. But I'm not a Levite, right, Abba? We are from the tribe of Benjamin!" He stared at his father expectantly, but his father appeared not to have heard him and kept reading his book.

"Joab!" Gveret Leah hissed. "Put that book away. I think it's about to start." He slid the book into the pocket of his jacket and grinned at her rather sheepishly. "He never stops studying," she explained to the others.

"Good job!" Gveret Ruth told him with a wink of her eye.

Just then there was a stir and everybody turned their heads to look in that direction. Since Rachel's side of the table had their backs to the activity, she stood up, swiveled her chair around, and sat back down so she could watch. In came a group of Levites with their long white robes. They gathered in a semi-circle in front of the room and began chanting psalms in four-part harmony. All around her, Rachel heard other male voices joining in, including those of Adon Jonathan and Samuel and Adon Joab. When they had all finished chanting the Hallel, they all sat down.

Young men bearing huge platters of food were soon spreading out among the tables and delivering the food. Adon Jonathan quickly reached for the unleavened bread that had been placed on the table and passed it around so that everybody could take some and say the blessings. Gveret Leah turned her attention to helping the two little ones to some food.

"I don't remember when I ate lamb before," little Samuel announced in the piercing voice of the very young. "But I do know why there's no bones in it!"

"Why?" asked Rachel, smiling at him.

"Because we aren't supposed to break any bones in the lamb, even by accident, so they take all the meat off the bones for us!"

"Good job, Samuel!" said his mother, squeezing his shoulder a little bit with one arm. With her other arm, she was bouncing little Deborah, who had apparently decided that she would rather play than eat. Gveret Ruth leaned forward and the two women began speaking in low tones.

As the food was served around, little Deborah scrambled back onto her own stool and put out a tiny fist for her utensils. Everybody became quiet and focused on their eating, and Rachel could once again hear the sweet harmonies of the Levites. "When do they ever get to eat, Adon Jonathan?" she asked Samuel's father softly.

"They eat in shifts," he explained. "During another seating, a different group of Levites is singing, and these men will be eating. Don't worry about

110

them! They and the Kohenim are taken particularly good care of by all the offerings, especially during a festival."

"You and Samuel are Kohenim!" Leah interjected. "Will you get to do anything special while we're here at the Temple?" Rachel realized that Leah must not have heard what Adon Jonathan had said to little Samuel earlier.

Adon Jonathan glanced at Samuel, then back at the twins. "Just ceremonially. All visiting Kohenim can participate in various offerings as they choose. Samuel and I will help with the mincha offering of incense and grain tomorrow. It's an honor, of course, which is why we volunteer, but as a practical matter, there are plenty of Kohenim right here in Jerusalem who already have all of the sacrifice periods covered officially."

"Were you ever able to do that before?" Rachel asked Samuel.

"Every time we're in Jerusalem," Samuel answered. "I wouldn't miss it! It's such a thrill to be offering sacrifices just as my ancestors have done for thousands of years."

"But I thought there was a lottery to determine which Kohenim have the honor of serving in which capacity. Since you're coming from outside Judea, can you just step into these roles?" asked Gveret Leah, looking up from her daughter for a moment.

"It IS just ceremonial, really just honorary," Adon Jonathan answered for Samuel. "You're right; there's a lottery that chooses which Kohenim will get to serve in which capacity each week. But when Kohenim from outside Judea come to visit, particularly during Festivals when there are so many of them, they are invited to oversee or observe. They don't actually do the tasks, but they can stand with the Kohenim who are performing them and watch the entire process take place."

"Some day, we'll even know how to do it ourselves!" Samuel added. "There are various steps for the incense or for the grain, depending on who is offering the sacrifice and what it's for."

Little Samuel wrinkled his nose, a puzzled look on his face. "But don't you get to offer the incense and grains when you're in your own country? Not just when you're here?"

Adon Jonathan smiled down at the little boy. "No, son, sacrifices are only permitted to be offered at the Temple. That goes back several thousand years. But I do have a special place for all of our neighbors where we read prayers and recite psalms back at my house."

The sound of excitement near the entrance gate was building and spreading to where they were seated. People were starting to stand up near the gate and were quickly followed by others at nearby tables.

"I was hoping for this!" said Adon Jonathan. "The king is coming to our seating! I had heard that it was likely but didn't want to say anything in case the plans were changed. Now you'll see some real pageantry."

Little Samuel announced importantly, "The king is from the tribe of Judah. His great-great-great-a million times-grandfather was King David." His father wrapped an arm around him and hugged him.

As the people sitting around their own table rose, there was another commotion. Rachel was glancing around to see what else was going on, when Leah poked her in the ribs with her elbow. "Look over at the Nicanor Gate!" she whispered excitedly. "Kohenim are coming out!" A small band of Kohenim came through the gate into the Court of Women, formed two columns facing one another, and a gorgeously attired man came down through the space between them.

"It's the Kohen Gadol!" exclaimed Rachel, also softly.

Little Samuel, whose father had hoisted him onto his shoulders, shortly made the piercing observation, "They're all barefoot!"

Adon Jonathan looked up at the little boy and smiled. "Yes, that's how the Kohenim work in the Temple. But try to keep quiet so you can watch."

"But what is the Kohen Gadol? I know it means Big Kohen in Hebrew, but I don't know how he's special." Little Samuel bounced on his father's shoulders, causing him to wince.

"He's the one in charge of all the Kohenim," Adon Joab said, loosening little Samuel's hands where they were gripping his neck. "And he has some special parts to play, like on Yom Kippur. Or right now, so watch!"

A small group of men in military attire had come through the entrance gate and also formed two columns. Down between them marched a small group of people, with a man in old-fashioned robes at the end.

"That's the royal family," Gveret Ruth said. "The king is the last one."

112

Samuel gave Rachel an impish smile. "He's your cousin; go over and greet him."

She shook her head at him saucily and replied, "The Kohen Gadol is YOUR cousin. Why don't you give him a big hug?"

They laughed but continued watching as the two retinues walked toward each other. The king and the Kohen Gadol each put their right hands on their hearts and nodded at one another. "You are welcome in the Temple, son of David," the Kohen Gadol said.

"Thank you, son of Aaron," the king replied, equally formally.

"Your table awaits you," and the Kohen Gadol stepped aside. They could now see an empty table closest to the Nicanor Gate, which the Kohenim had been blocking from their sight. "Your paschal lamb will be out immediately."

"Thank you again," the king said, nodding once more. Then he took his place at the back of the table, so that he was facing all the crowds of people standing around their own tables out of respect and staring at him. He waved at them and they broke into cheers and applause. Then he quelled them with a gesture, turned back to the Kohen Gadol, and said, "I would ask your blessing on all of these people and on us."

"Of course," said the Kohen Gadol. Shivers ran down Rachel's spine as he raised his hands, fingers joined to form a triangle. The community lowered their heads while he intoned the ancient words of the Kohenic blessing. Rachel couldn't help but weep softly, so moved by the grandeur of this moment.

The awed silence afterwards lasted only seconds, to be filled by the loud comments of small children in attendance, including little Samuel, who asked, "Was that really the king? Was that really the Kohen Gadol? I never saw them before ever!"

"Ever in your whole long life?" teased his father, bouncing him affectionately on his shoulders. Then he swung him back down to his chair. "I have to admit that I've only seen the king once before and I think I've only seen the Kohen Gadol from a huge distance on the Holydays. People don't get to see them a lot."

"You've met him, though, right, Adon Jonathan?" Leah asked softly.

"I have been presented to him once when I was serving at the Temple," he answered.

"I saw him once in the Sanhedrin," Adon Joab recalled. "There was a case that involved a group of us from Sefad and I was in the delegation that came down to hear it being discussed. I never got close enough to speak to him, though. He doesn't dress quite that fancy when he's presiding over the Sanhedrin!"

"But have you ever met the king?" Rachel asked breathlessly.

"No," he smiled at her, "we've only seen him ceremonially, from a distance. I think people who live in Jerusalem have a better chance of seeing him in person."

"But you said he's your cousin!" little Samuel said insistently. "Hasn't he ever come to your house even in your faraway country?"

Rachel leveled a look at Samuel, then smiled at little Samuel. "Samuel only meant that our family is from the Tribe of Judah. If we're cousins, the connection must go back several thousand years."

Little Samuel nodded solemnly. "Like I was just telling you, great-great-great. Just like King David."

Meanwhile, everybody at the tables around sat back down, so they soon did as well. Samuel helped himself to more cheese and put it on the unleavened bread he still had on his plate. He then picked up the platter of tomato and cucumber salad in front of him and passed it across the table to his mother, who helped herself and then passed it along to the twins. They filled up their plates. "I've had quite enough lamb," whispered Leah to Rachel.

"I wonder what is for dessert?" asked Rachel, looking around for the food-serving Levites.

"It's usually a selection of fresh fruit with yogurt," Gveret Ruth said, smiling at Rachel.

"I wanted cake!" shouted little Samuel. His father quieted him by bending over and whispering in his ear. Leah and Rachel smiled indulgently at him and then at each other.

"Little Deborah has been quiet for a long time," Gveret Ruth observed.

Gveret Leah glanced down. "She's asleep. I'm not sure how long that has been."

"Well, we're almost done, and then you can put her in bed. Where are you staying?"

"At an inn right near the Lion's Gate," she answered.

"We're in the direction of Jaffa Gate," Gveret Ruth said. "So if we don't see you again while we're all in Jerusalem, I wish you safe and comfortable travels."

"Thank you. I wish the same for you."

"Oh, here comes dessert!" Leah exclaimed, at which both mothers turned their heads. "It looks like papaya slices in the yogurt."

"I learned in school that you aren't supposed to cook a kid in its mother's milk," little Samuel announced, wrinkling his forehead like a little old man.

"The yogurt is made from goat milk, and a lamb is a kind of sheep, so they're not the same type of animal," his mother explained to him. "And they weren't cooked together, either!"

The group chatted a few more minutes as they ate their dessert, and then they all stood up and said their farewells. Adon Joab hoisted little Samuel up on his shoulders again while Gveret Leah picked up a still-sleeping small Deborah. Rachel and Leah followed Samuel and his parents toward the entrance gate, the girls pulling shawls around their shoulders as they stepped through because it was noticeably cooler outside of the Temple grounds. As they walked down the hill together, Rachel exclaimed, "THAT was an eventful dinner! Thank you again so very much for bringing us to Jerusalem."

"Yes, we're so grateful," added Leah, with a squeeze of Gveret Ruth's arm which hung near her as she walked. "There's just so much more comfort to the trip when we're not just all alone in Jerusalem!"

"Of course. We're glad to have you! You're giving me more people to talk to, too, than just these two big men." And she glanced affectionately at her husband and son, strolling just ahead of them and deep in conversation. "Tomorrow the men will serve in the Temple, so we can just walk around Jerusalem if we want and look at anything you like."

"Is it really far to where the Sanhedrin meets?" asked Leah. "I know we probably can't get inside, but I would love to see the building and the room where they meet."

"It isn't that terribly far from the Temple. The old location used to be built right into the walls. But the modern one is about two streets away. And you know, when they're not in session, we are welcome to go inside and walk through the building and even their assembly hall. Why don't we spend the morning looking around Jerusalem, if the weather is as mild as it was today? We could stop at the market and bring back some fruits, vegetables, and fish if we wanted to cook our own dinner tonight. And then in the afternoon, we can go look at the Sanhedrin and maybe be able to meet up with Adon Jonathan and Samuel. I think they are in recess during festivals. It could be a wonderful day."

"I'd really like to see the ruins they uncovered from King Herod's remodel," said Rachel. "Samuel said they have found more since the last time we were here."

"We should wait till we can all do that together, because I think the men might also want to see those," Gveret Ruth answered. "Maybe when we meet up before dinner."

"And then the next day is the first day of the Omer offering," Rachel mused. "I hope there's somewhere good to go where we can see all that."

The women strolled along, talking as they went, until they had reached their inn. They found the men waiting for them outside the front door. "Abba and I will be going back to the Temple for Shacharit," Samuel said to Rachel. "And then I think we're going to stay on the grounds and pray with the Kohenim until it's time for us to serve at Mincha. So we'll eat breakfast very early, probably before you get up. I'll see you again at dinnertime."

"Have a really fulfilling day!" Rachel said to him, trying to visualize what it might be like to be a Kohen right there on the Temple grounds. "I can't wait to hear all about it."

"Oh, you will, probably enough details that you will fall asleep," Samuel replied.

"I'd especially like to hear about if you get to see the shewbread. Abba and Jesse said that only Kohenim and Levites could see it, that it's inside where most men cannot even go."

"Okay, I'll watch for it," Samuel promised, smiling affectionately. "I have to admit that I've never really paid attention to everything around us with the Kohenim doing their rituals that I have to learn to help with and the Holy of Holies right there beyond us."

The group walked inside the enclosure to the plaza and gathered in a loose knot to say their good nights.

"So, ladies, why don't we meet around 7:30 for breakfast in the main dining room?" suggested Gveret Ruth. "We can just wear everyday dresses for sightseeing in Jerusalem. Meanwhile, get a good night's sleep."

"Good-night, Gveret Ruth," the twins chorused. They each hugged her, nodded at Adon Jonathan and Samuel, and went into the inn to find their room.

Chapter 20

"I can't believe we're really here, and without Abba and Ima!" gushed Leah as she unlocked the door to their room. "Even though we're here with another family, I still feel so grownup."

"Me, too," said Rachel, kicking off her sandals. "Pesach must be the most exciting time of the entire year to come to Jerusalem. And it reminds me that I do love lamb!"

"Oh, I never forgot," grinned Leah, hanging up her frock. "But wouldn't it be great to come just once and see Bikkurim?"

"We never have come for Shavuot, have we? I just remember three Pesachs now and two Sukkots."

"Abba and Ima brought us once when we were very little," Leah answered. "But we wouldn't be able to remember that time. I'd like to see Sukkot, too. Hey, what if we just stayed in Judea until then?"

"Oh, yes," laughed Rachel. "That would be a guaranteed way to please our parents!"

Leah unbraided her hair and started brushing it. "That reminds me, we really should call Abba and Ima and tell them all about tonight. It was amazing. Stunning that we saw the Kohen Gadol AND the king!"

"What time is it there? Do you suppose they're home?" The twins quickly made calculations, and then Leah pushed a button on her phone. Getting comfortable, they both lay back on her cot, heads on the pillow and feet planted so that their knees stuck up. The phone lay on the pillow between them. When their mother answered the phone, they breathlessly talked over one another, words spilling out as they each tried to describe the wonder and awe of the evening.

"One at a time!" Gveret Dina finally laughed. "But first let me get Abba, so you can tell us both. It does sound like you're having a great time at least!"

With Adon Shimson on the phone, the girls took turns relaying the events of the day and especially of the evening. Their parents were properly impressed with all of their adventures and wished them great explorations for the next day. The girls asked to have their love sent to Jesse, who had gone to bed, since his next tournament game was scheduled to be quite early the next morning. All the pageantry would have thrilled him.

"So it seems to be going well with Samuel," said Leah, peering closely into the mirror as she put lotion on her face.

"Sure!" Rachel said, startled.

"I was thinking there might be too much togetherness. Being on a trip can separate a great relationship from a mediocre one."

"Oh, no, I'm enjoying every minute. Being with him without having to stop for class or something, just open-ended. It's lovely. And I enjoy getting to know his parents better, too." Rachel yawned widely, covering her mouth a little late.

"I guess it's too late for me to call Sarah," Leah remarked to Rachel, pulling the blanket up over herself in her bed. "Maybe I'll catch her tomorrow."

"Great idea," said Rachel, rather absently. She was still sitting up in bed and typing on her phone.

"Who are you writing to now? I'm ready for the light to go off!"

"Adon Yehuda. He was interested in hearing about all the things that we will be doing on this trip. He said he wants to train my senses to be more observant. I hope he was teasing!"

Leah put her pillow over her head and turned her back to her sister. Rachel tossed a smile in her direction and finished up hurriedly. "I'm done now. This has been a busy day, and tomorrow will be another long and active day for us. Good night, Leah!"

"Good night, Rachel!"

Rachel turned out the light and mumbled her evening prayers.

Chapter 21

The next morning, fresh from their breakfasts, the three women tied on scarves and set out. They had stopped at the front desk of the inn and picked up a walking map of the area. "There is SO much history here!" exclaimed Rachel. "We have to stop at every single place between here and the market."

"Well, I don't know about every SINGLE place we pass!" laughed Gveret Ruth. "But maybe some kind of interesting variety. I was reading my travel map this morning. There is one site along the way that dates back to Hasmonean times and a few from Roman times, including a Nazarene ruin of some sort."

"What about from the time of King David?" asked Rachel.

"Our cousin?" Leah asked slyly, poking Rachel in the ribs.

"Those places are mainly right around here, in the Old City," Gveret Ruth replied. "That's where he built all of his official buildings. We can see some of them this afternoon and maybe be able to meet up with Jonathan and Samuel when they finish with Mincha."

"I found a database that gives all the history of every place we might visit," Gveret Ruth remarked. "That and the walking map should direct us to the places I had in mind. I think most of what I marked on my travel map dates back about 2000 years or so."

"Things were so interesting back then!" Leah exclaimed. "Pharisees and Sadducees and Nazarenes and Essenes and probably lots of groups I can't even remember!"

"Well, it's still interesting," Gveret Ruth remarked. "Just a lot less strife!"

"Scary back then, though," shuddered Rachel. "The Romans actually breached the walls of the city. They could have killed a lot more people, maybe even destroyed the palace and the Temple!"

"Well, they didn't," Gveret Ruth answered briskly. "And so here we are to this day. But look, the first ruin on our map!"

They turned aside from the road they were on and walked up a short path to a building that was surprisingly intact.

"How old do you suppose this is?" Leah asked in surprise.

Gveret Ruth consulted the database. "Oh, it's not particularly old comparatively. Maybe 500 years? It says it was abandoned in the year 5214. It was a schoolhouse where one of the later codifications of the Torah was done by a famous Rabbi who I never heard of and his students. Would you like to go inside? It's a museum now with a huge collection of all of the Law Codes through the ages."

"Sure! There's so much history in all the different Codes they tried to put together all these years. The Torah is pretty disorganized if you want to use it as a guide to live by." Leah said.

"And a lot is obsolete, too, as all the years have passed. I don't mind burning incense and grain, but UGH, cutting up animals and sprinkling blood all over!" shuddered Rachel.

"And the Kohen Gadol had that gorgeous gown with all those things he was wearing, and it would be all covered in blood!" added Leah.

"You girls do know where our lamb last night came from, right?" asked Gveret Ruth. "The lambs were ritually slaughtered, like all meat is, and they were cleaned and cooked on the altars. Just no sacrificial ritual and no sprinkling of blood. And a LOT more sanitary!"

"2 ½ shekels per student and 5 shekels per adult to get in," Rachel read from the sign posted near the door. "That's a lot more than the tax we had to pay last night!"

"Well, admission charges aren't set in the Torah, the way the tax is!" laughed Gveret Ruth, as the three went inside and paid their fees.

Rachel picked up the exhibition guide as they entered the first room. "I'll have to remember all the details to tell Samuel later," she said.

"He's interested in all the ancient law codes, isn't he?" asked Leah.

"These are the codes that are based on the Torah," Gveret Ruth said, looking up from the database. "Samuel is more interested in the REALLY old

121

law codes, the ones that predate the Torah. He believes that the laws in the Torah mostly had their origin in earlier codes of the Ancient Near East.

The morning passed pleasantly as they sauntered along, stopping here and there if something interested them. They were sitting on a bench beside the path enjoying a cool drink, grateful for a moment in the shade, when Rachel's phone rang. "It's Deborah!" she exclaimed. "Do you mind if I take this call quickly?"

"No, not at all," Gveret Ruth assured her.

She pulled the phone out of her pouch and stepped a few meters away behind a tree. "Hi, Deborah!"

"Am I interrupting anything important?" came the voice of her best friend. "Are you in the palace waiting for an audience with the king?"

Rachel laughed. "Hardly! Although we did see the king last night! Leah and I are doing some sightseeing with Gveret Ruth this morning while the guys are at the Temple. We're going to stop by a market to pick up some stuff for dinner and then we'll go back to the Temple and try to get inside the Sanhedrin before the guys are done."

"Oh, it sounds wonderful! I so envy you. They have to be the best guides. And you saw the KING!"

Rachel replied, "Yes, the king AND the Kohen Gadol! The royal family came in to eat the paschal lamb and the Kohen Gadol came out to greet them in person. And the Levites were singing Psalms and it was all just wonderful! And yes, his parents really are the best tour guides, and so truly kind all the time."

"Well, sure, you're practically their daughter-in-law!"

Rachel blushed and glanced around to make sure that nobody was nearby, even though nobody but her would have been able to hear this declaration. "Between you and me, I'm beginning to feel a little like that. Samuel's parents are definitely treating me that way! And I'm so thrilled at the chance to get to know them better on a daily basis. You know, just in case for some reason I'd have to fit into their family some day."

Deborah snickered. "Yes, maybe, some day. Stranger things have happened!"

Rachel made a mock groan into the phone. "I'm glad to hear that you're doing well, anyway. I've been missing you. It would have been fun, the three of us girls and none of our parents …"

"…AND Samuel," Deborah inserted slyly.

"That is one part of the trip I would not be sharing with you!" Rachel darted a glance at the two women who were sitting on a bench under the tree where they had been standing. "We're having a quick juice break and then we're going on. It's so hot here, all dust and hills. I think this is the most I have ever drunk in a single day. But I don't think I should talk very long because they're waiting for me now."

"I just wanted to hear how things are going and make sure you're all right," Deborah said.

"Just wonderful. Jerusalem is so much like I remembered – everything is sand-colored and it's all so dry but still just so beautiful. But what about things with you? Did you finally choose a dress for Solstice Ball?"

"Are you kidding? How could I do that without my best friend? We will go shopping as soon as you're back home, because you need one, too. Whatever color it's going to be! But what about you? Are you fighting much with Leah?"

"Things are wonderful! Leah and I are having too good a time to fight. Tomorrow we can watch them start to bring in the Omer."

"Have you worn your new dress yet?"

"Not yet, but I plan to wear it tonight. We're going to cook dinner in the common kitchen of our inn and sit out on the plaza to eat it."

"How I envy you! You'll have to give me all the details when you get back. But I'll let you go now. Love you!"

"Love you, too, Deborah!" Rachel broke the connection, put the phone back in her pouch, and stepped back around the tree to the bench. By this point, Leah and Gveret Ruth were standing by it and chatting while waiting for her. She joined them with a quick apology, and they continued on their way.

Lunchtime found the trio at the market. The twins decided to order chicken salads, but Gveret Ruth, who wasn't fond of anything that was fried, played it safe and had a vegetarian salad with cheese and tomato. They made faces as unleavened bread was handed out with each order. They all agreed that it was a big step up from street food and they were glad that they had held out. Then they wandered through the booths, admiring the exotic fruits and vegetables and grains and other products from all around the region, even beyond Judea's borders. They gathered a number of treats as well as the makings of a delicious dinner, had everything wrapped very securely along with a few ice packs, and started back to the inn. "We can leave these things in the refrigerator at the inn," Gveret Ruth decided, "and then go on to the Sanhedrin. I'll call Adon Jonathan when we get back to the inn and see if we can meet them at the Temple and go back together for dinner."

"I'm so glad we have the opportunity to look around the city," Rachel remarked as they walked along, rather more briskly this time since they were carrying food and were not intending to stop along the way. "It's nice to be spending some quality time in Jerusalem. We've never really gotten far away from the Temple Mount when we've come here before. Abba and Ima were always worried about us with all the crowds."

"I suspect you were a bit younger then," Gveret Ruth smiled at her indulgently. They turned one final corner and stopped in front of a beautifully landscaped complex.

"Oh, is this the Sanhedrin?" asked Leah. "I didn't realize there was anything back here. Didn't we learn in school that it's built into the northern end of the Temple walls?"

"The Chamber of Hewn Stone hasn't been used for the Sanhedrin for many years," Gveret Ruth replied. "With all the staff they require and all the modern equipment and files to keep, they outgrew it a few hundred years ago. This complex dates back only a little more than 200 years."

"'Only'!" laughed Rachel. "You have to be in Judea to think of 200 years as really recent."

Leah nudged Rachel as they walked up to the building, and they smiled at each other. A guard stepped out very quietly to block their further progress as they started up the stairway to the main door arches.

"Do you women have business with the Sanhedrin?" he asked them respectfully, while at the same time making it clear that they were not going to get past him easily.

"We were hoping that there might be some kind of tour so we could see inside," Gveret Ruth answered him.

"As a matter of fact, there is one in about 20 more minutes. You're welcome to look at the grounds meanwhile. I can sign you up – just the three of you?"

"Yes, and thank you so much."

"It's nothing." The guard picked up his phone and pressed a button. "Benjamin ben Isaac will be out shortly to lead the group. Two shekels each." He paused, attention shifting to the phone he was holding to his ear. "Yes, Benjamin, I have three more guests for the next tour. Fine, they can meet you here at the doorway in 15 minutes." Looking back at Gveret Ruth, he said to her, "There is a map that shows the layout of the grounds around the side of this building to your right. Please return it when you are finished. You should have enough time to get a good idea of the different gardens and water features back there."

As they thanked him and started walking away, Rachel grabbed Leah's elbow. "Did you notice the pin that he's wearing?" she whispered.

"Yes, he's Zoroastrian!" Leah answered. "I've never seen one in person before! I thought they were all farther east. There can't be too many in Judea."

"Well, this IS Jerusalem, after all. A capital city and a diverse population. But I didn't know they were around here, either."

"They're mostly in Babylonia and Persia," Gveret Ruth interjected, having heard these last words.

"And in India, of course. But there are little groups of them scattered everywhere else in these nearby countries, too."

"I'd sure like to ask him some questions, if that's acceptable," sighed Leah, looking back over her shoulder. "And see some of their rituals!"

"I don't think you'll have much opportunity for either of those, Leah. They're a bit secretive and their rituals are private," Gveret Ruth told her.

125

"They were such an influence on us!" said Rachel. "It would be nice to ask somebody who actually practices it what they do, how they differ from what we do, how much it's changed in thousands of years..."

"We'd better get back to the front," Gveret Ruth announced. "The tour should be starting any minute now."

They walked back around the building and joined a group of perhaps half a dozen other people. A man wearing a badge that said "Benjamin ben Isaac, Sanhedrin guide" came out through the door of the building and down the front steps to greet the small group. "Welcome to the Sanhedrin," he said. "Although this building was built only in 5548, we still use some of the traditional names for the various rooms. The main room where the Sanhedrin sits in council is still called the Chamber of Hewn Stone, as it was more than 2000 years ago. Please follow me inside. No photography is permitted, please. This is the working center of government for all of Judea and I'm sure that you understand that we cannot risk spies. Postcards showing various views of the different chambers and of the exterior of the building itself are available for purchase at the end of the tour."

The group entered the building and found themselves in a very imposing foyer. "You can still see the influence of Greek culture on our art and architecture," Benjamin remarked, as he led them into a corridor on the right. They passed various offices and eventually reached a double door at the far end of the building, which Benjamin opened with a flourish. "Behold the Chamber of Hewn Stone!"

The girls gazed in awe at the semicircular table that filled three sides of the room. The open end of the table faced many small tables all arrayed along one wall. "That higher seat in the middle is for the chief of the Sanhedrin," Benjamin told them, leading the way across the polished mosaic floor to the center of the huge table. He went on with his explanations, mentioning both how things had been done in the past and how they were done now.

The group continued walking around inside the building, Benjamin patiently answering questions he had likely fielded dozens of times before, until they had once again reached the grand foyer. They thanked him for a most fascinating tour of the building, went outside into the bright sunshine, blinking, and walked back down the stairs. Leah looked around for the Zoroastrian attendant but was unable to see him anywhere in the area.

They strolled around the corner and were heading up to the Temple. A distant figure waving toward them caught Rachel's eye, and as they got closer, she saw that it was Samuel with his father and another young man. "Oh, good, we're all together again!" exclaimed Gveret Ruth, seeming rather relieved. "I wasn't sure how easy it would be to find them, even though I told them where we would be coming from."

"Samuel has friend tracking on his phone," Leah told her.

The men having rejoined them, they turned and walked toward their inn together. "This is my roommate, Seth ben Ephraim," Samuel said, introducing the women to the third man who was with them. "He has family here in town, so I haven't seen much of him, but we ran into him leaving the Temple just now."

"Pleased to meet you," the girls chorused, then smiled at each other. Twins so often do that!

"Are you here on your own?" asked Gveret Ruth.

"No, my parents are at the inn, too, but they are waiting for our family back there, so I came to the Temple alone today. It was nice to run into Samuel and to be able to walk back with such enjoyable company."

Leah smiled at the flattery and took a more comprehensive look at him. He was absolutely gorgeous! She elbowed Rachel and nodded toward him, and Rachel too took a look and then raised her eyebrows at her sister in silent approval. That dark curly hair, those deep brown eyes that were almost black, a cute little moustache, his skin so tan... Samuel had done okay with his roommate. She felt less sorry for him that he was not able to have his own private room at the inn. She shot a furtive glance at Samuel, but he seemed distracted and was not paying attention to her. Not that there was anything wrong in checking out a good-looking guy!

"I need to call a friend back home," Samuel said, looking up from his phone. "I just heard that his father died."

"I am sorry to hear that. You go ahead and call him when we get back to the rooms," his mother told him, squeezing his shoulder affectionately. "We'll start dinner and we can all eat whenever you're done."

"What IS for dinner?" Samuel inquired, interested.

"We found a lovely piece of fish at the market, and some of the freshest vegetables you've ever seen!" gushed Rachel.

"But only healthy things, no treats?"

"Oh, you of the bottomless pit! You're starting to sound a little like Leah. Yes, we got some great-looking pastry that we can enjoy for dessert with a cup of tea," teased Rachel.

Having reached the inn, the little group separated with brief farewells and went off to their rooms to freshen up a bit. Gveret Ruth invited him to join them for dinner, but he demurred, saying that he was going out to meet his parents and cousins within the hour.

"Samuel is so nice!" exclaimed Leah. "His whole family is. His mother has just been wonderful to us."

"Yes, they're all great. I am incredibly lucky!" replied Rachel, hanging up her skirt and blouse from their morning excursion and putting on a fresh dress. "Did you happen to bring an apron? I totally forgot mine."

"You never do remember things like that!" teased Leah. "I brought three, so I'd always have a clean one if I spilled on one of them. We're here for a whole week and I assumed we'd be doing a fair amount of cooking."

"YOU are nothing if not compulsive, but I'm glad because I know I can count on you!"

"And what do you think of Seth?" Leah continued.

"I don't think I've ever seen a boy that good-looking before," Rachel confessed. "Those eyes of his ... If he flirts with me at all, Samuel might have to work hard to keep me."

"Well, I'm not so sure about THAT!" laughed Leah. "But you're right; he's an absolute work of art. I hope we see more of him."

Rachel looked at her sister thoughtfully. She wondered about the emotional commitment that Leah had to Joseph. Thinking back, she realized that she was not aware of a single time that Leah had sent as much as a text to him.

Hands and faces washed and aprons tied over their new dresses, the twins went down to the kitchen area in the inn that was reserved for guests to cook their own meals. Gveret Ruth was already there, herself in a yellow dress and matching apron, and their parcels from the morning were arrayed on the counter before her. "Guess who's here?" she asked as the girls entered.

"Who?" they chorused.

"Jacob ben Judah and his parents! Samuel and Adon Jonathan ran into them this morning at the Temple. I guess the guys texted each other, discovered they were all on the Temple Mount, and connected with my friend tracking app."

"Oh, how nice!" exclaimed Leah. "Where are they staying?"

"Maybe they can join us for dinner? We should have more than enough food," Rachel added.

"Samuel is calling Jacob right around now to invite them over. They aren't that far from us. Oh, and let me see your new dresses!"

The girls pirouetted in the kitchen, laughing. "Hard to see the fronts with these aprons on, but you can see the back at least," said Rachel.

"They're just so pretty! Wear them in good health."

The girls had still another surprise when Samuel came into the kitchen to alert them to the arrival of their dinner guests. At a nod from Gveret Ruth, who was just sliding the pan of fish into the oven, they went out with him and into the lobby. And there they saw Jacob, his parents, and behind him Deborah's brother Aaron and his mother Esther!

"Oh, my goodness!" exclaimed Rachel, looking up at Aaron. "I completely forgot that you were going to be here! I talked to Deborah earlier today and she never mentioned that you'd found Jacob and Samuel!"

"I knew they were both here, so I searched for them on the friend tracking app. Imagine my astonishment when I saw that they were in the same place! As for telling Deborah, I haven't talked to the folks back home yet," Aaron replied. "And at that point, we all agreed it would be fun to surprise you!"

"And hello, Gveret Esther," Rachel continued, hugging her best friend's mother. "It's just wonderful to see you here! And you, too, Jacob. You just aren't as big of a surprise!"

Jacob smiled at Rachel and then at Leah. Then he turned to an older couple standing slightly behind him. "These are my parents, Judah ben

Asher and Rebeka bat Samuel. These are Rachel and Leah b'not Shimson. Rachel is Aaron's sister Deborah's best friend. Oh, and here comes Ruth bat Eli, Samuel's mother. Do you already know each other?"

Gveret Ruth finished drying her hands on her apron and reached out her hand to Gveret Rebeka, who took it briefly. "I'm not sure we have met before, but it's lovely to have you here. People from back home do make things seem friendlier!"

"Yes, I'm so glad the men ran into each other at the Temple. The chances of that happening can't be that high, with all the people here in town for the festival!"

"Dinner is almost ready, no more than another half hour," Gveret Ruth continued. "So maybe we can just sit here in the lobby and share stories about the adventures we've been having."

Just as they were sitting down, Adon Jonathan strode into the room, and they all stood up again so that he and the guests could greet one another. Then they settled onto the various chairs and sofas that were arranged in a semi-circle near the huge bay window.

"This is a really comfortable inn," Adon Joseph remarked appreciatively. "We should keep it in mind for the next time we come here."

"We've stayed here several times before," answered Gveret Ruth. "We've always been quite comfortable here. It has the best guest kitchen facilities of any place that we'd looked at. And it was already set up for Pesach upon our arrival."

Meanwhile, Rachel was exclaiming to Aaron, "I still can't believe we're all here together in Jerusalem! I can't wait to tell Deborah all about it the next time we talk. Unless you talk to her first."

Aaron laughed. "Not very likely! No way I could compete with the two of you."

"Have you been anywhere today besides the Temple?" Leah inquired.

"Well, not being illustrious Kohenim like our friend here," Aaron nodded at Samuel with a grin, "we were mostly sightseeing today. But we wanted to stop and catch Mincha and maybe offer some incense. We ran into Samuel and his father as we were leaving."

"I'm so glad you did," Gveret Ruth told him, catching the last words they were speaking. "It will be good to have a nice visit with people from back home." She smoothed out her apron and went back into the inn's communal kitchen.

Jacob asked, "So where did you go today?"

Rachel answered, "Gveret Ruth took Leah and me to some of the ancient sites around here. Samuel isn't the only one who likes ruins!" with an impish glance in his direction.

"We were heading toward the market," Leah continued the story. "So we stopped at a few sites in that direction. A museum of various Codes of Law, and a Nazarene site, and one they think dates back to Hasmonean times!"

"I'm mostly interested in those little sects that flourished during the Roman occupation," Jacob remarked. "Not the main political movements like the Pharisees and the Sadducees, but strange little groups that came and went like the Nazarenes. And even more the Essenes, but they wouldn't have any sites in this region. What was the Nazarene site like?"

Rachel shrugged. "It's hard to describe because it wasn't that different from anything else that's 2000 years old. A lot of it was underground – catacombs and things. The guide said that they were persecuted throughout their history and eventually just faded away. So I guess they had places where they could go into hiding or at least protect their leaders."

"And the Hasmonean site?" asked Samuel. "I can't think of anything out in that direction that would be military."

"Oh, this was later than that," Leah answered. "It wasn't associated with the Maccabean battles. I think the guide said that it was more like during the time when Aristobulus was challenging Hycanus II. Maybe around the year 3700?"

"You have it all over me with that one!" Rachel grinned, stretching. "I can't keep the names or the dates straight. I'm amazed you remembered it all."

"Are there Essene sites to see, too?" asked Jacob.

"They're more over by the Dead Sea," Samuel responded. "I don't think much was known about them until they gathered together and moved out of Jerusalem so they could have a more holy existence. I do need to see more of Judea some day!" and he glanced at Rachel.

She said wistfully, "I only wish we'd been able to see some of the excavations. I know they're digging in various places right here in Jerusalem. But Leah and I do intend to get out to a site somewhere in Judea. We've never explored anything outside of Jerusalem."

Just then, Gveret Ruth came out of the kitchen again with a platter of vegetables. She smiled at them as she walked through the lobby and out the sliding glass door to the plaza. The twins jumped up and ran into the kitchen to help bring out the rest of the food. Last came the fish, which had lemon and za'atar on it and smelled wonderful. Laughing and talking, the group arranged itself around two of the tables that the inn provided on the plaza for its guests' meals. It was a beautiful evening and everybody felt extra sparkly, energized by being together with people from back home and yet within a short distance of the Temple during a joyous festival. Samuel winked at Rachel as he held up a piece of unleavened bread, something they both felt that they could live long, full lives without ever having to eat again.

When the dinner was over and they had cleaned up, they sat down around the tables again to chat. Nobody was in a hurry for the evening to end. Rachel said thoughtfully, "You know, we were talking today about how the Romans destroyed part of Jerusalem and were awfully close to destroying the Temple. What would have become of us if they had succeeded?"

"There wouldn't be any Judaism after that," Jacob remarked. "We did eventually give up animal sacrifice, but not for another 1500 years. If the Temple had vanished entirely, that was the entire focus of our religion at that point. What else could have held us together? We wouldn't have survived."

Leah shuddered. "I can't even imagine who we would be or what kind of lives we'd be living instead."

"Well, we have always won every time it counted!" Aaron laughed. "When we're backed against a wall, we fight really well."

"I don't know," Leah answered. "The First Temple did get destroyed, after all."

"I don't even like to think about it," Rachel said. "There would be no guarantee that any exile after they destroyed the Second Temple would have only lasted 70 years again. We might well have been lumped together as extinct, just ancient history, along with the Hittites and Moabites and all the other groups that came and went."

The adults had been listening quietly, but at this point, Adon Jonathan joined the discussion. "When I think of how much it means in my family to be a Kohen, how central the Temple is to our lives even with us spread all around the world now – I just can't contemplate the trajectory our history would have followed for the last 2000 years without our Temple."

They visited a while longer, and then Samuel's parents excused themselves and went to their room. The young people walked Jacob, Aaron, and their parents to the point where their paths to their own inns diverged and then came back and sat on the patio for a while. Eventually, though, Rachel became aware that she was tired and knew that the next day would be another eventful day, so she said her good nights. The others readily agreed that this was a good idea, and all went to their rooms.

Chapter 22

The next morning, Leah arose and went back out on the patio to watch the sunrise. Rachel joined her a little later, carrying two cups of tea. "So they're bringing in the Omer today," Leah greeted her, nodding her appreciation for the tea.

"Yes, another new experience for us. I can't wait! I wonder when Miriam will get here?"

"Didn't Samuel say what time of day they might be coming? Meeting them might be tricky with all the crowds already here and then the people from the countryside bringing in the barley offerings. Maybe they'll come here to the inn before we have to go anywhere."

Rachel leaned back and took a sip of her tea, hot and fragrant. "I guess we'll find out when everybody else is up. Have you been out here long?"

"No, maybe half an hour," Leah answered. "I came out to see the sunrise because I was awake anyway. Sarah called me about an hour ago, and it woke me up. I came outside because it looked so pretty."

"So what's new with Sarah?" Rachel asked idly, blowing on her tea.

"Her room is finished! She is going to pick out a color to paint it and she should be moved back in before we get home. But then they start the messy part on the main rooms of the house, and she'll be moving in with us for a few weeks."

"That is definitely exciting!" Rachel agreed. "I can't wait for us to see it."

"Hey, what about Shira? Are she and Eli here for this festival?"

Rachel shook her head. "No, in the end, they couldn't get away. But we're trying to make plans for a visit once we're past graduation." The sisters sat in companionable silence for a while.

"What do you remember about Zoroastrians?" asked Leah.

"Other than recognizing the pin that they wear?" teased Rachel.

Leah elbowed her gently. "No, silly! I'm trying to remember what we learned about them. They started in Persia, didn't they?"

"Yes, not long before the First Temple was destroyed. They have one supreme God. They used to believe in a lot of lesser gods, too. And they believed in good and evil. Our teacher said that they influenced us when we went into exile, but then we went further and developed ethical monotheism."

"Which is the belief that laws come from God, if I'm remembering right."

Rachel sighed. "I wish we'd had a chance to talk to that man a bit, although maybe he wouldn't want to be discussing his religion yet again with some more annoying tourists. I keep trying to understand the difference between monolatry and monotheism. I can only remember it long enough to take a test!"

Leah laughed. "I don't think Zoroastrianism was the first monotheistic religion anyway," she said. "Wasn't there a Pharaoh 500 years before that who was a monotheist?"

"Yes," Rachel mused, "Akhenaten. He instituted worship of the sun as a god over all others. But they reverted to polytheism after he died."

"And then they wiped out the records of all the changes he had made!" laughed Leah. "It doesn't pay to innovate if you're going to be overturned as soon as you die."

The girls finished their tea and went back inside to shower and dress. After the group had breakfast, they were all sitting out on the patio chatting when they started hearing music. "Oh, I think they're starting to bring in the Omer!" Adon Jonathan exclaimed. "Let's go stand on the corner and see if they pass nearby."

They rushed outside just in time to see the first of the crowd go by, bearing sheaves of barley and singing springtime and harvest songs. "Do they have to go through the Bikkurim formula?" Rachel inquired.

"No," Samuel answered. "Bikkurim happens at Shavuot, when the harvest is actually of first fruits and vegetables. Only barley is ready to harvest this early in the year, so it's just an offering."

"Look how festively they're all dressed!" Gveret Ruth exclaimed. "This must be such an exciting time for all the people in the rural areas around the city."

"It feels like a festival even more now," agreed Leah. "All the singing and commotion and people with their gifts!"

"I'm glad we're staying at this inn," Adon Jonathan remarked. "We've never been on the path before of the people coming in with the Omer. It's just so exotic! We don't have this kind of parade back home, that's for sure."

"Tirzah called this morning," Gveret Ruth said. "They will probably arrive in the Temple Mount area just after lunchtime and will meet up with us then. It will be so good to see them! I think it's been several years, and I do miss my sister."

"Sisters are special," agreed Rachel, squeezing Leah's arm.

"I think of Miriam as being about ten," Samuel laughed. "But she has to be fifteen by now and probably not a little kid who whines about being bored any more!"

Just then, they were joined by Seth and an older couple whom he introduced as his parents. They exchanged greetings, and Rachel noticed that Seth's father was just as good-looking and charming as his son. She wondered whether they would get a chance to know them a little better before they had to leave Jerusalem.

They all watched the parade a little while longer. It was fascinating, so many different people from so many surrounding communities joining together with a common purpose and marching from different directions to converge on the Temple. Seth and his parents, murmuring apologies, left for their planned day. And eventually it began to seem like too much of the same kind of thing, so by mutual consent, the group went back inside the inn, where they each got their books and gathered again on the plaza to rest and read.

"What are you studying?" Rachel asked Samuel, noting the cover of his book.

"It's a commentary from about 500 years ago," he answered. "It's a bit slower going because it was written in Hebrew like so many of them were through the ages, and that's different enough from Aramaic that I really have to focus on each word sometimes."

"I have a project due a few weeks after we get back," Leah announced. "So I'm reading this book of sacred poetry. It's in Hebrew, too."

"Oh, that's the class that Deborah is in, right?" asked Samuel. "I never really enjoyed poetry myself. I'm glad it's only an elective!"

"And this is still that endless book of essays that I'm supposed to 'compare and contrast' for my project, also due a few weeks after we get back," Rachel said, holding up her book.

Gveret Ruth laughed and looked over at her husband, who was studying a printed edition of Isaiah and not really paying attention to the conversation. "Well, I admit that I'm just reading a novel. There are advantages to not being in school any more. I'm on vacation, so I have that luxury!"

"What is it?" asked Leah, looking in her direction.

"The newest one by ben Shlomo," she replied. "His writing is so lyrical, and I couldn't wait for this one to come out!"

The chatter died down as they all focused on their books, enjoying being together and relaxing for a little while during an otherwise highly eventful trip.

A text popped up on Rachel's phone. It was from Shira, so she quickly opened it. "Hi! How's lover boy? Have you two run off into the sunset yet, or does too much togetherness make you want to strangle him?"

Rachel giggled. Samuel quirked a questioning eyebrow in her direction, but she just waved him off before texting back to Shira, "I can definitely see myself spending the rest of my life with him, but he hasn't asked me to."

"?!" came back almost immediately.

"Wouldn't it be romantic if he proposed to me right here in Jerusalem?"

"Sure would!"

Rachel cast a surreptitious glance at Samuel under her eyelashes. His nose was once again buried deep in his book. "You'll be the first to know!" She signed off with a heart and a smiley face and put her phone back down.

"Was that Deborah?" asked Leah, looking over at her.

"No, Shira."

"What's new with her?"

Rachel snickered. What if she were to announce right out loud what their conversation had been about? Might that force Samuel's hand? Or drive him far away? Out loud, she said only, "Nothing, really. Same old." Then she stared at Samuel, falling into a daydream.

Chapter 23

Some time after lunch, Rachel and Leah were back in their room, Rachel rebraiding Leah's hair, when they heard a knock on their door. "My cousin Miriam is here!" Samuel called to them through the door. "We're all going to sit in the lobby for a while because of course Ima has to feed everybody even though we just finished eating!"

"Okay, we'll be right out!" Rachel called back to him, giving a gentle tug to Leah's braid before tying a blue ribbon on the bottom to match Leah's dress.

Shortly thereafter, the girls strolled into the lobby, where they saw the four adults standing and talking near one of the coffee tables, with Samuel a little bit outside the circle but looking on intently. They didn't see the teenaged girl at first but then noticed her near one wall of the lobby, looking at the pottery on display there. Samuel was the first to spot the girls and introduced them to his aunt and uncle, who greeted them warmly. When he introduced Miriam, she ducked her head and mumbled something they couldn't quite understand, and they remembered that she was said to be shy, or at least in front of her mother.

"Let's go outside," Leah suggested, hoping that would make her feel more like opening up. "Unless you're starving and can't live without a cooky and some tea!"

"Okay," Miriam told her shoes, and the three girls left by the front door. Rachel caught Samuel's eye, but he shrugged helplessly and jerked his head toward his parents, and she understood by this that he was trapped with his relatives for a while.

"So you live in Jerusalem, right?" asked Rachel, smiling at the younger girl. "Is your home far from here?"

Miriam answered softly, not quite making eye contact. "Far enough that we needed to take transport. Abba and I could have walked, but Ima has bad knees and wouldn't have been able to do it."

"What is there to see around here that we don't know about and shouldn't miss?" asked Leah.

Miriam looked up excitedly then. "Oh, I know just the thing to show you! Have you ever been to the Mount of Olives?"

"No. Isn't that north of here?"

"Well, actually more like east from here. There was a celebration there a few weeks ago, so you've missed it, but I can show you the ramp that leads from the Temple to the Mount of Olives when we go out there this afternoon for the offering of the Omer."

"Why do they need a ramp?" asked Leah. "Isn't it awfully far?"

"And what's up there that you would have a celebration for?" Rachel chimed in.

Miriam laughed, and her whole face lit up so that they realized she was actually quite pretty. "It's only about 4000 cubits from the Temple, not all that far. And I think I'll keep it as a surprise until we're there. If we have a break, we can walk alongside the ramp to the mountain, and I'll show you the spot and tell you all about it."

"We should," Rachel mock-grumbled. "They'll be burning the barley for ages, and Samuel and Adon Jonathan will have to stand there and watch the whole thing. I bet we can get away and nobody would even notice!"

"I think they'd be glad for us to have something to do," Miriam said. "It seems like it isn't going to be as hot today, but we'll cover our heads and carry water just in case."

"Sounds like fun!" Leah said, and Rachel nodded and smiled as well.

The front door of the inn opened and Gveret Tirzah called out, "Girls! Oh, there you are! Come on in and have some goodies!"

They nudged each other and giggled as they walked back inside to join the rest of the group. Leah caught Rachel's eye and grimaced as she noticed the platters. Cookies made with ground-up unleavened bread instead of ordinary flour were so heavy and dry. Rachel winked back at her and passed her the nearest platter.

Shortly afterwards, Gveret Ruth and Gveret Tirzah were in the inn's kitchen, washing dishes and very deep in conversation, while Rachel was dumping cooky crumbs into the trash and preparing to hand them the plates that still needed to be washed. Miriam had disappeared but came back in carrying her backpack, from which she pulled out a few water bottles. There was a fountain with purified drinking water in it next to the sink and she began filling the bottles. Leah was packing dried fruits and nuts into a small bag. "Would anybody want any unleavened bread?" she asked.

"UGH! Cookies were enough! Let's not eat that more than we actually have to!" Rachel replied. Miriam smiled without looking up.

"What's going on?" Gveret Tirzah inquired, interrupting herself in what seemed to be a long story she was telling her sister.

"I'd like to take them up to the Mount of Olives," Miriam explained.

"We'll be standing around forever otherwise, watching the barley burn up," Rachel added.

"Oh, to see -"

Leah quickly broke in, "Don't tell us! Miriam says it's a surprise for us!"

"Okay, that's fine. If you can make the trip there and back within two hours, before we leave the Temple," Gveret Ruth said. "I'm sure you realize that you won't have Samuel with you."

"Yes, we're aware of that!" laughed Rachel. "Nothing can pull him away from his pride in being a Kohen!"

"And they're safe with me anyway," Miriam added. "I have been there dozens of times and I know my way around very well."

When everybody was ready to go back to the Temple, the three girls tied on head scarves and each took a water bottle. Leah clutched her small bag of snacks, and off they went. There were still stragglers in the streets rushing along, singing, and carrying yet more sheaves of barley. They let themselves be swept up in the sparse crowd and were soon in a holiday mood as they were being propelled toward the Temple grounds. Pushing their way in through the Temple gates almost with volition, since they were still being drawn along by the crowd, they came to the Court of Women. Here, Adon Jonathan, Samuel, and Adon Joel continued on into the next Court, from which they could observe the burning of the sheaves of barley as the culmination of this annual offering. The three girls separated from the women at this point and managed to elbow their way "upstream" back out of the Temple enclosure.

At this point, Miriam took the lead and walked them around the Temple wall, first northward and then eastward, to the opposite side. She called their attention to a golden ramp that was directly ahead of them, then pointed eastward to a nearby peak and said, "That is the Mount of Olives. This ramp leads there."

The twins looked at each other and shrugged; Miriam was clearly not ready to give them any insight into this excursion just yet. Leah opened her water bottle and took a sip of water, and then they set off, adjacent to but, following Miriam's example, carefully not walking directly on the ramp. The ground was well trampled here, and it was obvious that there had been a lot of people following this same route. They continued up the side of the mountain, taking occasional small drinks of water so as to make it last, until they reached a huge clearing, where the ramp ended. Here Miriam finally stopped, sitting on a large rock and indicating that the twins should find nearby rocks to sit on. "Let's have our snack now," she suggested, looking at Leah. "That was rather hot work!"

As Leah started opening the bag of dried fruits and nuts and distributing the contents, Rachel burst out, "So where are we? This must be the place where the celebration happens, but now can you tell us why? What it's all about?"

Miriam smiled. "Do you know about the red heifer?"

"Yes, it's something that is burned to ash, and then the ashes are mixed with water and used to purify people who have come in contact with a corpse and are impure," replied Rachel.

"Right," nodded Miriam. "The red heifer isn't allowed to be sacrificed inside the Temple enclosure, so they slaughter and burn it up here. The golden ramp is how the Kohen Gadol walks between the Temple and this site when they're going through that ritual."

"And we haven't actually done that for almost two hundred years," Leah added. "We still have some ashes from the last one that was sacrificed. I know they're watching carefully for the next one, but no suitable candidates yet. I think there have only been sixteen of them, according to the tales."

"And you're right again!" Miriam said. "During the month of Adar, just a few Shabbatot ago, the portion that was read from the Torah was about the rules of the red heifer. So people come up here and have a huge feast every year to commemorate this, even though most years, we're not actually sacrificing a red heifer because we don't have one. It's a kickoff event of some sort to the three summer festivals, the way I always see it. I went to it with my two best friends this year. It's too bad you missed it, because it's always fun to have a reason to celebrate."

"So IS there actually some kind of ceremony or ritual with the Kohen Gadol doing anything symbolic?" asked Leah.

"Not really. He does walk along the golden ramp with the crowds on both sides of it walking alongside him until he gets to this place, but there's no killing or burning going on here most years. It's basically another excuse to eat and drink and sing!"

"That is SO exciting!" exclaimed Rachel, who had been looking down at the view of the Temple Mount from their vantage point. "I wonder when there will be another red heifer. Are the ashes we're still using really left from the previous one?"

Miriam shrugged casually. "There are ceremonial ashes in an urn that they use, but it's hard for me to believe they're still from the last red heifer. Every few years, a candidate calf is born, but so far none of them has stayed entirely red for the first few years of their life. You can't even have two hairs that aren't red! There's one right now outside Shiloh, but it's only two years old, so the Kohenim keep an eye on it, but nothing is happening yet, and most of the time, they do fizzle out."

Rachel was leaning back against a tree, her eyes half-closed, and mentioned, in a teasing tone, "There is the best-looking guy staying at our inn. He is Samuel's roommate, Seth ben Ephraim. We haven't seen much of him because he's here with his parents and they have family in town." She looked over at Leah and winked.

Miriam perked up. "Maybe they'll be around when we get back to the inn. I am definitely in the mood to meet some gorgeous guy."

"Oh, I don't know," Leah drawled. "We saw him first!"

Miriam laughed. "Well, Rachel won't be any competition because of Samuel, and I think I can take you on any day, Leah."

"He IS awfully good-looking," Rachel said. "I'm not so sure I wouldn't give you a run for your money!"

Miriam looked back down the hill, from which the Temple was clearly visible. "You can't make offerings back where you live, can you?" she asked. "They can only be performed at the Temple and that's too far for you to get to routinely. What kind of rituals are observed in Anatolia?"

"They're done at your uncle's house," Rachel said proudly. "He has a big enclosure in the back where he leads songs and prayers, a few psalms, readings from the Torah. That kind of thing."

"And then afterwards," Leah added, "we get to eat wheat or barley pancakes cooked in olive oil."

Miriam shuddered. "That sounds gross!"

"They're meant to represent the grain sacrifices that are offered here at the Temple," Rachel explained. "You're right; we aren't permitted to offer sacrifices away from the Temple, but we do have reminders so that we feel connected."

"That does make sense," Miriam agreed.

Leah glanced at her phone and then suggested, "Speaking of offerings, the mincha offering might be over soon. We should probably start heading back. We wouldn't want to be walking down this trail after dark."

The three stood up, brushing crumbs off their dresses as they picked up their backpacks and water bottles. "It's such a beautiful day!" noted Rachel, tying on her hat. "Even without the amazing history here, the weather just doesn't feel anything like it does back home. Was it already warm enough to be up here during the celebration?"

"Not as warm as today, of course, but the spring rains are done by then and it's certainly warm enough to be outside as long as you would need to be," Miriam replied. "And doesn't food taste a lot better when you eat it out in the sunshine and fresh air? Thank you for bringing the snack, Leah."

"Sure," laughed Leah. "Everybody who knows me already knows that I don't like to go very long without eating! I always do enjoy dried fruit and nuts, so I hope you do, too."

"I do," agreed Miriam. "And almost anything is a welcome break from unleavened bread products."

"AND it's only the second day of the holiday..." groaned Leah. Rachel gave her a quick one-armed hug and the girls headed back down the mountain toward the Temple once again.

"Do you suppose it's okay for us to walk on the golden ramp a little bit, or even just to step on it? Just to see what it's like?" Rachel inquired within moments. "There isn't anybody else around and it's not like the Kohen Gadol is suddenly going to show up to sacrifice a red heifer."

Miriam hesitated. "I'm not aware of any actual law against stepping on it, but it's just customary that it belongs only to the Kohen Gadol. I wouldn't feel comfortable touching it myself, especially as a woman."

"Well, then, we shouldn't," decided Rachel, and she turned her face forward once again.

The girls turned on their phone tracking functions and were soon reunited with the rest of their party. "So what did you think?" asked Gveret Ruth, having been briefed by her sister and her son as to what the girls were up to.

"It was astounding!" Leah gushed. "It's one thing to read about the red heifer in the Torah and to know about the rituals involved. But to see it right in front of us as something that is actually done and that everybody basically takes for granted is just an amazing thing to me."

"And me, too," agreed Rachel. "I can't believe the centuries – millennia, really – of history in the very air around us here!"

"People have been in your own land for almost as long," pointed out Miriam.

"Well, that's true, and we do know about it from school and from visiting communities around us like Hamiskoy where the indigenous people of our region live. They are certainly keeping the old ways alive. But they aren't OUR ancestors' ways from thousands of years back!"

Gveret Tirzah put in, "I'm so glad that you girls had a chance to see that place while you were here. It would be harder to see it clearly if there were crowds everywhere because of the celebration."

"Yes, that's true," Gveret Ruth agreed with her sister. "I've only been up there during the festival myself, so I'm not sure I'm completely clear about the layout."

"It was fascinating!" Rachel put in. "Thank you so much for the great surprise, Miriam."

"Yes, thank you once again," Leah echoed. "We are so lucky to be here with such experienced local guides."

"But I wonder if we would ever be able to see them actually sprinkling somebody with the ashes," Miriam mused thoughtfully.

"It's not done as a public ceremony," Adon Jonathan answered her. "And I think in practice, it's only used for Kohenim who have incurred corpse impurity just before or during their service in the Temple. The ashes are used pretty sparingly, really."

"And that would be in the Temple anyway, right? This site is only where they actually slaughter and burn the red heifer?"

"Yes, Miriam," Adon Jonathan said. "So even if it were more public in nature, you'd be stuck back in the Court of Women and wouldn't be able to see it anyway."

"I'm really so glad we got to go up there today!" Rachel enthused. "It makes everything that we study come so much alive to see the places where these things really take place."

"We didn't have nearly as good a time," Samuel mock-whined. "Watching people burn sheaves of barley one after another is not that exciting after a while." Rachel pretended to slap him.

"Well, anyway, we're together again now, which means it's probably time to start thinking about dinner," Gveret Ruth said. "Will you be able to stay and join us, Sara?"

"Not this time, I'm afraid," Adon Joel said. "I have a meeting later tonight and I want to be home to change and get ready for it. So we're going to have to leave shortly. But how lovely it was to spend an enjoyable day with you!"

"Yes," echoed Gveret Tirzah, "it truly was. And since you'll still be in Jerusalem another few days, we have been talking about coming out to meet you once more, either tomorrow or the next day. Miriam has class, so it would probably be just the two of us if we decide to do that and it's okay with you."

"Oh, we would LOVE that!" Gveret Ruth said, hugging her sister. "Let us know as soon as you decide. If it's Sixth Day, maybe you'd even be able to stay longer and spend Shabbat with us."

By this point, they had reached the inn and stopped by Adon Joel's car parked out in front. "Okay, I will definitely call you either way. Love you!" replied Gveret Sara.

"Love you back!" Gveret Ruth said, with a hug.

Rachel and Leah hugged first Miriam and then Gveret Sara. "It was so wonderful to meet you all! I really hope we do see you again," Leah said.

"And you, too, Miriam," said Rachel, with an additional hug of the younger girl, having become quite fond of her in the brief time they were together. "Why don't we exchange numbers, so we can keep in touch? And then you'll know when we're able to make another trip to Jerusalem."

Miriam readily agreed, handing her phone to Rachel, and they hugged again after the transaction had been completed.

They stood on the path and waved until the car was out of sight, then turned and walked into the inn. "Might as well just eat our leftovers for dinner," suggested Gveret Ruth, "since it's just us. We'll probably be eating out all day tomorrow."

As Samuel stepped back to let Rachel in ahead of him, he whispered to her, "So did you think that Miriam is shy?"

"Not with us!" she laughed. "But I did see the difference around her parents."

"I'm so glad you girls got along. She's a real doll and we don't see each other in person all that much."

Meanwhile, Leah was asking Samuel's parents, "What is on the schedule for tomorrow?"

"There are several options we've been considering," Adon Jonathan replied. "There are a few lovely hikes in the hills around the city. You girls hiking up on the Mount of Olives put that into our minds. Or we could see more museums or more public buildings or a matinee of one of the plays – theatre is really excellent in Jerusalem."

"That could be a real novelty!" Leah said.

"We'll have to do some research," Gveret Ruth said, "because not all of the plays are in Aramaic. Some are in Greek and there is one theatre that portrays updated versions of Bible tales and actually does all of its dialogue in Hebrew!"

"If it's Bible stories, we could probably follow that," Rachel noted.

"And we do have a few more days," Samuel mused, "although First Day won't really count at all since we have to get to the airport and leave to go back home. But I really am looking forward to spending Shabbat in Jerusalem."

"Shabbat in Jerusalem of course is lovely," Adon Jonathan said. "With the extra offering and the extra songs and prayers. Although you three would normally have classes coming up on First Day next week, I'm glad that we're staying here instead. You'll just have to miss a few days."

"I am REALLY not ready to go back to the university already!" Rachel exclaimed. "It would be one thing if we were home during the festival like we are most years and just used the time to catch up on our work or be with friends. But being here in a different world will make it so disorienting to go back again like nothing ever happened to us."

"I know what you mean," Leah agreed. "But I'm eager to see our friends again. And of course, the school year is almost over anyway. Solstice Ball is in just a few weeks and then our final trimester after that. Too amazing to think about!"

While they were still standing in the lobby area talking, Seth and his parents came in from outside. Leah noticed him first, blushed, and elbowed Rachel in the ribs.

"How nice to see you again," Gveret Ruth said to the three newcomers. "What adventures have you been having today?"

"My cousins took us to Shiloh," Adon Ephraim answered. "So exciting to be in the midst of that chapter of history. There's a whole museum there where the Tabernacle once stood. And the altar is still there, too, now that

148

they've excavated it. We really hadn't seen much outside of Jerusalem on our past few visits."

"How interesting!" Samuel said.

Rachel stood very still and stared at Seth, her eyes opening wide. She cast a quick glance at her sister and then resumed her thoughtful scrutiny of Seth.

Leah, also looking at Seth and so not noticing her sister, said, "We had an adventure of our own. Samuel's cousin Miriam took us up on the Mount of Olives where they burn the red heifer to make the ashes."

"THAT would be something worth seeing!" Seth agreed, looking directly at Leah, who lowered her eyes. "That's where that golden ramp behind the Temple leads, right?"

"Yes," she answered. "You aren't allowed to walk on the ramp itself, but we followed it all the way up the mountain, the way the crowds go on the festival."

Seth and his parents excused themselves and headed into the main part of the inn, Seth glancing back to say, "Good-night, ladies! I'll see you in the room later, Samuel."

After the door closed behind them, the group resumed their previous discussion about what they might want to do the following day. Rachel started getting the impression that there were no pressing plans that anybody had in mind. She tried unsuccessfully to catch her sister's eye, and then she looked down at her phone, typing in busily. Every now and then, she paused for a moment and looked unseeingly into the distance, lost in thought.

Just then, Adon Jonathan's phone rang. He stepped a little away from the group and took a brief call in a hushed voice. Putting his phone back into his pocket, he rejoined them and said to his wife, "That was one of the Kohenim at the Temple. They have invited me to join the group early in the morning who take out the ashes from today and kindle the fresh fire for that next day. I'll stay for shacharit and breakfast afterwards, if that's okay with you."

"Of course, what an honor!" Gveret Ruth replied. "We'll be fine. We'll just eat breakfast here and probably wouldn't go anywhere anyway until mid-day, so you should be back by then."

"I suppose I wasn't invited to help," Samuel remarked, "but if it's okay, I would like to walk over with you and join in shacharit."

"Certainly!" Adon Jonathan said. "It's not as if we were able to see this kind of thing every day back home! And you can wear regular clothes, too, just as I will. No need for special priestly garments just to be together in prayer."

"But if you're providing priestly service, wouldn't you have to wear special garments?"

"No, you wear casual clothes when dealing with the ashes and only change into the priestly garments afterwards if you are going to serve. Very practical!"

Leah looked at her sister, who appeared to be totally lost in thought. "You've become really quiet," she observed. "I don't think you've said a word in a long time."

Rachel looked up from the floor tile she was gazing at fixedly. She glanced first at her sister, then turned beseechingly to Gveret Ruth. "Would it be possible for us to make our day trip tomorrow? If Leah is willing to come, that is. I had been thinking about possibly going to see the excavations at Jericho, since that isn't very far from here, but Seth gave me the idea of seeing Shiloh as well. Or maybe instead. I would so much love to see the foundations of the tabernacle that they're uncovering there and everything else about that site! It was the capital for hundreds of years before King David moved the capital to Jerusalem."

Adon Jonathan answered, "It's up to Ruth, of course, but my concern would be having you take buses or trains all over Judea by yourselves."

"I think we could figure it out," Rachel said. "I put the app on my phone for taking the bus before you ever invited us to join you, when we thought we were coming here on our own, just in case we'd have a chance to see anything beyond Jerusalem."

Leah put in quickly, "I'd love to go with you, Rachel, if Gveret Ruth agrees."

Gveret Ruth put a knuckle to her cheek. "If you're sure you'll be okay alone on the bus system, and you can be back well before dark so I won't worry about you, I don't see why you can't have the side trip you've been hoping for."

Rachel impulsively hugged her. "Thank you! I'll get up early in the morning to do some research. We can join you for breakfast and then leave right after that."

"It's good that Seth and his family went there today," Leah remarked. "Sounds like it's a perfect place for us to go investigate."

"I'm glad I didn't have to share my room with a stranger," Rachel remarked, thinking about Seth. "Although Seth seems nice enough, but it's good to have your best friend and twin sister in your room with you!" Leah smiled and blew her a kiss.

"It's a busy time of year," Samuel shrugged. "The inn is not going to let a bed go to waste. And the little I've actually seen of Seth, he is very nice and I've enjoyed being with him."

The girls burst into giggles and Samuel looked at his parents, puzzled. "You would just have to sit there and stare at him and it would be pleasant enough," Leah explained. Samuel shook his head, at which his mother clarified, "He is an unusually attractive young man."

"Ah!" said Samuel, grinning. "That's not something I paid any attention to."

"Just like admiring any work of art, of course," Rachel put in.

"Well, of course," nodded Leah, pulling a hyper-serious face.

And then they both giggled again. Samuel gave them a look, rolling his eyes. *I can hear it as plainly as if he said it out loud: GIRLS!* thought Rachel.

"Why don't we all get some rest, so Rachel can get up early," his mother suggested, "and we womenfolk can meet for breakfast?"

The girls hugged her, nodded to Adon Jonathan and Samuel, and started to go inside. "Wait, Rachel," Samuel called out to her as she was walking away. He waved a hand toward the street beyond the gate of the inn. She looked at Leah, shrugged, and joined Samuel walking out into the night. Leah sank down onto a chair rather than continuing to go to their room, as she watched her sister disappear through the gate.

Chapter 24

As soon as they were out of earshot of his parents, Rachel asked Samuel, "What is it?"

"You're taking away a whole day of our trip to go off on a jaunt of your own!"

"You're going to be at the Temple all day anyway! You won't even notice I'm away!"

"Yeah, well…" Samuel stooped down and picked up a pebble from the dusty ground below.

"What's really on your mind, Samuel? Don't think I didn't see that look earlier."

He drew a long breath. "So you've talked a lot about going to Greece, right? But you've never seemed that serious about it to me, because in the next breath, it's all about the Hittite ruins right in Anatolia. It's never seemed like you were considering moving very far away for your career." Another deep breath. "But now we're about to graduate, and we're not just daydreaming like children any more, AND you have a whole new obsession with Judea that sounds awfully real to me."

"Nothing's really decided," she offered, rather weakly.

"But this is as serious as I've ever heard you about where you might want to have your career, and I have to tell you I'm not crazy about it. Jericho is a big risk in my mind. You will probably be enthralled with it and then you'll be moving heaven and earth – oh, I know you! – to make sure that you have some kind of great job here."

"You're projecting way into the future!" she answered.

"I'm not so sure. Once you set your mind on something, there's no looking back for you. And it does feel like you've set your mind on Judea."

He turned and stomped back into the courtyard and then disappeared into the inn, leaving Rachel with words dying on her lips.

Rachel slowly walked back in herself. Spotting Leah waiting for her, she sank into the chair next to her. "Don't even ask," she said.

"Is he mad about something?"

Rachel sighed. "He's afraid that I've already made up my mind to spend my whole adult life in Judea and leave him behind."

"Well, haven't you?" Now it was Leah's turn to turn her back and walk into the inn. Rachel followed slowly behind her. She caught up with Leah just before reaching their room and grabbed her hand.

"Please, Leah, let's just enjoy the trip while we're here. And being together. None of this is happening any time soon, if it even ever does. Let's just call our best friends and tell them about our day. We've been having such good times together!"

Leah smiled at her tremulously and then nodded once. She turned and opened the door, letting Rachel in first. "We sure are. We have a lot to tell them. And I really have trouble being mad at you!"

Once in their room, they flopped onto their beds and simultaneously reached for their phones. Leah got through first and exclaimed, "Hi, Sarah, I have so much to tell you!"

Rachel was laughing at her sister but interrupted herself when her own call went through. "Hi, Deborah, I have so much to tell you!"

The girls burst into giggles again and then turned their attention to their separate conversations. They kept overhearing what the other was saying about their day up on the mountain with Miriam and interjecting more details as they were reminded of what else had transpired. They finished their conversations around the same time and started unbraiding their hair while they caught each other up on the doings of their best friends. Both were tired, so this conversation did not last very long, and the lights were soon off. Rachel fell asleep almost immediately, but Leah felt thirsty and decided to go into the kitchen for a glass of water.

As she was turning off the faucet, she heard footsteps behind her and turned around to see who was coming into the kitchen. It was one of the maintenance people for the inn. He nodded at her and went to a closet to pull out a mop. As he turned back, Leah caught a glint of metal from his jacket illuminated by the light coming through the window. It was a Zoroastrian pin!

Impulsively, Leah asked him, "Do you speak Aramaic?"

He nodded and said, "Yes," with no discernible accent. "I am the third generation in my family to be born in Judea," he added, "so I grew up speaking Aramaic. Is there something I can do for you?"

"I have never met anybody who was Zoroastrian before," Leah confessed. "Would it be too terribly personal if I were to ask you a few questions? I'm so curious!"

"No, that's fine. You'd be amazed how many people just treat me like another piece of furniture. But you're recognizing me as a person! I'd be very happy to answer anything that I can." And he smiled at her.

"My name is Leah," she began.

"And I am Omar."

"So we've been taught that it was Zoroastrian influence while we were exiled in Babylonia that was responsible for Judaism becoming truly monotheistic."

"Yes, that's my understanding," he nodded. He indicated the chair next to her with a tilt of his head and she waved him into it. Then he continued, "What we were taught is that Judaism had a main god like all the other Canaanite people – El, Baal, Yahweh – really all the same. But there was also a mother goddess who was your god's wife, and there were other lesser gods with various responsibilities toward important things like rain and fertility. Your religion did TEACH that there was only one God, but that's not how the ordinary people actually lived. Your prophets railed against it all the time and in fact blamed the destruction of your First Temple on the fact that the people were unable to be monotheistic. There was even a pillar to Ashera right inside the Temple grounds."

"I wonder why it was so different in Babylonia?" Leah mused.

"I think it's the geography, really," he replied. "Judea and many of the countries in the region are dependent on rain for their crops to grow. We were blessed with the two rivers, flooding seasonally and keeping the land between and around them very fertile. I think that's the same reason Egypt was able to become an empire, too – they had the annual flooding of the Nile and the fertile land on both sides of it and weren't dependent on rain, either. So you had to pray for rain and expiate your sins when it was dry for a long time, while we never had to think as much about the weather."

"That makes a lot of sense!" she exclaimed. "But – and you'll forgive me, I hope – we're also taught that we're exceptional somehow. But if we were exposed to monotheism in Babylonia and that's when we began to pray only to Yahweh, why are we considered first or special?"

"First, you need to realize that your culture is actually older than ours. Your King David reigned somewhere around the year 2800. Our religion was founded maybe 400 years later."

"I didn't realize that! I thought your people were so ancient."

"Persia of course is ancient, but it was polytheistic. There was a prophet named Zarathustra who founded Zoroastrianism. And then of course, as with any other new idea that people have, it started spreading through the region. Your ancestors were exposed to it while they lived among us for 70 years and carried it back to Judea when they returned to build this Temple – the monotheistic one."

"And then?"

"There are many similarities in Jewish law and Zoroastrian law, especially around marriage. But there is a way that scholars think that Zoroastrianism was not purely monotheistic either. It does believe in some sort of universal force. But it has elements of dualism in it – there were the divine twins, one good and one evil, and there are ways that you could see them as different gods. Your God has absorbed both good and evil within the one entity. You don't really have the dualism embedded in your religion. But we influenced you with our ideas about a resurrection, final judgment, and a Messiah to come some day and establish one way of living for all people. We do have a strong belief in a savior to come in the future and rescue the entire world from evil, and that influenced you while you were living in Babylonia."

Leah blinked. "You sure know a lot about this!"

Omar laughed. "I'm a minority living among people who are not my own. We are taught all these things in our schools to help keep our pride and our identity strong."

"So what makes Judaism special, then?" Leah persisted.

"Your monotheism was the first ethical monotheism known in the world. Before that, kings — who were maybe divinely appointed or even divine themselves, but still kings — handed down the law to their people. If there was any kind of revelation in a belief system, it was directly from the god to the prophet. Yours was the first to have a revelation directly from your God to the entire people, and your laws dictated directly by your God. It wasn't so much that you came to believe that there was one god as that you believed that the source of proper behavior was from that one god."

"Really fascinating! I can't wait to tell Rachel all about it. She's even more interested in ancient times and people than I am."

"Rachel is the friend you are traveling with? I see another young woman with you."

"She is my twin sister."

"I wouldn't have guessed that!" he said in surprise. "She doesn't look at all like you."

"We are not identical twins," Leah told him.

"And those are your parents and your brother as well?"

"No, our parents and our brother are at home. These are very dear friends of our family who agreed that we could accompany them to Jerusalem for the festival. The son is my sister's boyfriend. If they hadn't invited us, we were going to travel alone."

"Unchaperoned," Omar murmured, making a face of disapproval.

"Yes, I guess so, although that's not as big a thing in my country as we have found it to be here."

They continued chatting for a while. Leah finished her water and surreptitiously rubbed her eyes, but Omar noticed. "You probably need to get back to bed, and I have to finish my duties before it's time to set up for breakfast." They said their goodnights and Leah slipped back into her room and into bed. Rachel never stirred.

Chapter 25

The next morning, Leah was out on the patio very early once again. Her heart was pounding expectantly and she kept turning her head toward the doorway that led to the lobby and then the inside of the inn every time she thought she heard a sound. And then there really was a sound, and she looked up yet again to meet Seth's eyes.

"You couldn't sleep, either?" she asked.

"Samuel woke me up when he was getting ready to go to the Temple," he answered. "He was trying to be quiet, but I was really finished sleeping by then anyway. I like to watch the sunrise."

"I do, too!" gushed Leah, and then reminded herself to tone it down a little. "It's already glowing a little bit over there in the eastern sky, so it should be pretty soon. Sit down and watch it with me."

Seth picked up a chair and carried it nearer to the window, which was also a little farther away from Leah. "I think it's going to be another lovely day."

"Yes, this seems to be the best season in Jerusalem," Leah agreed. "Not too hot and not raining."

"So where is home for you?" he asked, settling into his chair. If he was facing her slightly more than he was facing the window, she was not about to comment.

"We live in Anatolia," she responded. "A city on the Hospitable Sea named Trabzon. What about you?"

"We live in Adana. Not far from the Mediterranean."

"Oh, I've heard of that!" Leah exclaimed. "That's a really old city! I know it was mentioned in Hittite tablets 4000 years ago."

Seth nodded. "Yes, it does have history. Closer to Jerusalem but quite far from you."

Leah suppressed a little sigh and then glanced at the sky. "Oh, look, it's just starting!" The sun itself was not yet visible, but there was a distinct brightness quite low on the horizon to the east, and the clouds were ranged around this point in brilliant shades of red and orange.

Seth swiveled around in his chair and also started watching out the window. Once the sun was fully above the horizon and the red had changed to a white too bright to look at for long, Leah asked shyly, "Would you like a cup of tea? I was just about to make myself one and sit here a little longer."

"No, thank you, but do go ahead. I think I'll stay another few minutes and then go in and wash up and get dressed for today."

Just then, Leah heard footsteps behind her. She turned around to see Rachel approaching. "Two early mornings in a row!" her sister greeted her, and then her eyes fell on Seth and her eyebrows rose. Leah colored and then rose to hug her sister.

"Good morning, Rachel," Seth said, also rising. "We were just watching the sunrise. I'm going back in now, but I'm glad I had a chance to see you this morning."

Rachel nodded at Seth and he went back inside the inn. Then she turned to Leah and burst out, "So you're sitting out here with a man without a chaperone?"

Leah giggled. "Yes, I'm a disreputable woman! Although all we did was sit across the whole patio from each other and watch the sun come up. I didn't even make him a cup of tea. But would you like one?"

Rachel said, "Sure! Pomegranate would be wonderful. Thank you!" When Leah came out of the kitchen a few minutes later, Rachel added, "So I know you have gotten his whole life story. That's how you are! Where are they from?"

"All the way across Anatolia from us," Leah pouted. "In Adana."

"You're such a flirt!" Rachel teased her. "I can't believe how fast you get to know people, especially men!"

Leah struck a simpering pose. "We all have our talents!"

Rachel sat down and waited while Leah was making their tea. When Leah returned, handing her a steaming cup, she said, "I've been texting with

Adon Yehuda, and he suggests that the place that makes the most sense for me to see is Jericho. It will give me a good idea of the sites and problems that I would find if I were working in Judea. The tel there goes down for many layers of civilization. So I think that's what I want to do, even though it was tempting when we heard about Seth going to Shiloh."

Leah shrugged. "Whatever you decide. I'm just going along as your companion."

"He thinks we shouldn't even try to visit more than one city in just one day. The important thing is to get the flavor of archaeology in Judea."

Leah scratched an insect bit on her arm. "He definitely has your best interests in mind."

"So now I have done a whole lot of research on various sites and I've decided what I'd most like to see."

Leah looked at the ceiling of the lobby in mock astonishment. "Why am I not surprised?"

Chapter 26

Breakfast was over. Rachel and Leah had changed into their travel frocks and their hiking boots. They reassured Gveret Ruth multiple times that they were confident about how to use the bus app, which gave step-by-step directions to get them to Jericho. Yes, they were set for cash. Yes, they had water bottles. Yes, they would call if they ran into even the tiniest bit of trouble. Yes, they would do everything in their power to make it back before dinnertime or else call.

"I am responsible for you," Gveret Ruth reminded them, apologetically, once they had run through this entire litany. "You're adults, of course. But you're given into my care in the absence of your parents and I take that seriously. I do hope you find the day rewarding. I can't wait to hear about everything you see!"

The girls walked toward the nearby bus shelter, enjoying their freedom. "I can't believe Gveret Ruth thinks we can't make it on our own," Leah said.

"I know. I've studied the app and the instructions lots of times, and I have complete confidence in our abilities to navigate."

Leah nodded toward Rachel's necklace, which was hanging outside her frock. "Then you might want to tuck that in again, since you don't need it."

Rachel blushed and closed her fist over her necklace, caressing it surreptitiously as she slipped it back under her frock.

The transit app planned out a trip for them that involved two buses with minimal walking or waiting. They were quite proud of themselves for this. As they settled into seats on the second bus, Leah asked, "What is so special about Jericho?"

"It's the oldest city in the world," Rachel answered promptly. "It goes back about 12,000 years, to Neolithic times. Excavations are finding layers of different civilizations going back through all the ages. It was destroyed by earthquakes several times and also was conquered by different waves of people through the years. One thing I read about that I'm really looking forward to seeing is the difference between where they built with mud brick and where they built with stone."

"So the walls that Joshua knocked down were defensive?"

"Actually, the walls were first built to protect Jericho against flooding. It is below sea level."

"And what do you mean by mud brick and stone?"

Rachel waved a hand around quickly. "Just the different influences. Lands that had been conquered by the Egyptians built with mud brick. That's what we used when we were slaves in Egypt. We'll find out more when we get there."

"This all does sound fascinating. And a substantial change for you from Greek ruins, which I think are mostly what we have in Anatolia."

Rachel furrowed her brow. "Well, in the interior, of course we have the earlier civilizations from about 3000 years ago. The Greeks mostly stayed on the coast and didn't get much into the interior beyond the mountains. You know, Hatti, Hittites, people like that."

The app beeped, and Rachel pushed the button to request the bus to stop at the next shelter. She told Leah, "I engaged a tour guide to take us around the sites through their visitors' webpage. They'll take us in a vehicle directly from one place to another and save us a lot of time getting around. That way, we can see the most possible."

"Are there any Judean ruins here?" asked Leah.

"Well, there are a few Hasmonean sites — a synagogue and a fort. I did request to see those."

They trudged up the hill from the bus shelter to the Visitors' Center, where they met their guide. He took them in a motorized cart to the first excavation on Rachel's list. She soon fell into animated conversation with him, peppering him with questions, using jargon that Leah didn't even understand. Leah lagged behind, looking around at the view, the juxtaposition of ancient ruins with a modern city. The day passed quickly, at least from Rachel's perspective, as they visited various sites and Rachel continued to ask all sorts of questions. Leah gamely followed after her

161

everywhere, marveling at how much her sister seemed to come alive, almost vibrating, as the day went on. At one point, she stopped to take a sip of water, then found herself having to catch up as Rachel and the guide had continued ahead, not even looking around for her as they got back to the vehicle. The guide delivered them back to the Visitors' Center, and Rachel was surprised to find out that the time was almost 15:00. How swiftly the time had flown for her!

As the girls strolled down the hill from the Visitors' Center to the bus shelter, Rachel was enthusing. "All those layers that they've excavated, each one a whole different culture! I never realized how many different nations conquered Jericho over the course of time! And when the guide told us that mud brick is delicate and the vibrations of people marching around blowing horns really could make it all collapse, I just about jumped out of the golf cart!"

Leah said nothing in response, just kept her eyes on the bus shelter, which was now just steps away. She slid onto the bench there while Rachel, shading her eyes, looked down the road toward the horizon. "Our route home is just the reverse of how we got here," she noted, consulting the app that had planned their trip. "We should make it back in plenty of time for dinner."

On the entire trip home, Leah looked on, bemused, as Rachel bubbled over with all her observations and feelings. She was incandescent with joy. 'This is it; this is where I need to have my career!" she kept exclaiming. This elevated level of energy had not diminished in the least as they walked into the inn – or rather, Rachel burst into the inn. She cornered Samuel and his parents in the lobby and recounted the entire day for them.

After a while, Leah began to feel almost invisible. Rachel definitely could get all wrapped up in her experiences, but it seemed as if Leah had not been there and was not present now. Had her presence even made any difference on the trip, save for a pair of ears to be regaled by Rachel's babble? Samuel, too, was uncharacteristically quiet, merely watching Rachel with thoughtful eyes. It seemed to her that the more she extolled the wonders of the sights they had seen, the less he shared her enthusiasm. He excused himself to use the restroom and did not return. Leah slipped out soon afterwards. Rachel continued with her diminished audience, having so much more to recount.

Leah had gone into their room to change clothes for the evening, after taking a quick shower to wash the travel dust off her skin and hair. She was pulling on her new yellow dress when Rachel danced in. Rachel braided Leah's damp hair and then began to wash and get dressed for the evening herself. Then she sat down on her bed and pulled out her phone to text Adon Yehuda and send him photos from the excursion. Leah stepped out of the room, not sure that Rachel was even noticing her absence.

Rachel left the room shortly, apron over her arm, and looked for Leah in the lobby and out on the patio but did not see her. So she stepped into the kitchen, tying on her apron as she did so, and saw that Gveret Ruth was already there. "Have you seen Leah?"

"I saw her going outside a little while ago. Do you want to cut up the cucumbers tonight?"

"Sure!" And Rachel took the platter of cucumbers, got a knife out from the utensils provided by the inn, and began to slice them. "I have really mixed feelings about going home again," she confessed.

"I do, too, and I don't even have classes to go back to when we get home!" laughed Gveret Ruth. "This is such a special, sacred place, like nowhere else on earth, but my home is also like nowhere else on earth and I do tend to be most at peace when I'm there."

"I'm glad I got my project started and could get away for this week," Rachel continued. "I won't feel as pressured when I get home and there are still a few weeks before it is due. I am having a wonderful time here and will never stop being grateful that you and Adon Jonathan asked Leah and me to join you. But I do like my own bedroom at home!"

Gveret Ruth started fanning out slices of cheese on another platter, which already had a stack of unleavened bread in the middle. "I know what you mean. And while we're confessing our deepest secrets, is it okay to tell you that I can't wait until Pesach is over and we can eat some real bread?"

The two women laughed and continued preparing the evening meal, Rachel occasionally glancing out to see if Leah was anywhere in sight. They

163

carried the platters out to the patio, where Adon Jonathan and Samuel were already sitting at a table and chatting.

"Tirzah called and said they'd love to take a hike with us tomorrow – they know just the place," Gveret Ruth told her husband.

Rachel put her platters on the table and went back to get a pitcher of water. When she returned, everybody was sitting around the table and helping themselves. "It isn't like Leah to be late for a meal!" Rachel declared. She walked over to the door and looked around in front of the inn for a few minutes, then shrugged and came back to the table. "I don't think she will starve, but I'm a little worried because she didn't seem like herself while we were getting ready for tonight."

"You do have a way of closing out everybody else when you get so enthusiastic, you know," Samuel said. "Leah probably just wanted a bit of a break."

"I do, I know that," Rachel acknowledged. "I've been called self-absorbed more than once."

He gazed her for another minute, shook his head once or twice, and then turned to his plate.

Meanwhile, Leah was a few streets away, strolling with Seth. She had come out of the room telling herself that she just wanted a breath of fresh air but secretly hoping that she would run into him, and he was in fact sitting in the lobby reading as she came through. He looked up at her with a quick smile. "Going outside?"

"Yes, just for a little walk before we eat dinner," she answered him. "What are you up to?"

"I'm waiting for my parents, and we're going to go over to that chicken restaurant on the next street for dinner when they get here. I'm a little early; they should be out here in 15 minutes or so. May I join you on your walk?"

Leah hesitated, warring emotions within her heart. She was not really sure whether she should be alone with this man whom she hardly knew. But this might be the last time she would ever see Seth, so what could happen and what harm would there be? She looked into his eyes timidly and he flashed a winning smile at her, which was sufficiently persuasive that she nodded and turned to go outside. Seth followed her and they soon turned the corner, admiring the various gardens as they passed homes along the street. Seth pointed across the street after they had turned a second corner. "That's the restaurant, over there," he said.

"Looks nice," Leah murmured. Why did she have no ability to converse with this person suddenly? She was never at a loss for words!

A few blocks farther along, they came to a small park at one corner. "Oh, let's go in here," Seth suggested. "It's so nice to see something green when almost everything is just this sand color." She walked along with him willingly – she was completely at ease with him by now and wondered what could ever have been so alarming – and even sat down on a park bench after he had done so with only a momentary pause. They chatted for another few minutes about the surroundings and their trips, and then Seth moved closer to her on the bench. "Do you know how pretty you are?" he asked.

Leah blushed and looked down. "I know my mom thinks so!" she joked, parrying his words because she was not accustomed to compliments from men.

"When I first saw you, I thought you had the prettiest eyes I've ever seen. They're the color of – I don't know what it's called, but like that ring you're wearing."

They both looked down at Leah's right hand, where it rested on her thigh. She was wearing the ring she had bought earlier in the trip. The stone in it was smoky quartz, which she told him. "My family calls my eyes 'amber,' but smoky quartz seems close, too."

Seth picked up the end of her braid and wrapped it around his hand. She shivered a little as he did so. "I wonder what it looks like when you let it down," he said. "You always keep it so tightly bound up in this braid."

"We all do," she said, rather inanely.

"But it's your hair I'd be curious to see, not all the girls' hair!'

Leah felt a little odd. Joseph had never talked to her anything like this before. If Samuel talked like that to Rachel, it certainly was not in her presence. This was something new, and she found herself mesmerized by the way things were proceeding.

There was a long beat while Seth gazed at her steadily. She tried to meet his eyes, but her own faltered before his. And then: "Has anybody ever kissed you before?" he asked, looking at her as if she were the only person alive in the entire world besides him.

"No, of course not," Leah stammered. "I've only had one boyfriend, and we never got to that stage. What about you?"

"I haven't ever had the opportunity, but I'm sure it would be so nice. And I can't imagine anybody I would want to try it with more than you!" He reached out to take her hand where it lay on her lap. She instinctively pulled it away – a man couldn't TOUCH her! – but he smiled and gently reached for it again. This time, she let it lie passively in his grasp. Then he leaned toward her and kissed her softly on her lips. It was an amazing feeling, nothing like kissing her family or friends. Nothing like her most intense daydreams. Leah took in the sensation for a minute but then sprang up and, in great confusion, started walking back toward the inn. Seth chuckled but fell into step beside her.

When they rounded that final corner before the inn, by silent mutual consent, Seth hung back for a minute while Leah continued on. She walked in through the lobby, nodding at his parents who were now standing there, and on into the patio. Rachel saw her come in immediately but could not catch her eye. Leah was looking down and looking embarrassed or even guilty. Her face was as red as Rachel had ever seen it. Gveret Ruth smiled at her and said, "We've just started! Sit down and join us."

Leah washed her hands quickly in the kitchen and then took her place next to Rachel. Seth walked through the patio, nodding politely at everybody, and vanished into the inn. Leah quietly accepted the platters as they were passed to her so that she could fill up her plate. She said nothing throughout the rest of the meal and then, pleading a headache, went off to their room. Rachel followed her almost immediately.

"What is going on?" Rachel demanded. "Where were you?"

"Interesting that you've noticed," Leah snapped back.

Rachel put her hands on her hips and glared at Leah. "And just what is that supposed to mean?" she demanded.

"I'm invisible! I'm just an extra in your play that stars only you!"

"Like when? We've been together on this whole trip. We've had fun together!"

"Fun, yeah. As long as I go along with you like a good companion and we do what YOU want to do. Tell me, Rachel, what's in it for me if you move to Judea and start living your dream life?"

Rachel was silent for a long moment. She bit back a sarcastic answer while she pondered how this must all feel from Leah's perspective. Then, in a gentler voice, she said, "I'm sorry that I have been so into myself and excluded you. But really, Leah, it isn't like you to disappear. Especially at mealtime!"

"I disappeared for you long ago today. I might as well not have been in Jericho with you. Do you even remember that I was there?"

"Leah!" Guilt struggled with impatience as Rachel stared at her sister. "And you're not answering me! Where were you?"

Leah had already started changing into her night clothes. She kept her dress over her head a minute or so longer than it needed to be there, hiding her face while she thought frantically. Instead of answering directly, she asked, "Has Samuel ever kissed you?"

"No, of course not!" Rachel answered instinctively. Their brief squabble vanished entirely from her mind. "We're very careful to follow the strict rules about what a man and a woman can do when they aren't married or even engaged. WHAT have you been up to?"

Blushing hotly, and addressing her bare feet, Leah mumbled, "Well, Seth kissed me. And Rachel, it was amazing!"

Rachel was torn among feelings of curiosity, repulsion, and great love for her sister, who was clearly so excited. "How in the world did this ever happen?"

"After we changed, I went out to take a quick walk before dinner. I really did plan to come back in time to help Gveret Ruth and you. But then I ran into Seth waiting for his parents – well, I was actually hoping I would run into him! And I didn't see anything wrong in letting him just come on my walk with me. He said he only had 15 minutes. And before I knew it, we were sitting on a bench in a park a few blocks away and he kissed me!"

167

"He is SO forward!" Rachel exclaimed. "He is such a flirt, such a charmer. He must kiss all the girls he can!"

"Oh, no, Rachel, he told me he'd never kissed a girl before and he really wanted to try it with me!"

"Well, now you're ahead of me in experience! So –"curiosity winning out, "what did it feel like?"

"Like nothing else! Nothing like I have ever imagined!" Searching for words, she continued, "I felt like it was making my heart sing and my stomach jump."

"What happened next?" asked Rachel.

"I got to feeling embarrassed and I jumped up and started right back for the inn," Leah said. "But I think that's why we're not supposed to kiss boys or even let them touch us. Because I have to admit that what I really wanted was another one, more and more!"

"I can understand that!" Rachel nodded, musing about how hard it was to be near Samuel without ever feeling his skin against hers. "And I'm so glad that your good judgment took over and you stopped it right then and there. Now you'll never see him again and it will just be a memory."

Leah sighed and looked sad. "Yes, I'll never see him again. I think he could really be special…"

Rachel was not so sure. "I don't know, honey. He is such a charmer! I haven't been able to take him as sincere when he says all those things to us."

"But we talked and talked while we were walking, and he's really different than how he's been acting around us. He's serious and smart and so nice."

"AND gorgeous!" her sister put in. "Those eyes …"

"Well, yes, there is that!" laughed Leah. "Oh, well, it really IS a memory. I wonder how many other people I'll be able to share that memory with?"

"Certainly not Abba. Or even Ima. Probably only Sarah."

"She's pretty rigid in following our ways, though. I may not be able to tell her!"

Rachel asked hesitantly, "What about Joseph? Is there a chance that this is just an exciting adventure away from home and you will go back to him? You've been dating him for a few months now."

"You were right about him and me," Leah said. "There isn't a real spark with him. I feel like we're just buddies sometimes."   By now, Rachel too had her nightgown on, and she slipped beneath her blanket. "Well, you've had an eventful day, for sure. And now tomorrow is our last full weekday and then our first Shabbat in Jerusalem, so let's get some sleep so we can enjoy every minute of it."

Leah walked over to Rachel's bed and hugged her sister impulsively before turning out the room light and then climbing into her own bed. "You are one in a million!" she exclaimed. "I really hate it when we're not getting along. Good night, and let's have a great time tomorrow and make some more memories. *Together.*"

The next morning, Leah once again woke up early. She glanced over at her sister's bed. It was too dark to see, but the soft sounds coming from that direction made her aware that Rachel was still sound asleep. It would be so easy to slip outside again, maybe meet Seth, maybe enjoy more sweet kisses with him before saying goodbye forever. It was unfortunate that they had had so little time together that no relationship had truly been formed. She daydreamed about this for a few minutes, then resolutely lay back down and dozed until she heard Rachel stirring. She crawled into her sister's bed and they put their arms around each other. "I'm so glad to find you here," Rachel murmured.

"Nowhere else to be!" Leah declared briskly but untruthfully. "What should we wear for our last day of sightseeing here?"

"We'll be hiking and then we'll come back and have to immerse and change quickly for Shabbat, so those lightweight dresses that never ever seem to wrinkle, I think," Rachel replied, and they sat up on the edge of the bed, smiled at each other, and then rose to start their day.

Adon Joel and Gveret Tirzah arrived at the inn for the promised hike shortly after breakfast. "Too bad Miriam couldn't come," Gveret Ruth said to her sister.

"Yes, she sent her regrets. She really enjoyed her day with Rachel and Leah. It was almost like she was a different person," Gveret Tirzah agreed.

"It definitely sometimes seems like we have two different daughters!" Adon Joel shook his head in disbelief. "She is so quiet – really almost withdrawn – when it's just us. And she turns on a light and bubbles when she's with her friends. We saw that when she was with the girls the other day. I wonder which is the real Miriam."

"You are so good with her," Gveret Ruth observed. "I hope you don't worry that you stifle her. She wouldn't be the only teenager who behaves differently with adults than she does with people around her own age."

"Thank you," Gveret Tirzah said, squeezing her sister's hand.

Grabbing hats, snacks, and water bottles, they set off for the mountains.

Several hours later, Rachel gasped, "Stop! Wait! Rest break!" as she reached around for her water bottle. "I'm just not used to going up these steep hills and in all this heat!"

"This? This is nothing," Adon Joel winked at Adon Jonathan. "You should try this in Fifth Month. And on a REAL mountain!"

"Ugh, I am with her!" protested Leah, stopping as well and turning toward her sister as she took out her own water bottle. "I know it's supposed to be a blessing to die in Judea, but maybe not today?"

Samuel laughed, trying to disguise his own panting as best he could. "You girls are just too soft!" he teased. "You would never make it in any kind of army."

"That wasn't my ambition anyway," Rachel retorted. Her glance lingered on him for a moment longer. What WOULD it be like to kiss him? Then, face flaming, she quickly turned away before he might have a chance to read her mind. But several more times during the day, she looked at him thoughtfully with that same question. She began to notice that he had almost pulled away from her, that he was not as focused on her as he usually seemed to be. Was she scaring him away with these thoughts? Something was definitely going on in that head!

Gveret Tirzah, puffing gently herself, said, "We do this at least twice a month and it still wears me out, so don't let these strong men fool you. But we're almost at the top, and I think you'll agree that the view is really worth all this."

"At least we have a day of rest coming up," laughed Leah. "We can sleep in then. Or sleep pretty much anywhere – on rocks, say."

Adon Joel turned his face up the mountain once again and prepared to lead the way. "It really is no more than 15 more minutes. I think you can all do it. Wait till you see how coming down is actually harder – you have to be careful the whole time, and it can really hurt your knees. You're resisting gravity."

"Well, at least if somebody is as old as you are," Gveret Ruth teased her brother-in-law affectionately. Everybody obediently fell into line once more and continued the arduous ascent.

"You guys aren't making coming back down anything to look forward to," protested Leah, still screwing the lid back onto her water bottle, trying to eke out a few more seconds of rest.

Around a few more trees, a scramble over one final huge boulder, and they were suddenly at the edge of a relatively level meadow. Bees and butterflies added motion to a floor covered with flowers and leaves of many colors, themselves moving subtly in the slight breeze. Everybody exclaimed over the beauty of the place, but Adon Joel walked through to the other side and climbed up on a tree stump. "Just come over here and take a look at the view, and then we can rest here for a while before we need to start back down."

Adon Jonathan looked at his watch as he headed in that direction. "I think we need to start getting ready for Shabbat at 13:00," he declared, "so if it takes as long to get back down to the car as it took to get up here, we have almost 20 minutes here."

"It's a little quicker," Gveret Tirzah replied.

"Abba, Ima, you can talk all you want, but you really do need to see this view!" Samuel finally interrupted them.

"What is it, Jerusalem?" asked his mother, walking over the last few cubits to join him.

"No, it's the other direction. We're on the northeast side of Har Hatzofim," Gveret Tirzah told her. Gveret Ruth soon stood between her sister and her son, looking down over the fertile terrain below, all different shades and shapes of green, various contours, water winking bluely here and there – an incredibly beautiful vista.

Rachel sighed and glanced over at Leah, which she had been doing surreptitiously for much of the hike. She found her sister chewing vigorously. "What are you eating NOW?" she asked.

Leah laughed. Her penchant for snacking was no secret from anybody who knew her. "Just some dried apricots," she replied. "Want some?"

"No, thank you. I think I'll just have more water."

"Be careful with your water," Adon Joel cautioned them. "There's nowhere to refill your bottles up here or anywhere on the way back down, and you will probably need some water even going down, since it's getting so much warmer now."

Rachel, who had only just begun to loosen the cap of her water bottle, smiled at him, shrugged, and put it back into her backpack. "I have plenty," Samuel announced to her, but she shook her head. "Let's save what we both have and see what we need for the hike back down."

"Which can begin around now!" Adon Jonathan said, turning around from the view to face the rest of the group. "Same way back down, or is it a circuit hike?"

"Same trail," Gveret Tirzah nodded. "Just don't let gravity run away with you and be gentle with your knees."

With that, they crossed the meadow once again and headed down the trail.

Chapter 27

Just a few hours later, Rachel touched Leah's arm lightly as they relaxed in the mikvah. "Are we really going home so soon? Is Jerusalem just going to be a memory for us until the next time we go?"

"And we have to think about school?!" Leah chimed in.

"AND our friends and pottery with Gveret Judith and everything else that's been on hold for festival week but is all going to start up again!"

Leah shook her head incredulously. "It's already becoming like a dream! But not every place gets this whole week off."

Rachel asked, "What happens with your volunteering in Hamiskoy? When does it begin? You haven't missed any of that, have you?"

"That wasn't going to start until next week anyway. They were still working on the building itself for the craft studio. Next week is when we get to decide what goes into it and how to set it up. And then a few weeks later is when classes and meetings begin."

"And you still want to teach charcoal drawing?"

"I would only be assisting with that. I'm not the most talented or experienced volunteer they have, and they are using a lot of people just to help out the instructors or keep the place organized and cleaned up. The instructors are mostly Eleusinians anyway, to teach the ancient crafts and to serve as role models."

"I wonder why we call them Eleusinians?" Rachel mused.

"It's a generic term that's completely incorrect. It's named after the Eleusinian Mysteries in Greece. It just means the people who engage in nature worship or really any form of polytheism."

Rachel glanced away, then back again. "We all do different things to make the world a better place, all to help other people. Everybody has different skills and interests."

"But not you and me!" Leah protested. "We are twins, after all."

"Are we exactly the same on ANYTHING we do? Not really."

"True," Leah acknowledged. "Although it's nice that there ARE some things we both like. It's been fun taking pottery with you and I'm glad we're going back for that!"

"Don't rush our time here! We still have all of Shabbat ahead of us," Gveret Ruth reminded them.

The girls put on their prettiest white frocks and prepared once again to braid each other's hair. Gveret Ruth pulled out some fresh flowers from her tote bag and they gratefully accepted those and braided them into their hair. Gveret Ruth next pulled some kohl out of her bag, and all three women carefully lined their eyes, beautifying themselves for the start of Shabbat. As they left the mikvah, they could hear the sound of the shofar announcing that all business must cease in anticipation of Shabbat, and they smiled at each other in anticipation.

The inn prepared a Shabbat meal for all of its guests. People whom they had only acknowledged with a smile in passing gathered around all the tables, covered with white cloths for the occasion. There were candles on every table to be lit by each family group. Unleavened bread stood in baskets on each table, waiting to be blessed so as to launch the meal. Trays of roasted chicken and roasted fish, grilled vegetables and fresh fruit, and bowls of mixed green salads stood on serving tables. Rachel and Leah joined Samuel and his parents at their table. Leah looked surreptitiously around but did not see Seth or his parents anywhere. She stopped looking when Samuel made a comment about being able to spread out in his room now that his roommate and family had left to go back home before Shabbat. She knew they would be parting at some point but rather wished she had had the opportunity to say goodbye. Once again, she regretted having become involved with him so late in their stay. She would just be a brief spring lark to him, if he remembered her at all. She stared gloomily at her hands.

Her thoughts were interrupted when her sister said, "Leah, I'm going back to the tables to get some more fruit. Can I bring you anything?"

"I'd like more of those mushrooms, if you don't mind. They were delicious."

"They were indeed. Maybe I'll get myself some, too."

As Rachel walked away, Gveret Ruth asked Leah, "Have you enjoyed yourself here? Is it different from how you were planning when you expected it to be just the two of you?"

Leah answered truthfully, "You made the trip so much richer with all that we did together. Rachel and I would never have done all of that exploring on our own, and certainly not enjoyed such great cooking! I was a bit worried" – quick glance at Samuel – "that I might feel a little left out with Rachel and Samuel being here together, but it was wonderful and I never felt that way at all. You were a great mom to us!"

"I'm relieved. I was concerned myself that you might feel excluded."

"Well, I have to admit to you that I did feel a bit that way, but not because of Samuel."

Gveret Ruth opened her mouth to say more but stopped when Rachel returned to the table. Samuel, who had been deep in conversation with his father and had not been paying attention to the women's discussion, looked up and gave his mother a quick smile. Rachel set a tiny bowl of mushrooms on Leah's place and then sat down with some strawberries and mushrooms at her own place.

"This has definitely been a wonderful trip, Ima! I'm so glad we have been able to do all the things we've done this time," Samuel said.

As the group was finishing its dinner, people around them began singing grace after meals, and they joined in, feeling incredibly special to be doing it here in Jerusalem, so near the Temple. When they had finished, serving staff came to remove their dishes and they stood up and moved away from their table to give them more space. Leah smiled and nodded when she noticed Omar working a few tables away, and he gave her a little wave.

"What is the schedule for tomorrow?" asked Gveret Ruth.

"Samuel and I will go up to the Temple for shacharit and stay there all day for all the Shabbat sacrifices," Adon Jonathan replied. "You women are certainly welcome to spend the full day up there with all the women who are still in town. We will be busy all day, though, so we won't be able to see you until after Havdalah."

"Maybe we'll go down just for the sacrifice services and come back here to rest in between," Gveret Ruth said. "And then when you get back after it's dark, we'll have to pack, because we'll be leaving very early in the morning. My sister did say they'd be willing to drive us to the airport so that we can see each other one more time."

"Oh, that's lovely!" exclaimed Rachel. "They are all so nice. We really had a fun time with Miriam, and it will be fun to see her again."

"She probably won't be with them, Rachel. It will be First Day and she'll be back in school. But I'll make sure that word gets back to her how much you enjoyed being with her, and maybe you'll all be able to stay connected after we get back home."

The next morning, Adon Jonathan and Samuel left early. Rachel and Leah were still asleep, but by the time they came out for breakfast, Gveret Ruth told them that the men were long gone. The inn provided a light breakfast buffet, and the three of them chose yogurt and fruit and sat down at a table on the patio. It was another beautifully sunny day with a nice breeze. "I could get used to this," Rachel remarked. "It is ALWAYS sunny and warm here!"

"Well, of course, it rains in the winter and can get a lot colder, but yes, Purim until Sukkot is generally dry and sunny here," Gveret Ruth answered.

Their meal finished, the three women headed toward Jaffa Gate and the Temple compound. Many more people than they had expected were heading in the same direction, and they were part of quite a crowd by the time they reached the Court of Women. The realization struck them all that many people must have come for the festival and remained in town through Shabbat. The overall mood of the throng was celebratory, even joyous.

Standing there among the women, peering over the heads of the crowd in order to catch a glimpse of what was occurring on the elevated platform where the altar stood, the girls were humbled to be participating in a ritual that in some configuration had been going on for thousands of years in this same spot. The crowd fell silent as of one accord and the Levites could be heard singing. Grain was ceremonially mixed with oil and spices and then flung upon the flames, which shot up into the sky brightly as the offering was burned. The words of the Kohenim could not be heard, but the power of the moment was palpable. Leah's hand found Rachel's as they stood as part of a crowd all experiencing the same thing and yet at the same time intensely alone with their awareness of the sacred moment. It felt transformative to them. An honor to be there and at the same time, a moment of utter humility.

The Kohenim withdrew to their area behind the altar and the Levites were left reciting Psalms, culminating in the Psalm written specifically for the day of Shabbat. Rachel shivered a little. The Levites withdrew, the sound of their chanting slowly fading as they backed behind the partition, but the women remained completely silent and immersed in the experience for another few moments. Finally, Rachel once again began to hear little murmurs.

"Unbelievable! This is nothing like how I feel when Adon Jonathan is conducting services back home," Leah whispered to Rachel.

"I know. It's a whole other kind of thing, a peak experience for me for sure. I had no idea how powerful it would feel. Have we never come to the Temple for Shabbat before?" Rachel asked.

"We must have! We always stay for several days when we come for one of the festivals. I can't believe Abba and Ima would stay away from the Temple on Shabbat. I don't know why it's hitting me this way this time."

"Maybe being older, maybe all that we've seen and learned this time, maybe being with Kohenim and more in tune with what goes on behind the scenes at the Temple?" suggested Rachel.

The crowd was starting to move toward the gate. Gveret Ruth was already starting to head that way, so the girls turned and followed her so as not to get separated. As they worked their way down the hill and toward the Jaffa Gate, Gveret Ruth suggested, "Let's not head right back to the inn. It's early for lunch anyway. Let's just stroll around the Old City for a while and enjoy this beautiful sunshine and the peaceful feeling of Shabbat."

Accordingly, they walked around the Old City, admiring the shops, most of which were closed for Shabbat, as well as the ancient architecture. Children were playing everywhere, running up and down the ramps or jumping off the steps. Sometimes the buildings would block the sun, and other times there would be bright sunshine and a bit of the breeze that always blows in Jerusalem. Finally leaving the Old City, they wandered through a few nearby neighborhoods. People were out in the streets, walking or clustered in little knots and talking to each other. Flowers and trees were in bloom everywhere. A very serene morning.

Finally, Leah mentioned, "I'm getting hungry," and they agreed to head back to their inn. They found a dairy buffet set up for the guests and took their plates outside, where they sat on lawn chairs and continued to enjoy the day.

"Does anybody want to go back for mincha and maariv?" asked Rachel. The consensus was that all three of them would rather take a nap, although they definitely wanted to go back to the Temple for Havdalah. So Gveret Ruth went to her room, followed a few minutes later by Rachel and Leah, who went into their own room. They flopped onto their beds. Leah immediately turned her back toward Rachel and closed her eyes. Rachel picked up a book from her nightstand and began reading. She luxuriated in the sense of nowhere to be, nothing she was expected to be doing, not having to interact with anybody for a while. A gentle breeze stirred the sheer white curtains in their open window, and even that there were no sounds of traffic, only singing and distant voices talking and children playing, was quite relaxing. It was not very long before she laid her book down on her chest and closed her own eyes to join Leah in slumber.

She had a sense that some amount of time had passed when she suddenly opened her eyes again. Yes, that was tapping on their door. She put her book back on the nightstand, stretched briefly while smothering a yawn, and then tiptoed over to the door, which she opened a crack. Seeing nobody there, just a cleaning cart in the hallway right outside, she opened it a bit wider and caught sight of Gveret Ruth receding down the hallway. She slipped out of the room, closing the door as soundlessly behind her as she could, and speedwalked down the hall, whispering, "Gveret Ruth!"

She turned and looked at her and smiled. Then she pointed toward the plaza outside, so Rachel nodded and followed her out there. "I'm sorry if I woke you," she said, softly. "My sleeve brushed against your door as I was walking by. I had to squeeze by that cart. I think everybody else who's at the inn is asleep. Let's just take a little walk."

They strolled around the area of the inn for a few moments, enjoying the flowers and trees and the songs of birds they could never quite seem to spot. As the sun started sinking lower in the sky, Gveret Ruth said, "We had better go back. The others are probably awake by now and wondering where you are! And we'll want to get back to the Temple before it gets dark. Samuel will have to find Jonathan and we ladies will have to find our way into the Court of Women and maybe a good spot so we can see the Havdalah service."

Samuel and Leah were sitting out on the plaza when they returned. They had been conversing but broke off abruptly upon spotting Rachel. It was so sudden and obvious that she self-consciously began to wonder whether they had been talking about her. And what could they possibly have been saying? She cast her mind back over the previous few days but could think of no grievances that her sister and her boyfriend could possibly have against her.

Leah said, "I've been awake for ages and I'm already mostly packed, just what I'll need for tonight and tomorrow. You'd better catch up with me!"

Rachel laughed and said, "That won't be too hard. We never really got very UNpacked. I will have plenty of time before we have to leave."

With that, the foursome left the plaza of the inn through the gate and headed back to the Temple Mount. Passing once again through the Kiponus Gate, they found long tables set up in the court as before. They looked around for the family they had been sitting with for the festival meal but did not spot them. Gveret Ruth turned her head quickly and said, "Oh, there's Jonathan, waving at us!" and the others spotted Adon Jonathan and were soon making their way to the table where he was standing. Wine, candles, and spices were set on every table for those gathered around it to make Havdalah together. Two young couples joined them, which filled their table. The Levites came out and surrounded the courtyard. In addition, one or two stood near each table. They began singing, and the people soon joined in. The sun was setting while they sang. Leah reached for and squeezed Rachel's hand, and she smiled at her. *Whatever is on her mind, it can't be THAT bad.*

When the brief Havdalah service was over, the Levites lit their way with torches through the gate and down from the Temple Mount. Lost in the intense experience, the fivesome made their way to the inn without speaking. Once inside the courtyard, they bade each other good night just with gestures and went off to their rooms.

Rachel sat cross-legged on her bed and texted Adon Yehuda. His comments on the observations that she had been sending him throughout the trip had been tremendously supportive. She particularly valued some of his responses that had caused her to notice things with more attention. She owed him a great deal of thanks. Finishing her grateful note, she shut off her phone and lay back to sleep in Jerusalem for the final time on this spectacular trip.

Chapter 28

The twins got up the next morning, dressed in their travel frocks, which the inn had laundered for them, put their final items into their backpacks, and walked slowly to the plaza for breakfast. They were suddenly in no rush to go back home. This was an experience such as Jerusalem had never been before, possibly because they had gone through it without the protective buffer of their parents around them. Life would be more this way in the future, more time spent functioning on their own without their parents to guide them. It was a thrilling and also sobering thought.

As they served themselves fruit and yogurt at the breakfast buffet, they heard Samuel behind them calling out, "Uncle Joel! Aunt Tirzah! Hi, we're over here!"

"Oh, good, we're really getting a ride to the airport," Leah whispered to Rachel. "I really was not up for taking a bus with our backpacks and all our stuff."

Gveret Ruth came running out of the room she had shared with Adon Jonathan, her wet hair streaming behind her, and hugged her sister hard. "I can't bear the thought of not seeing you for another few months," she said.

"You're still sure you aren't coming back for Shavuot?"

"No, we just can't do it this year. But we are definitely planning to be here for Sukkot. It just seems like such a long time to be apart!" And the sisters hugged again.

Adon Jonathan entered the room, smothering a yawn. "Maybe for once I will be able to sleep on the flight," he muttered. Then, catching sight of Adon Joel and Gveret Tirzah, he went up to hug them. "Thank you so much for taking us to the airport and thank you especially for spending time with us. We'll be back for Sukkot and hope we can spend even more time together."

Gveret Tirzah moved farther onto the patio in order to hug the girls. She asked, "Are you sure you're twins?"

The girls giggled as they looked at each other. Both were wearing frocks appropriate for a long time on an airplane, but Leah's was bright yellow with lace trim while Rachel's was heather blue. Leah's backpack was hot pink with sequins embellishing it, while Rachel's was tan. Leah resembled her mother more in facial features, while Rachel favored their father. All that they had in common was the fact that they were about the same height and their dark braids.

"So our parents tell us!" Leah answered impishly.

"And please give our love to Miriam," Rachel added. "We really did enjoy getting to know her a little."

"We certainly will," Gveret Tirzah promised, then turned to her brother-in-law. "Are you ready to get going?"

"Oh, yes," he replied. "I'm so glad you have a van big enough to carry seven people comfortably. That's not what you would expect with an only child."

"Miriam is an only child only when it comes to bedtime!" she laughed. "With all of her activities and teams, we are constantly ferrying groups of girls all over the place."

"Well, we really are glad we got to know her, and I know that I for one plan to keep in touch with her!" Rachel said.

The short drive to the airport just outside Jerusalem passed quickly. Before long, they were finding their seats on the airplane and strapping themselves in. "Where's Samuel sitting?" asked Leah.

"He's about three rows in front of us," Rachel replied. "His father is sitting with him and his mother is across the aisle."

"I guess I was busy finding our row," Leah said. Although what she had really been doing was looking out the window of the airplane and fantasizing about staying down there with Seth instead of flying home without him.

"It just might be that you don't have radar for Samuel like I do!" Rachel laughed.

"You said it, not me!"

"I wonder when we'll be able to go back to Jerusalem ourselves?" Rachel mused.

"Abba and Ima said before we left that the whole family might be able to go, either for Sukkot or for next Pesach."

"Maybe they'd be willing to spend more time in Judea the next time. There are so many other digs I need to visit."

Leah laughed, then teased, "And maybe even look at some ruins in Rome and Athens along with all the ruins in Judea!"

Rachel tossed her head. "I can't help that I'm so interested in the ancient past!" Then she smiled at her sister and added, "Maybe …"

Leah stretched out her legs and looked at her shiny yellow shoes, then glanced over at Rachel's earth-toned sandals beside her. "We really are different in so many ways. Our interests, for one. And I like really bright, sparkly things and you're much more subdued."

"We're different," Rachel agreed, "but you are still my best friend in the whole world!"

Just then, a serviceperson started pushing a cart down the aisle of the airplane. Leah pulled her foot in a little farther and started looking over the cart. Only beverages? There had to be some snacks coming. She craned her neck to look farther down the aisle and heard her sister giggling. "Yup, we're different, all right!" Rachel choked out. "I'm not wondering where my next snack is coming from!"

"Got me!" laughed Leah, as she shifted a little in her seat and lowered her tray table in readiness for whatever she might be served.

Soon after the carts had cleared the aisles, Samuel passed by. He stopped for a second when he saw the twins. "Can you believe we're already going home?" he asked.

"In some sense, I can't," Rachel answered. "Re-engaging with our daily routine, friends and school and all, seems inconceivable after this amazing vacation."

"By the way, what color do you like on Rachel?" Leah demanded.

Samuel looked nonplussed but didn't take long to reply, "Blue, I guess."

"Thank you! You may go now," and Leah waved dramatically down the aisle. All three of them laughed as Samuel shrugged and walked away. "You can almost hear him thinking, 'What are girls ever talking about?' But at least you know now which dress to buy for Solstice Ball!"

"I THOUGHT that's what you were up to!" Rachel laughed. "It's between a peach dress and a blue dress anyway, although I had yellow and green in mind just in case."

"No such problem for me," sighed Leah. "I'll be going stag again. That's the downside of breaking up with Joseph. Maybe I should hang on just through the end of the school year. No, that wouldn't be kind. Do you want to do the twins thing?"

"NO!" answered Rachel emphatically. "Or at most, the same dress but different colors. We're not eight!"

"Good, I was hoping you wouldn't say yes! I found an emerald green dress that I already want, and Sarah has already approved of it. Now I can buy it."

Rachel smiled at her sister and then, having finished her snack, laid her head back and closed her eyes. And so passed the rest of the flight home: dozing, eating, reading, and chatting.

Chapter 29

Once the girls had settled back into life at home again, they both found circumstances that differed from those surrounding them before the trip. A few days after their return,

Leah was outside reading a book for one of her classes, when she heard somebody calling out to her. Looking up, she saw Joseph ben Asher across the street, waving at her. She waved back and he sauntered over to where she was sitting.

"How are things going, Leah?" he asked her.

"Just fine. It's as if we had never been in Jerusalem. I'm already back into my usual routine."

"I've missed you so much! Let's walk over to the sweet shop and get a piece of pie."

Leah looked at him and realized that there was no particular magic there. Seth had made her fully aware of the special feeling that there could be between two people, something she had never really sensed with Joseph. "No, thank you, Joseph. I need to finish this before dinner, because I have to write an essay about it tonight."

"Well, maybe tomorrow, then. I want to hear all about your trip. It seems like it's been months that you've been gone."

Leah looked directly into Joseph's eyes. "I'd be happy to get together with you, but you need to realize that it will only be as friends."

Joseph looked down for a few seconds, and then he looked back at Leah. "Did you meet somebody else over there?"

Leah laughed in surprise. It had been an acquaintance of such brief duration, and yet it had affected her so profoundly. "Yes, I guess I did!"

Joseph scuffed his foot on the ground for a few seconds, staring at it, before he spoke again. "Okay, if that's what you want. But we have always had good times."

"Thank you for understanding."

Joseph shrugged slightly as it if really did not matter to him, not meeting her eyes. Then he walked back across the street. Leah watched him for a moment and then returned to her book, but she found that she could no longer concentrate, because her mind was astounding her with memories of Seth and the realization that he had insinuated himself far more deeply into her life than she had suspected at the time. Just when they were starting to get to know each other, they had had to separate.

The bigger change occurred in Rachel's life, although it was so subtle that it took her a week or more to become aware that anything was different. But eventually it occurred to her that she wasn't seeing as much of Samuel. He didn't call her and he didn't drop by. She saw him between classes at lunch and on other occasions when the group of friends all met, but she had no time alone with him since returning from the trip. Thinking back, she called to mind some of the distant signals she had been getting from him the last few days of their trip.

Hesitantly, she broached the subject to Leah. Leah sat down on the bed beside Rachel and said, "We actually talked about it near the end of the trip. It was the day you and I went to Jericho. You came home on fire with your new ambition to be an archaeologist in Judea, and Samuel wasn't sure where that left him. Adon Jonathan really wants him to take over leading Shabbat and festival services for the community in the next few years, so he feels like he's stuck here. And frankly, Rachel, we were both feeling a little hurt, with you so excited to move so far away and leave us both behind. But neither one of us wanted to say anything to bring you down while you were so on fire."

"I never really thought about what it might mean for Samuel and me," Rachel said slowly. "I've just been so focused on finally having a definite idea of what I want to do and planning to work toward that. And yes," seeing Leah open her mouth and anticipating what she was about to say, "I know we've talked about this before. My self-absorption."

186

"Well, I wasn't going to say it quite that baldly, but yes. Sometimes when you're fixated like this, you move forward without interruption, on a path that's too narrow for anybody else to go along with you."

"So has he dropped me? Are we breaking up? Is he just taking time to think?"

Leah sighed. "I don't really know. I haven't seen much of him myself. But we can listen to the grapevine and let some time go by and see what happens. The main thing for you to be thinking about yourself is whether there's a place for Samuel in this new life you're planning."

Is there a place for Samuel? Rachel thought. *Isn't he always going to be there?*

Chapter 30

Some time later, Sarah agreed to meet Leah at the diner for ice cream sundaes; they both felt they needed a break from their studies. They invited Rachel to join them, but she declined, hoping that Samuel might come over at long last. What had gotten into him? Why was she too afraid of his answer to ask him directly? A dreary future stretched out before her.

Leah got into her car and drove over to the diner, where she encountered Sarah just getting out of her own car. Once inside and seated at a table near the back wall, Leah looked over at Sarah and smiled. What fun it was to spend time with her best friend again! They placed their orders and continued to chat. Suddenly, Sarah broke off and stared at a point closer to the front of the diner. Leah turned around, following the direction of her gaze, and saw Samuel and Batya, just then sitting down at another table. Batya, in her usual silk, had her hair properly braided in the back, but she had allowed little tendrils to remain free of the braid and they framed her face most fetchingly.

"What's our responsibility here?" asked Sarah. "Do we have to tell Rachel? Do we march over there and demand that they tell us what they're doing here? Maybe it's just something innocuous."

"Rachel is my twin sister. Of course I will tell her that we saw them together. And then she can confront Samuel and find out what's going on – if anything is at all."

"But they've been together for years and years!"

Leah nodded. "They were best friends before we even entered our teens. And then they started dating as soon as Abba gave her permission. I can't believe he would turn his back on what they've had for all those years so easily. Do you know, he hasn't come over or even called or texted Rachel in weeks and weeks. Not since we got back. If I go over and smack him right now, will you be my witness that it was in self-defense?"

Sarah tilted her head and stroked an imaginary beard. "That seems like a hard position for a judge to believe. But how awful for Rachel! What is Samuel thinking?"

"Well, let's not stare at them any more, or they'll notice us looking," Leah suggested. Just then, a server set their sundaes down on the table and they picked up their spoons in anticipation.

As was their custom, the girls shared bites of each other's sundaes and continued chatting, although each of them occasionally sneaked a peek at the table where Samuel and Batya were sitting. The whole mood of their meeting was dampened with what was going on just a few tables away. Batya was very obviously flirting with him, and Samuel, staring at her in fascination, did not seem to be rebuffing her.

Finally, finished with the ice cream, Leah couldn't stand the charged atmosphere any longer, so they got up to leave the diner. She noticed that Batya and Samuel were still seated at their table and they would have to walk past them to go outside. The way he was gazing into Batya's eyes, perhaps he wouldn't notice. They had to take the chance. She led the way, head down, walking as quickly as she dared without calling attention to herself. But as they passed the table, Samuel, who was seated facing them, raised startled eyes to them and turned a little red.

"Good!" said Leah to Sarah, as the door closed behind them. "He knows he got caught. That will make it easier for Rachel." She turned and shook her fist in his direction before following Sarah to the street. Their cars were parked on the street in front of the diner. Leah drove home in a daze, pondering what she might say to Rachel. She decided that she needed a cup of tea to unwind before starting her schoolwork. Dinner would probably be ready shortly anyway.

Nobody was in sight as she entered the living room. Gveret Dina was in the kitchen making final dinner preparations. Hearing the door close, she came out and hugged Leah. They wandered into the kitchen together, talking. Rachel entered shortly afterwards, carrying a knife that she had just sharpened at her mother's request. She too hugged her sister.

"You can just relax with your tea, if you want, dear. Rachel and I have everything under control. In fact, there's almost another hour before the roast is out of the oven, so go ahead and have a cup of tea with Leah if you want, Rachel."

Rachel followed Leah into the living room. "Well, as you can see, Samuel didn't come over. AGAIN," she said. She took a breath and then changed the subject. "What flavor sundaes did you get?" Then she looked more closely at Leah. "Okay, I can tell that something is going on with you. Tell me now!"

Leah had trouble meeting Rachel's focused stare. She swallowed and looked away.

"What happened? Did you have a fight with Sarah?"

Leah cleared her throat and then looked directly into her twin's eyes. "We saw Samuel and Batya together at the diner."

Rachel's eyes opened wide and she placed her right fist over where her necklace rested underneath her frock. "Maybe it's just a school project?" she suggested. "What should I do? Do I confront him?"

"He knows I saw him," Leah told her. "And he looked embarrassed. But now that he knows you probably found out about it, you have nothing stopping you from asking him what's going on. Believe me, it took a lot of restraint for me not to punch him on his nose!"

Rachel smiled weakly. "I guess I'll call him. We don't meet for coffee in the mornings any more, and you noticed that he wasn't even at lunch with all of us. So I can't just count on running into him."

"I'm sorry to have to tell you this kind of thing," Leah said, coming over and hugging her sister's shoulders. "But I can't know something this important and NOT tell you about it."

"Oh, no, you did the right thing," Rachel reassured her. "I will call him right now. But would you mind leaving the room? It might make it easier for me."

"Of course not!" said Leah, patting the top of Rachel's head before turning and walking out. She closed the door behind her so Rachel could have more privacy.

190

Rachel picked up her phone and stared at it for a few moments. Then, with a decisive shake of her head, she punched in Samuel's number. The phone rang three times before he picked it up. "Hi, Rachel," he said softly.

"Hello, Samuel. Ummm..."

"You don't have to figure out what to say to me. I know that Leah saw us at the diner."

"Yes, I was wondering what's going on."

"Yesterday between classes, I ran into Batya. We said hello, and she said she'd like to get to know me a little better since she's becoming such good friends with you. You know, get to know the people who are close to you. She also mentioned getting to know Leah better. She even laughed and said your families were all tangled up anyway, now that your brother is dating her sister."

Rachel rolled her eyes at the notion of her and Batya becoming good friends. Then she prompted Samuel, "Okay?"

"So she suggested that we meet for coffee this morning. The carpool got there late and I only had about 20 minutes until I had to go to class, so she said maybe we could meet at the diner after school this afternoon and continue our conversation."

"What did you even have to talk to her about?" asked Rachel. She screwed her eyes up tight and yanked her necklace out so hard that she was momentarily concerned that she had broken the chain.

"Oh, you know, just the preliminary getting-to-know-you chatter. She was very friendly, and of course she's so pretty that I didn't mind looking at her for a while. So I agreed to meet her at the diner. And then..."

There was a long pause, until Rachel, against her will, felt that she had to prompt him. "And then?"

"Oh, Rachel, I could see that she thought it was a date! It really caught me off-guard. I kept trying to talk to her in more friendly way, not acting like I was romantically interested or anything, and then Leah and Sarah walked by and I felt so exposed! I assure you that I didn't plan any of this."

"So what now?" asked Rachel, squeezing her eyes tightly shut.

Another pause. "You and I have never said we were exclusive. It has just kind of happened that way. Batya is nice and she's so smart and I might want to see her sometimes. Just as friends."

"I'm not anybody's jailer, Samuel. You are free to see anybody you want." There was a long pause, while she wracked her brains trying to think of something else to say. Finally, unable to stop herself, she blurted out, "It feels like you've been avoiding me ever since we got back from Jerusalem."

"I suppose I have," he said, with no further explanation. Had he been seeing Batya? Or other girls? She said nothing and waited for him.

When he spoke again, there was a note of pleading in his voice. "Don't take it too hard, Rachel. None of this really means anything. You wouldn't care if it were some guy I was getting to know instead of some girl!"

"Sure, Samuel. Thank you for being so honest with me." She severed the connection without waiting for his response. Then she lay back on her pillows and started to cry.

Some time passed. She really was not sure how much. Then there was a cautious knock at the door. She walked over and opened it. Leah and Jesse were both standing in the hallway. Leah took one look at Rachel's red eyes and hugged her. Jesse walked into the middle of the room and stood facing his sisters unsmilingly.

"Tell Rachel what you told me!" Leah said.

Jesse looked at Rachel, anger blazing from his eyes. "Noa has told me that Batya's hobby is stealing other girls' boyfriends from them. She brags about it! She'll stoop to whatever it takes. And then she drops them once there's no more challenge."

Rachel's face turned white. She had no weapons against this particular adversary. She looked at Leah with mute appeal.

"Samuel is so committed to you, Rachel. He has been forever! This is at worst something that will just fizzle out — novelty, you know. A pretty girl. But in the end, you are the one he loves. You have to be! All these years you've been together!"

Rachel sighed. "So we think, Leah. So we think. But don't forget that I haven't really spent any time with him since we got back from Jerusalem. I don't think it's something as innocent as you're making it sound. And meanwhile, I don't want to think that Samuel might get hurt." Then she looked over at Jesse. "Thank you so much for sharing that with us, Jesse. I know it was embarrassing for you to talk about, but it was vital information for us to have."

"Embarrassing?" he chuckled. "It would be a challenge to see if she wants to take me away from Noa!"

"JESSE!" the sisters exclaimed in unison.

He laughed again and then looked at them, once again serious. "I was brought up better than that, of course. Noa is a wonderful person and I would never want to hurt her. Although – an older woman! - if she were to take the initiative…."

"Your usefulness in this room has reached an end," declared Leah, shoving him out the door.

The two sat down on Rachel's bed and looked at each other. "Maybe it really is just a dazzle," Leah suggested.

Rachel shook her head sadly and recounted the whole conversation to Leah. "No," she concluded, "it sounds like more than that. He seems like he's really starting to like her."

"A passing fancy!" said Leah, more decisively than she was actually feeling inside. After all, she had seen the two of them together. Samuel could hardly take his eyes off Batya. "And then it will all be behind us, and after all, you're going to Solstice Ball with him in a few months." Then she bit her lip. Why couldn't she ever think before blurting things out?

Rachel looked up, startled. "I wasn't even thinking about that. Solstice Ball! Do you think that will still be on? Will he take Batya instead? How awkward would it be if they're together and you and I still wanted to go. Oh, Leah!" She dissolved into tears again as Leah sat beside her, unable to think of a single consoling thing to say.

Chapter 31

The time dragged on somehow. The twins had handed in their midterm projects. Rachel had not seen Samuel alone since Jerusalem, although he still joined them from time to time when they were together as a group; he at least had the decency not to bring Batya on these occasions. She had no idea how much he was seeing Batya. If Jesse had any information on that, he was not sharing it. As a result, Rachel thought of herself as single and put all of her energy and focus on this final year of her formal education. They would be graduating at the end of Sixth Month, just a few months away. So if she was okay, totally immersed in her classes, why was she checking her phone every few hours? Why was she looking off into space instead of paying attention to whatever was going on around her?

Classes were challenging, particularly those that she had with Batya. She avoided Batya, trying not to make eye contact with her. But before and after class, as some of the girls gathered and talked to each other, it seemed that the peal of laughter or the voice that she heard was always Batya's. All she could do was clench her jaw and get through the time somehow.

Outside of her nonexistent love life, everything seemed to be back to normal. But Rachel began to notice that there was not much of a sparkle in Leah's eyes, and it worried her a little. Leah never acknowledged that anything was the matter and did all of her work and chores with her usual energy but seemed to lack that edge of enthusiasm that was usually hers. Being home was indeed rather anticlimactic after their adventure, so Rachel decided to say nothing and just keep watching her.

Then one day, Leah came home from her weekly choral program and found Rachel waiting for her quite excitedly. "What's going on?" asked Leah, as she began changing out of her school uniform.

"Guess what?" Rachel burst out dramatically, giving a little dance step. Her light blue cotton dress flared a little as she spun back around and grabbed her sister's hand.

"What?" asked Leah, dubiously. She shook out her uniform and began to pull a yellow cotton dress off of a hanger. "We're both home for the day, right?"

"Yes, yes," Rachel answered impatiently. "Samuel forwarded a text to me. And that's all he did! Not even a personalized message, just forwarded the text!"

"Who was it from?" Leah asked indifferently, tugging at a wrinkle to make sure it was not set in too deeply so that she would not be able to wear the dress.

"Samuel got a message from Seth yesterday!"

Leah did look up then, but with very much the expression she might have had at age six, hoping that the wrapped gift she had just been handed was the doll that she wanted so much but fearing that it might not be. "Seth …"

"Seth ben Ephraim! His roommate when we were in Jerusalem for Pesach! Now you'll know how to contact him if you want to!" Rachel said impatiently, flinging her hair back over her left shoulder.

"What makes you think he would even want to hear from me? It was probably just a holiday lark for him. He never even asked me for my number." Leah dug out a nail file and began to smooth out the nail that she had just broken pulling the dress over her head.

"For one thing," laughed Rachel, "because he ASKED about you! He asked Samuel if you have a boyfriend back here or whether you might be interested in writing to him."

Leah looked out the window, staring past the trees that were in full leaf now and arched beautifully against the early summer blue of the sky. Rachel followed her sister's gaze, idly searching for the birds whose twittering she could hear. She was not able to catch a glimpse of any of them. Then she looked back at Leah, who was now looking at her with a rosy face and tears in her eyes.

"I'm conflicted," Leah whispered. "We both behaved a little badly, both too forward. I think I never expected to see or hear from him again.

Somehow what we did wouldn't matter." Pause, sidelong look, and then, "Partly, I wanted to have an experience that you hadn't already had yourself. But now being in touch with him might be embarrassing. Or he might have expectations that I have low – standards. I just don't know. I had no idea that I would be missing him so intensely!"

Rachel gasped a little; she had not guessed that pining away for Seth might be the cause of Leah's flattened mood lately, since Leah had never behaved that way over any other boy of their acquaintance. "Start from scratch, or not quite," she suggested. "You know each other, you like each other, you have a lot to learn about each other, and you're not in some exotic place now but here in your home country. You don't ever have to mention that one last walk."

"You're right, of course. I hope he can put the memory aside, too, and expect to treat me with respect. I don't want him to think that I kiss boys as soon as I'm alone with them."

"You can probably figure all that out in advance of ever seeing him in person, if you do decide to meet. It would be best if he could come here, so we could all keep an eye on him."

"You're so wise, Rachel!" Leah gave her a quick hug. "Okay, forward me his address and I'll contact him. IF you think I should write first. Maybe we should just tell Samuel to give him my information? I'm so confused!"

Rachel hesitated, wanting to text Samuel but having trouble finding the courage to do so. Common sense won out, leading her to say, "Let me call Samuel. Then if Seth really wants a connection, it's up to him!" Rachel picked up her phone from the nightstand and started tapping on it. Having told Samuel what they had decided, to Leah's smiling approval, she hung up and said, "Now come with me to pick up Jesse from his ball game. We can buy him ice cream on the way home."

The sisters squeezed hands as they rose and hurried out of the bedroom. Rachel was quite impressed with the change in Leah's face. She was grateful that Seth had reached out to Samuel and that Samuel had told her about it right away so that she could help her twin. Now at least one of them might be happy with a man.

As they were returning from the ice cream store, Leah's phone dinged. She and Rachel exchanged quick looks, but she wanted to be alone in the privacy of their room before she checked to see whether it was from Seth. It did seem far too soon for him to have been contacting her already, which made it easier to resist looking.

When they got back home, they found that their parents had just returned from their meeting. The family stood in the kitchen chattering for a bit while their parents made tea. Then all three children excused themselves and ran up the stairs to their bedrooms. Rachel turned her desk chair around and sat down in it facing Leah, who had crawled onto her bed with the pillows pushed against the headboard supporting her, kicking off her shoes as she made herself comfortable.

"Well?" Rachel demanded impatiently. "Was that already Seth?"

Leah pulled out her phone and glanced down at it. "There are actually TWO messages!" she murmured before diving down into them. "The first one is from Samuel, telling me that he did send my contact information to Seth. And the second one IS from Seth. Oh, Rachel! I'm scared to open it!"

"If you don't, I'll do it for you," teased Rachel, knowing that this would never happen.

"No, no, I'm doing it right now!" There was a pause as she read whatever was on her screen for a while. Then she looked up, her face completely transformed by a bright smile. "He thinks of me often! He hopes that I am willing to enter into correspondence with him so we can get to know each other better! He asks how you are doing."

"Very proper and polite," Rachel nodded approvingly. "I think this could be a wonderful thing for you! And you look happy for the first time since we got back."

"Too bad he doesn't live here and go to the university with us. We could even have gone to Solstice Ball together," Leah commented, putting her phone down with a decisive snap.

"You aren't answering him?"

"Not right away!" laughed Leah. "I can't be *too* eager, right?"

"Well, since you don't need my brilliant advice any more, I think I'll get started on my schoolwork," Rachel said, turning back around in her chair to face her desk.

"I should, too," Leah observed, but Rachel noticed that she didn't go to her own desk for quite some time.

Chapter 32

Rachel lay back on the reclining chair on Deborah's patio, eyes closed against the spring sun, which was gentle but still quite bright. In similar postures lay Deborah, her brother Aaron, and his closest friend Jacob. She and Deborah had begun a conversation up in Deborah's room, but then they decided it was too nice a day to stay indoors now that it was fully summer. Continuing the conversation, she said idly, "No, I'm not over him in the slightest. I keep thinking this is just a break and we will be back together again."

"It's so hard to tell with you sometimes," Deborah said. She picked up her cup and took a sip of iced tea before continuing. "I guess you just keep it all inside and focus on other things."

Rachel wound her braid around her finger. "Not much I can do. Samuel is dating Batya now."

Jacob jerked his head around to stare at her and then sat up entirely. "Batya bat Reuven?"

"Yup, that's who we're talking about." Sigh. "I keep trying to hate her, but I just can't."

"But she's dating Judah ben Shmuel! You know, the president of the senior class. That's been going on for months!"

"Then do you know what's going on with Samuel?" Rachel asked, her voice almost shrill. "I know you're friends."

Jacob shrugged. "I don't see much of him myself lately. I think he's just going through some stuff."

"Guys!" Deborah expostulated. "You can't ever count on them for details that matter."

Rachel closed her eyes again and sank more deeply into her chair, letting the conversation continue to waft around her like white noise as she pondered this new turn of events. She held her phone in her hand, resisting the urge to text Samuel anew each minute. His absence from her life made her fully aware of how much she needed him there with her. *I take him for granted. He's always been by my side, so I have assumed he always would be. Loyal Samuel, waiting there for me, while I'm fixated on my brilliant future and not on him. He deserves better.*

When they returned home, Rachel sought out her mother. "Ima, this is killing me!"

"Samuel?" her mother asked.

Rachel nodded. "Apparently, he isn't dating Batya after all. Nobody is really sure what's going on with him. It is tearing my heart out. But Ima!" Rachel seized her mother's arm. "This is nonnegotiable. There are things in life I've been able to give up, even the senior seminar. And I haven't really had a lot of regrets about that. But I think my future is in Judea and that's something I'm not willing to give up."

"Then it might be that you'll be giving up Samuel," her mother said, wrapping her arms around her daughter and holding her gently.

It might be that I have to give up Samuel? I'll be in Judea and he'll be back in Trabzon? She sighed, feeling the color go out of her world.

Chapter 33

Leah pounced on Rachel as soon as Rachel walked into their room. "I had another text from Seth. He graduates the same day we do, and then, after that but before the holidays, he is coming to Trabzon for a workshop!" Her eyes were shining.

"Is it just because of you, or is it a workshop he would have come to anyway?" teased Rachel.

"Who cares? Now I have something to look forward to! We can spend more time together and see if there's actually anything between us."

"You've already shown more sparks with Seth than you ever did in months of dating Joseph," Rachel commented. "That says a lot."

"He didn't even say what the workshop is about, but I know he's interested in art like I am, so maybe it's related to that."

"Will he be staying in a hotel?"

"No, he said he would stay with Samuel. It seems like they have grown quite close."

"Maybe that means I'll get to see a little more of Samuel than I have been," Rachel sighed. But she got to see Samuel sooner than she expected. When she was crossing the central courtyard on campus several days later, heading for her next class, she spotted Samuel leaning against a tree, his eyes fixed on her intently.

Samuel wet his lips a bit, cleared his throat, and then spoke. "I knew you'd be here and I came here to find you. Rachel, I can't tell you how much I've missed you. It's like somebody removed my arm and threw it in the Hospitable Sea."

He had obviously made this exaggerated statement to elicit a laugh from her, but she was in no such mood. She furrowed her brow. "But then what happened, Samuel? What were the last few months all about? You weren't with Batya?"

"Oh, no, not at all. I saw her once more after we talked about her, and that's only because she showed up at my house unannounced all ready for a lovely chat on my back deck."

"But you said we were both free to date other people. You said you wanted to see her!"

Samuel could not meet her eyes, and she saw some color spreading across his face. Could it be embarrassment? Shame? "I was just feeling guilty about needing to think things through and wondering why we COULDN'T be free to date other people if we really wanted to. I don't have any interest in her as a girlfriend when I have you. Rachel, I love you!"

Rachel was startled. He had never said that to her in so many words before. "Then what was going on?"

"A lot on my mind," he said. "We really need to talk about it, and soon. But not here and now, when you're about to be late to class. I just couldn't wait to see you and reconnect."

She sighed. "If it weren't my last trimester, I'd be tempted to cut the class! Oh, Samuel, when can we talk? This has been killing me."

He nodded very slowly. "This is your last class, right? And I'm done for the day. Let's meet for coffee, but let's take it outside so we can talk on a bench undisturbed." He reached over and brushed a leaf off her shoulder. "See you then. I just couldn't stand not seeing you anymore."

Her class seemed interminable. Repeated peeks at the time on her phone didn't succeed in making the time pass any faster. She dutifully took notes but was convinced that she had missed half of what the instructor had said – and would have to review her notes to figure out what the other half had been.

Samuel was already at the coffee shop when she got there, a half-finished cup of coffee in front of him. He pushed it away and silently went up to the counter to order two cups of coffee to go. Then he led her outside to the nearest shaded bench. He cleared his throat, opened his mouth, and seemed to be trying several times to say something, but no words came out.

"Please, Samuel, I can't wait another minute. What's on your mind?"

"I asked you to meet me because I believe in what we have between us. I believe we can work anything out together." Long pause, then, "Ever since you went to Jericho that day, you've been driven," he began. "It's all you ever talk about now. I know, I know –"he held up a hand to stop her pending interruption – "I haven't been there to hear you myself. But Jacob and Aaron tell me."

"You're right, Samuel. I've been completely focused on myself and my future."

"It isn't only that. It's also sheer geography. You are planning to move to Judea after we graduate and spend your life there. I will be remaining in Trabzon taking over my father's duties as Kohen."

There was a long silence. Rachel sipped her coffee and stared at the leaves on the tree opposite their bench. The sun was still relatively high in the sky, since it was near the summer solstice, and it filtered through the leaves and dappled the grass below. She closed her eyes and tried to breathe slowly and evenly.

"I don't know what to do about that," she finally said, breaking the silence. "This would be a lot to give up, much more significant than the senior seminar. Or even going with your family to Jerusalem for Pesach. I've already started applying for fellowships so I can continue learning at a more advanced level while I work at a site. More likely the Galilee than the Negev, just because of the climate. But I feel like I've already made my peace with saying goodbye to Anatolia as a place to live."

"And putting me aside for a while," Samuel said, "how would you do without Leah?"

"Well, I've learned that I don't need her right at my side to be able to survive. That would have held me back a few years ago, but not any more. I would miss her terribly, and we would have to be visiting each other all the time, and probably talking multiple times a day, but she intends to stay in Anatolia and work at some place like Kayra Han." She swallowed hard and looked away for a moment. "I'm afraid Judea isn't something I'd be able to give up."

Another pause. Then Samuel said, "Leah and I talked about this in Jerusalem."

"Yes, she did mention it to me."

"And I think she's feeling a lot more bereft at the thought of your moving out of the country than you realize. Or than you're feeling."

"It's harder to be the one left behind. I will be in a new life and having new adventures and fulfilling my dreams, and she will still be here, but without me."

"Well, not quite that dramatic a contrast!" Samuel laughed, without much humor. "She'll be starting a new life in a new place, too, Kayra Han or wherever she ends up. But you seem to be moving toward a permanent separation from her – AND from me – without a second thought."

"Samuel …" She looked over at him. He had rested his elbows on his knees and was cradling his head in his palms. She took another sip of coffee to collect her thoughts. In a softer voice, she continued, "You're right. I've been forging ahead with my plans. My passion for this has blinded me to everything else. I admit that I haven't given a lot of thought to leaving people behind. I had a vague idea you'd be thrilled for me."

"This is big. This is your career. This is your whole future. But Rachel, I have been dreaming of spending the rest of my life with you, and I was thinking that I was in your future, too."

Rachel looked up, startled. On the same day, he had told her that he loved her and essentially hinted that he wanted to marry her. How could they separate from each other? He reached behind the bench and tweaked the end of her braid gently. "I want to make this decision hard for you!" he said. "I am not giving up easily!"

She met his eyes with new understanding. "So this is what you've been wrestling with the past few months?"

"Yes, I needed some time away from you to think things through. When you're with me, you're like a bright light that blinds me to everything else around."

"That's downright poetic, Samuel! But I am coming to understand. I could hardly stand these few months. I can't even begin to imagine being without you for the rest of my life."

Samuel finished his coffee and tossed the cup into the recycle bin at the side of their bench. "I don't even want to imagine that. Think it through. Not every one of us gets our greatest wish fulfilled. You can make a fascinating career right here on the coast and make a significant contribution to science. You can visit different sites on occasion. And I would do my utmost to keep you happy so that you never felt you were missing anything crucial."

"Or –" significant look – "You could make a meaningful life in Judea, with me."

"Rachel, we've talked about this before. Abba expects me to follow in his footsteps, take over his congregation. But you've given me some ideas to explore."

Rachel looked away. "Now it's my turn to think. But let's not avoid each other while we're working through this."

"No more," he promised. "Let's be together while we can, even if it turns out that we have to separate in the future."

She looked at her phone. "It's almost time to meet Leah and go home."

"One more thing, while we're clearing the air." He rubbed his nose nervously. "Batya. What that was all about was trying to see whether I could make a life with a different girl, find happiness with somebody else. That it didn't have to be you or nobody. So I admit that I was interested in her and did consider myself to be dating her, although as I told you, we only saw each other those few times. Then I even looked at other girls. But it wasn't worth it. I didn't even want to get started, since none of them was Rachel bat Shimson."

"It means more to me that you're honest with me than that you try to protect me. Thank you for telling me that. It honors me. Let's think, together and on our own. Nothing has to be decided for another month or more." She added to herself, *Only I really don't think this is something I'll be able to bend on.*

Samuel stood up slowly. "Okay, I will see you soon. I'd like you to stay after services on Shabbat, have lunch with my parents, and we can spend the afternoon together."

"That sounds good. But – " impulsively – "this means we're still on for Solstice Ball, right?"

Samuel laughed and pulled her braid once more. "You ARE such a girl! I keep forgetting that you want to flounce around with a pretty dress and nice hair and jewelry and dance until your feet are killing you."

She just looked at him. And, as he turned to walk away, leaving her in suspense briefly, he called back over his shoulder, "Of course! Wear blue!"

Chapter 34

Rachel sat cross-legged on Deborah's bed. Deborah herself was lying on the floor next to her bed with her feet flung up over its edge. "We've been over this and over this," she said. "Making a life in Judea is what your entire self is pointed toward right now. Samuel is stuck in Trabzon tending to the community as his father's successor. What solution could there be?"

"Like we've been saying, it only works if somebody gives up their life plan. I am pretty much obsessed with Canaanite ruins, and in Anatolia, we have mostly Hittite and Greek ruins. The ancient history of our people and their homeland is what I NEED to know more about. Samuel is a Kohen and has duties that go back to ancient times."

"Maybe he could become Kohen Gadol and live in Jerusalem," Deborah suggested jokingly.

"Not funny! And anyway, he's not in the line of succession. This seems like one of those problems that has no solution. I can't see myself ending up anywhere else any more. Judea is my future."

"No solution that makes everybody happy, Rachel. But there is a solution if you just think about you having to decide. You will either stay in Anatolia, probably near Trabzon and marry Samuel, or you will move to Judea."

"Gee, thanks, Deborah," Rachel said sarcastically. "You've made it so much easier for me now!"

Deborah kicked Rachel's left knee lightly. "That's why you have a best friend!"

"He loves me! He talks about spending our lives together! And my feelings for him have only grown year by year. I feel especially close to him after spending that time in Jerusalem with him and his family."

Deborah shrugged. "I haven't met anybody yet that I have those kinds of feelings for. But when I do, I hope there are no complications standing in the way of making a commitment to him."

Rachel slid off the bed onto the floor, and Deborah spun around so that she was sitting next to Rachel. Rachel closed her eyes and put her right hand over them. "I usually make my decisions with my head. This one calls for my heart. But oh, Deborah, my heart wants both!" She reached inside her dress and pulled out her necklace. She brought it to her lips.

"What would your grandmother have advised you?" Deborah asked, watching this familiar ritual.

"She would want me happy and fulfilled. She would probably say there are plenty of men and I should go to Judea and live out my destiny."

"You aren't really the 'plenty of men' kind of woman," Deborah observed. "It's only ever been Samuel for you."

"And I've already really hurt him by my indifference. I just get so focused and then I run right over everybody I care about!"

"I call it passion," Deborah admonished her. "And it's actually one of your best attributes. You have passion for the things you do and you have such joy in doing them. Most people I know don't really have either of those."

"Thank you. But I think the people on the receiving end don't feel quite that way. Poor Leah has been trampled over our whole lives."

"And yet she competes with your mother and Samuel for being your biggest booster."

"I need to be more aware of the people I care about."

"Well, then there's me. I wasn't going to say anything, but you realize you'll be leaving me behind, too, if you leave Trabzon."

Rachel hung her head and put her hands over her eyes. *There is no way to get out of this with everybody winning.*

Rachel's phone rang. She looked at it and said, "And there's my mother now!" She completed her call and then said to Deborah, "She wants me home now. Thank you for everything. I love you!"

"I love you, too, and I will completely support whatever you do, even if it means you'll be leaving me far behind."

208

They hugged and then Rachel ran down the stairs, calling out goodbyes to Deborah's mother and brother, and out to her car.

After dinner that evening, Rachel decided to seek Adon Yehuda's advice. She texted him and waited for a little while. When she had still not heard back from him as of breakfast the next morning, she decided she would drop by his office. She entered the old stone building where the faculty offices were and climbed the stairs to the second floor. Rounding the corner to his office, she noticed that there were several people talking in the hall outside his door. She nodded at them in greeting and then turned to face his door.

A sign hung on the door, a sign that assaulted all her senses, took away her breath and her ability to think for a few seconds, and began crashing her world. "We are sorry to announce that Adon Yehuda suffered a heart attack last night and passed away. Funeral information to be posted shortly." The words were typed in red, presumably to make the sign more noticeable, but to Rachel, it appeared that they had been written in blood.

And now what? Rachel had come to rely on his wisdom and support in these last few months. Even after her graduation, she was counting on seeking his advice as she made her way through life, starting her professional work wherever that might be.

There were two chairs in the hallway outside his door, as there were outside the door of every instructor. Ignoring the small crowd that was gathered there and exchanging expressions of shock and disbelief, she sank onto one of these chairs and supported her suddenly heavy head in her hands.

What do I do now? How can I be left on my own? Oh, Adon Yehuda, I have so many things to work through! You were always supposed to be there for me.

Chapter 35

Rachel went through the rest of that day in a daze. Somehow, she got through all of her classes. Another instructor covered Adon Yehuda's class, and she flinched as she walked in hesitantly. She wasn't even certain that she would be able to sit through his class, and it seemed to her to be a travesty that somebody else would dare to teach it. *As if he were replaceable.* Even the other classes were constant reminders to her, since the students were buzzing about this unexpected event in every class. Rachel was able to control herself during classes but frequently burst into tears during the breaks between. As the news spread across campus, it didn't help that she kept getting texts from so many of her friends who were aware of how dear the professor was to her.

Toward the end of the day, she went back up to his office to see whether the information about his funeral had been posted yet. Walking down that hall and knowing that he was not behind that door and never would be again felt like a knife twisting in her heart. But Rachel wanted to do him the final honor of attending his funeral.

And indeed, there was a new sign, giving the details. The service would be at 11 the next morning, in the university chapel. Burial would be private, family-only. She wasn't sure she could stand there and watch people shoveling dirt on Adon Yehuda anyway. Yes, it was a high honor to be burying one's own dead, but she couldn't face the thought of covering his coffin with dirt. *How could he breathe under all that?* This brought a flashback to her grandmother's funeral, the only other one she could remember attending. She'd almost had a moment of panic when the mourners all lined up to shovel dirt on the lowered coffin and was unable to do it herself. *I've had so little experience with death.*

The next morning, Leah determinedly stated that she was accompanying Rachel to the funeral. "But you never even met him!" Rachel demurred.

"Funerals are for the living. They make no difference to the dead. I will be going there to support YOU. You shouldn't have to be there alone, Rachel."

Rachel hugged her sister in silent appreciation. The two drove to the university and parked in the separate lot behind the chapel, still not exchanging any words. Rachel was immersed in her thoughts and memories and was grateful for the deep compassion that her twin sister showed her.

The service passed in a blur. Rachel knew that she was making all of the correct responses, standing and sitting when she was supposed to, but all of her attention was fixated on the plain pine coffin standing to the side at the front. *That's all that's left of Adon Yehuda. How does that happen to people? And what becomes of me now?*

There were other instructors and students there, some of whom she knew and many of whom she did not. They too were just background noise for her. When the group left the chapel and went into the adjoining social hall for the traditional mourners' meal, Rachel shook her head at Leah. Inconceivable that she was able to make it through something like that. Leah put her arm around her sister and escorted her back outside and to the car. The whole ride home, Rachel kept her eyes closed, feeling the tremendous burden of making her life decisions falling squarely on her shoulders alone.

They had just reached their home and were getting out of the car when Samuel's car pulled up behind them. Rachel closed her door and waited on the sidewalk until he had gotten out and joined her. He was clearly bursting with excitement over something. But he made a visible effort to control himself, saying first, "This has to have been so painful for you. It makes a real hole in your life."

She lowered her head as fresh tears sprang to her eyes and nodded silently. Then she cleared her throat and looked into his eyes. "Thank you. It helps me not feel so – bereft – with you here for me."

Samuel seemed like he was no longer to contain his emotions. He grabbed both her hands and spun her around right out there in public.

Rachel was left breathlessly laughing and a bit amazed at this uncharacteristic behavior. Surprised at herself, too; how could she be brought out of heartbreak to be present there with Samuel so abruptly? It was a lesson about their relationship that she would have to contemplate later.

"I was accepted! I can't believe this!" he cried out.

"What were you accepted to? Where did you even apply? I don't know anything about this!" She drew a shuddering sigh and then looked up at him. Leah, with a squeeze of her shoulder, walked past them and into the house.

"Because it was a secret in case it didn't work out. But it did! I'm so happy that we can stay together! I did everything I could to make that happen."

"I'm happy for us both, then," Rachel said, "but I still don't know what you're talking about."

Samuel took a deep breath and stood there, still holding both her hands, eyes shining. "There are half a dozen vacancies, more or less, each year at the Temple. They take in young Kohenim as interns and train them to serve at the Temple in rotation. I applied a month ago when I found out about it and told them all about my experience, helping at the Temple in First Month and helping Abba at home. And I got accepted!"

Rachel pulled her hands out of his grasp, took a step backwards, and stared at him. "What does this mean?"

"It means we can be together! I would have to reside in the Old City for the first year, while I'm being trained. After that, I could live anywhere and just stay at the Temple for my week of service each year. And you can go to graduate school there and then out in the field or whatever you would do but be centered in Jerusalem, at least for that first year." He drew a deep breath. "It means we can be together!" he repeated, gazing at her.

Rachel reached out to hug him but then looked around at where they were, outside in public, and resisted. Then she asked, holding her breath, "And your father?"

"Since it's service at the Temple, he says he would never stand in my way. There is another Kohen on the other side of the city who has three sons, and they could well take over and serve our neighborhood, too, when my father decides to step down."

"Can you come in with me? Ima called me home for dinner and that's why I'm just arriving."

"No, I have to go home and help my Ima with something. But I couldn't wait another minute to tell you!"

"I'm so glad you did."

Then he hesitantly asked, "Would you mind keeping this to yourself for now? Mainly for political reasons. I don't want to risk this getting around the community and potentially hurting Abba."

"Even Ima? Even Leah? If I swore them to secrecy?"

"I'm not the one who would be hurt if anything got out."

"Sure. I can just talk less about my decision and most people won't notice or care."

Rachel skipped into the house with a lighter heart than she had been feeling since all this started. Her first instinct was to run to her room and text Adon Yehuda. Memory slammed into her all over again, showering her with a fresh sense of loss. She would never be able to tell him anything any more. He would never know what was going on her life from now on. But then she wiped her eyes and thought about what Samuel had just told her. *Now we can begin to build a real future together!*

Chapter 36

On Sixth Day, the twins went to get their hair done and pick up their new dresses at the dressmaker's studio. Solstice Ball was going to be on First Day! They returned home and each packed a little overnight bag, having made plans to spend Shabbat with their best friends and then get ready for the dance with them. Rachel smiled as she packed her nail polish. This was not a color that Deborah had seen yet! Abba drove them each to their respective best friend's house and the long-awaited Solstice Ball weekend was suddenly upon them.

Up in Deborah's room, Rachel and Deborah sat on the navy rug together, Deborah's jewelry box open between them, looking through everything that they had seen dozens of times in case something caught their eye as a suitable adornment for the dance. Deborah suddenly looked at her clock and said, "There's only an hour until Shabbat. We should go down and help Ima with dinner."

"Sure!" said Rachel, putting a necklace with a single blue stone in it aside. "May I borrow this one?"

"Of course, if I can borrow your pearls that I spotted in your bag!"

They both laughed and then ran lightly down the stairs to help Gveret Esther with her dinner preparations. She smiled at them and motioned toward the closet where spare aprons hung, and they tied them on and started helping.

At the dinner table a little later, Aaron gave them a look and then commented, "I don't even recognize either one of you with your hair so fancy. Shouldn't you just jump in the shower so that you will look more like yourselves? Samuel won't even know who you are, Rachel!"

Rachel smiled at him. "I think he might know who I am!"

Aaron smiled back. In a more serious voice, he said, "I'm so glad you're back together. You really belong together."

"And what about you?" Deborah demanded, pointing her fork at him. "Are you sure you might not make a mistake and pick up some other girl instead of Sarah?"

"I'm pretty sure of myself!" Aaron drawled. "She'll be the one with the spot of paint on her nose because she's been painting that one wall of her own room that she's taken so long to decide about. She thinks that's a lot more fun than just moving out of the house during all the construction. YOU would have done that, Deborah. You'd want to stay all tidy and perfect and wouldn't go anywhere near a mess, let alone paint your own room."

Deborah stuck her tongue out at him. "Yes, that sounds like a perfect description of me, all right!"

All three laughed, since Deborah was usually the first one to get into the middle of any activity. "Have you seen their addition yet, Rachel?" Deborah then asked, turning to her best friend.

"No, not yet. I get reports from Leah, though. I think they intend to have it all done within the next week and then throw their house open so everybody can see it at long last."

"I think it's really lovely that Solstice Ball is on First Day and then the very next day is your birthday," Gveret Esther observed.

"Yes, and we've finally figured out what we want to do! 23 is our last birthday while we're still students, and we wanted to do it right. We'll spend the morning at the club, swimming and playing tennis and working out. The afternoon will be at the spa. And then in the evening, our whole family will come over for a special dinner."

"And Sarah and I will be taking them out for lunch the next day, just the best friends," put in Deborah. "I can't wait until my own birthday, but that isn't for another few months. I would like to make big plans, too."

"What might you want to do, honey?" her mother asked curiously.

"I'm not sure yet. Some of the girls go to a restaurant with a group of their girlfriends, and that sounds like something I might do. But Rachel's plans are so different that I need to rethink!"

215

"You can see how our day goes," Rachel suggested, "and then make your decision. You do have a little time."

"Will you see Samuel at all?" Gveret Esther inquired.

"Yes, he's coming over in the evening to join the family for dessert and then he'll stay for a bit afterwards. We might watch a movie together, just him and the immediate family."

"Too bad Seth isn't going to be around!" Deborah said. "How are things going with him?"

"Well, it's early days yet! They only just got in touch the other day. But Leah says that they're really hitting it off and getting to know each other so much better. I hope he does come to visit some day, and you have a chance to meet him, Deborah."

"He's really nice?" asked Gveret Esther.

Both girls laughed. "It's more than that. He's the most gorgeous boy I've ever seen!"

"I hate to interrupt," Aaron put in, not looking particularly sorry, "but I was hoping I could get some more potatoes if somebody would be quiet long enough to pass the platter down to me."

They all laughed, and the meal continued most enjoyably. When Adon Joseph and Aaron left to go pray, the girls went back into the kitchen to help Gveret Esther clean up and continued their chatting. Then they went back up to Deborah's room to wind down for a while before going to bed. Deborah pulled out two brightly-colored silk scarves to wrap around their heads and protect their hair. The lights went out and the girls quickly fell asleep.

The next day was a whirl of getting ready for the dance, talking, and laughing, interspersed with typical Shabbat activities. It took forever for the sun to set, and then it suddenly seemed too soon and unexpected when there was a knock at the door. Deborah opened it and Leah and Sarah pushed their way into the house. All four girls were giggling and laughing. Aaron had left a little earlier to pick up Jacob and Samuel, so they felt completely uninhibited and quite festive. Also, looking at one another and catching occasional glimpses of themselves in the mirror, they were feeling very grown-up. Gveret Esther and Adon Joseph came into the room, making all sorts of admiring comments, and took several photographs of the four girls. Rachel made sure that her borrowed necklace was shown off to advantage in each one. Then Gveret Esther led the way to her car and they were off!

"I could have driven, you know," Deborah muttered rebelliously, not quite softly enough for her mother not to hear her.

"Oh, honey, it makes such perfect sense. This way you don't have to worry about parking downtown, finding your way home late at night when you're tired, or anything else. I am happy to pick you up whenever you're ready to come home – as long as it is before 1!"

"It does make sense," Sarah piped up from the back seat. "We're grateful for the ride, Gveret Esther."

"Yes, we are," the other girls quickly chimed in. Deborah shrugged elaborately, but since she was not feeling particularly aggrieved, she said nothing more about it. Her mother drove them to the hotel and pulled up in front.

"Before you go inside, let's have one final photo!" Gveret Esther insisted. The girls lined up obligingly, fully aware of the pretty picture they made. First there was Sarah in her tailored pale yellow chiffon dress that left one shoulder bare. Next to her stood Leah in emerald green, all ruffles and beaded bodice, her brown hair hanging straight and shiny. Then came Rachel, in a baby blue silk dress, princess waistline, her own brown hair falling in ringlets over her shoulders. She was wearing a circlet of white flowers like a crown on her head. And standing at the far right was Deborah, resplendent in a fairytale dress of the softest peach, a matching ribbon holding together her auburn curls.

Rachel had one fleeting thought – *I would love to have sent this picture to Adon Yehuda. He deserved to share some of my happiness, too. Not just my angst.* But she brushed it aside and focused once more on the here and now.

They went inside, found the ballroom, and spent the first few minutes admiring how elegantly it had been decorated. Then they moved into the crowd and started looking for other friends and for the boys they knew. Before she was able to find Samuel, he spotted them first and made his way over through the gyrating crowd. "Hi," he said, shyly, offering her a box. She opened it to find a lovely circlet of fresh blue and white flowers for her hair.

"Thank you, Samuel," she said to him, handing it to Leah, who deftly fastened it into her hair.

"You look – really – " he broke off helplessly. The other girls giggled, but Rachel just smiled and thanked him.

The evening passed in flashes of music and color and so much talking and laughing, and of course dancing. Little groups of young people would form and break up over the course of the evening. It felt like everybody there was their friend. Rachel and Leah had hardly any opportunity to speak privately with each other. But just sharing glances now and then meant so much. Rachel wondered whether this really was going to be the end of being together on a daily basis.

Sarah came running over and squeezed Leah's arm. "This is just amazing. Students, friends, all sharing the excitement. Isn't that Joseph ben Asher over there?"

Leah squinted and nodded. "Yes. It would have been so much easier if it had worked out with him. But the few hours I spent with Seth showed me that it was time to move on."

Deborah joined them and said, "Isn't this dance a lot of fun? I'm so glad I came! It's our last big hurrah before we go out into the adult world and start making our marks."

Now Rachel giggled. "Only you have that long-range view, Deborah! All the rest of us are just listening to the music and having fun with our friends." Then Samuel came by and reached his hand out to her, and Rachel returned to the dance floor with him.

Sarah, Deborah, and Leah remained at the side of the room, talking, and laughing. Just then Aaron walked over and drawled, "Want to dance some more, Sarah?"

She smiled up at him, nodded her head, and walked off with him.

Deborah and Leah had talked for another minute or so when Leah noticed Joseph looking their way. She impulsively smiled and waved him over, feeling badly that he was standing there alone and really didn't know

218

many of the other kids since he had graduated the previous year. He smiled back at her gratefully and came over to them.

"Hi, Joseph," Leah said to him. "Deborah, this is my neighbor Joseph ben Asher. Joseph, this is Rachel's best friend, Deborah bat Joseph."

He nodded at her politely and chatted with them for a few minutes. Then he excused himself. Leah, looking over her shoulder, noticed him asking a girl she didn't even know to dance. Oh, well, at least his heart wasn't broken!

And then the dance was over. Rachel, flushed, the flowers askew on her head and missing a few of their petals, tired but incredibly happy, went to find her sister and their friends. Gveret Esther dropped Sarah off at her home and brought the other three girls to her own home, since Leah's car was there. Both girls hugged Deborah as well as Gveret Esther and were soon on their way home, exhausted but beaming, regaling each other with tidbits from the evening as they drove along.

"It looks like Joseph was attracted to that girl in yellow," Rachel observed. "Good thing you don't really like him!"

"That's for sure. Seth definitely changed the way I look at him or any other boy for that matter!"

"Well, I'm glad. And I'm glad that Seth will be here pretty soon and you'll have a chance to see how things stand with him."

"Just think," Leah mused, removing her makeup while Rachel was brushing her hair. "When we wake up next, we will be 23!"

"That's amazing," Rachel agreed. "Your age changes and yet you feel completely the same. I wonder what exciting things are coming our way next?"

Leah turned off the light without answering and nestled into her pillow. That casual remark was going to come back to Rachel not even 24 hours later, but for now, she too snuggled into her pillow and was soon asleep.

Chapter 37

All too soon, it seemed, there was a knock on their door. "Come in," Leah said, sleepily, and pulled herself up a little on her pillow. Rachel turned over and peered toward the door with one eye. In walked Jesse, wide-awake and cheerful and fully dressed. How could THAT be possible? And he was carrying two bouquets of flowers. Right behind him were their parents, each bearing a lovely breakfast tray loaded with all sorts of delicacies. Both girls sat up and smiled, as the three walked farther into their room. The family called out, "Happy birthday!" and distributed hugs, as they set the trays on their desks and handed them the flowers.

"Thank you, thank you!" exclaimed Leah. "You really went all out." Their mother sat down on the side of her bed and put her arm around her.

"Well, it isn't every day that I have two people in my house having a birthday!" laughed their father, spinning Rachel's desk chair around toward the beds and sitting down on it. Jesse contented himself with sitting on the floor.

Rachel looked around. "Don't we usually open presents around this time?"

"PRESENTS for young women who are all grown up?" Ima asked in mock shock. "What could you possibly want? I think we just sent you to Jerusalem and then to a formal dance?"

Rachel looked sheepish. "I guess it's just a leftover from childhood. Of course, you don't owe us anything. This celebration is really quite enough."

Abba shrugged. "Well, but since you specifically mentioned presents, perhaps you would be interested in these." And he pulled two envelopes out of his pocket, glanced at them, and handed one to each of the twins. They looked at each other and then tore them open. Leah was given a gift certificate to the advanced drawing program that she had been looking over repeatedly but was unable to justify spending that much money on herself for one workshop, and Rachel was given a gift certificate to an outfitter that provided all the necessary clothing and equipment for a budding archaeologist. The girls leaped out of bed and threw their arms around their parents, then hugged their brother for good measure, just to watch him squirm.

"You have an hour until you are supposed to be at the club," Ima remarked. "Stay there for lunch, which Abba has already arranged. Then the spa is at 14:00. You don't have to be home until maybe 17:30, just before the family arrives, because you are NOT expected to help with dinner on your birthdays."

"THAT is a treat!" Rachel smiled. Leah, her mouth already crammed with a large slice of orange, nodded in agreement.

The girls waited until the rest of their family had left their room before they threw back their blankets and sat on the edge of their beds. "Okay, I guess it is time to get dressed," Rachel announced, sleepily. "We can shower at the club before lunch. We can't go to the spa all dirty and smelly."

"Nice of Abba and Ima to give us this festive day and buy us both those workshops we couldn't afford," Leah said, standing up.

"Yes, I really wasn't expecting anything," Rachel said. "Mostly just teasing like a little kid might. But when will you have time for your workshop? You're doing that internship right after graduation, and then it's the holidays."

"They run them throughout the year. There's one in Ninth Month and one in Tenth Month. At some point, the internship will end and I'll be looking for a real job. Just not sure how long a term they're going to offer me." Leah continued, "We'll have to do something especially nice for Abba and Ima. More than just helping with cooking and cleaning up."

"Let's think of something special," Rachel agreed. She leaped out of bed herself. "Meanwhile, it's time to put on our workout skirts and get ready to go over to the club."

Leah started changing out of her night frock. She looked up a moment later as a moan escaped Rachel's lips. Rachel had a wild look in her eyes. "I can't find my necklace!"

"Do you remember taking it off?"

Rachel thought back to the day before. "YES! I borrowed a necklace from Deborah and took mine off to put that one on. I probably left it at her house."

"That's not something you're going to want to wait to find out about. You'd better call her right now."

Rachel did call Deborah, who searched her room quickly and said she could not find it. "I'll look more thoroughly when we're not on the phone, and I'll also ask Ima," she said.

Rachel was shaken but really had no choice. "Okay, but let me know right away."

Leah shook her head mournfully. "Not a good thing to happen today, on our birthday. I hope it doesn't spoil things for you. You don't think it's an omen of bad luck or anything, do you?"

"No, not at all. It has been a way of keeping Savta close to me. It makes me feel safe and protected. But I just feel – empty without it. Not in danger. Vulnerable, but maybe more emotionally than realistically?"

A few minutes later, while braiding Leah's hair, Rachel asked, "Is anybody else going to be there?"

"You mean our friends? No, I thought it should just be us."

"That sounds fair. It will be a fun day!" She deftly tied on the yellow ribbon that she had been holding between her lips, then turned around. "My turn."

Leah picked up the soft expanse of Rachel's hair and remarked, "By the way, I had birthday greetings from Seth this morning."

"How did he know it was our birthday?"

"Samuel must have told him. They are writing and talking all the time. Even more motivation for him to come here and visit!"

"Do you know when his art workshop is going to be? What if you've already started your internship?"

"No, I already looked it up," Leah said, reassuringly. "It's right before the holidays, and my internship wouldn't start until afterwards."

The day flew by with one exciting event after another. They tried out different exercise machines, played tennis until they were laughing too hard

222

to see the ball any longer, and then went for a swim, carefully covering their heads so as not to get all of their hair products into the swimming pool. The shower afterwards was long, hot, and luxurious. Then they changed into clean dresses and headed for the dining hall for lunch. Afterwards, they melted into chairs as they indulged in all of the spa treatments they had lined up in advance. And then it was time to go back home.

"THIS was a day to remember forever!" sighed Rachel, swinging her legs into Leah's car.

"It sure has been!" her sister agreed. "And now we're about to be wined and dined by all of our relatives. I can't imagine planning a day that would have been any more perfect than this one."

"Well, as Abba said, we don't have birthdays every day. And especially when our lives are about to change forever, with school behind us."

Just then, Rachel's phone buzzed. When she read Deborah's text, her face paled and she looked beseechingly at Leah. "I almost forgot, because we've been so busy. Deborah can't find my necklace anywhere, and Gveret Esther looked as well and has not seen it."

"Did you give them back the necklace that you borrowed?"

"Yes, it's in the box where it belongs, and I have my pearls back. But my necklace is nowhere to be found. I feel like I'm lost without it. Isolated. A strong wind could just blow me away."

"Well, we're home now. Can you put on a happy face for now?"

"I'll do my best. I don't want to spoil all of their pleasure. Or ours!"

When they came into their house, Uncle David, Aunt Ruth, and their cousins were already there. Enticing smells were winding their way out of the kitchen, and Leah gave an exaggerated sniff and winked at Rachel. "It's going to taste even better because we didn't have to do any of the cooking!" she whispered to her.

They fell into the arms of their family. Uncle David pulled back very pointedly. "You're adult women now," he remarked, "and maybe you're too old to be hugged."

Everybody laughed, but Rachel stuck out her bottom lip. "It isn't worth that price," she said, not entirely joking. Whereupon he drew them both into the circle of his strong arms at the same time.

As they were all talking at once, there was a knock at the door and Gveret Dina opened it to more family still, including their grandparents. Adon Shimson waved them all into the dining room, Gveret Dina and her sister Gveret Tamar having disappeared into the kitchen to bring in the food. Laughing and chattering, the family sorted themselves around the long table. Little Eve sat opposite the twins, who had placed themselves in the very middle of the table so as to be able to talk to anybody there at any time, staring at them with wide brown eyes. At only 8 years old, she idolized these grownup girls who were so kind to her, so pretty, and seemed to have all sorts of self-assurance and understanding of adult ways.

"It's hard to believe how old you are!" exclaimed Gveret Tamar, looking at them fondly. "You were in Judea all by yourselves for Pesach."

"Well, hardly by ourselves, Aunt Tamar," laughed Rachel. "We were very well supervised by Samuel's parents."

"Where is Samuel?" asked Uncle David, glancing around the table.

"He'll be here for dessert," Gveret Dina answered. "We all agreed that this dinner would be family only."

"I haven't seen him in a long time," their grandmother remarked. "Such a nice young man."

"He is that!" agreed Rachel, turning to accept a platter of sweet potatoes and apples from her sister.

"And what happened with your kickball tournament?" Gveret Tamar asked, turning to Jesse.

"We went all the way to the championship game," he answered, not looking up because he was so intent on shoveling the food into his mouth. "But then we lost that one. It was close, too. A real heartbreaker!"

"But Jesse did score two of the points in that final game," his mother said, proudly.

"Oh, Ima!" He threw her a look that was meant to silence her. "That doesn't mean much if we lost the game."

"This roast beef is wonderful," their grandmother said, loudly, in a transparent effort to change the subject.

"Yes, Ima, everything is so good," agreed Leah. Rachel, having just put some green beans into her mouth, could only nod in agreement.

"And then cake and ice cream for dessert!" piped up little Eve, holding up pudgy fists in celebration.

"Well, not ice cream," her mother admonished her softly. "The twins have always preferred frozen yogurt."

The child looked momentarily chagrined, but then rallied and said brightly, "I hope the cake is chocolate!"

"Actually, we both like white cake," Rachel said to her gently. "I hope that's okay."

Eve's smile did not even diminish. "Hey, cake is cake!"

The twins stood up as everybody finished their meal and sidled out behind their assembled family to the end of the table, where they started collecting plates. "Now, Ima, we have to do SOMETHING!" Leah told her firmly, as Gveret Dina started to protest. "After all, if we're young women now, we can't be pampered like little children."

As they were rinsing the plates in the sink, they heard another knock at the door. Leah looked at Rachel and smiled. "That must be Samuel!"

"I hope so," Rachel answered her, blushing a bit. "It was strange to go through this entire day and not see him or even hear from him. We only just reconnected!"

"Not even a phone call?"

"He sent me a message this morning that I found when we woke up," Rachel replied. "But I haven't heard or talked to him since."

"He might have had a lot to do today himself," Leah suggested.

The girls dried their hands on a towel and stepped back into the dining room.

"Ima, wasn't that Samuel at the door?" Rachel inquired of her mother, not seeing him in the room.

"Yes, he came in, but he's gone off with Abba for a few minutes," Gveret Dina answered her casually. The girls slid along the wall behind the chairs and back to their own places. Gveret Dina and Gveret Tamar disappeared into the kitchen just as Adon Shimson came into the room, followed by Samuel.

"Happy birthday, Rachel! Leah!" he mumbled, not entirely looking at them.

He was all dressed up as if he were going to the synagogue, and so Rachel exclaimed, "Why, Samuel, you look so good!"

"Thank you," he replied, coloring briefly. Eve stood up and moved her chair a little to the side, while her older sister brought in another chair for Samuel, and he took the place opposite the twins but did not sit down. He stood there uncomfortably until Gveret Dina and Gveret Tamar came back into the room, each bearing a cake. Gveret Dina nudged Gveret Tamar in the side and they both stood quietly next to the table. "Rachel," he said, in a lower voice that she almost didn't recognize, "you are a woman now. Your student years are almost behind you. I am hoping that you will do me the honor of becoming my wife." He held up a small box.

Some of the surrounding family started to whoop but were quickly shushed by the others. They had to hear how she might answer!

Rachel stood up at her own place and reached her hand across the table, which he clasped warmly in his. His touch was even more electrifying than she had fantasized. "Yes, of course I would, Samuel! Thank you so much for asking me while I'm surrounded by all my loved ones." Dropping her hand briefly, Samuel opened the box and slipped a small gold ring on her finger. Rachel pretended to glare at Adon Shimson, demanding, "Abba, is that what was going on? Did you know in advance?"

"I don't think he knew until tonight, when Samuel asked his permission," her mother answered. "But I have known for at least a week. You can't imagine how hard it was to keep such a huge secret! I couldn't even tell Leah, because she might have looked at you differently or acted differently and given it away."

"Ima!" Rachel said, in mock anger, but with a radiant smile hovering around her lips. "I count on you to tell me important things like this."

Samuel was still standing, both hands pressed against his heart, shining eyes fixed on Rachel. *He looks at me with such love!*

"Are we having cake soon?" piped up Eve, who was somewhat interested in the goings-on but even more so in the two decorated cakes standing just meters away from her. Everybody laughed, as Rachel reluctantly withdrew her hand from Samuel's grasp and they both sat down. "Are you going to be a beautiful bride soon, Rachel?" she added.

Rachel blushed and looked at Samuel, then Leah, then her mother. "I guess I am! I really wasn't thinking that far ahead yet. You will have a wedding to go to soon, Eve!"

Everybody applauded as the two women set the cakes in front of the two girls. "Here you go, girls! Let's cut the cake. We can all move into the living room to talk about all of this."

The girls served the cake, and then each cut a final piece and handed it to the other. As they exchanged plates, Leah whispered for Rachel's ears only, "You'll find out what it's like to be kissed tonight!"

Rachel blushed again and picked up her dessert fork. "Could be!"

And that is exactly what happened. Samuel hung back a bit as everybody made their way into the living room, waiting for Rachel. He caught her hand as she approached him and leaned in and kissed her. "I am the happiest any human being could ever be!" he exclaimed, to the cheers of the assembled family.

"I'm not so sure!" Rachel laughed up at him. "And I'll tell you, you have made this birthday the best one ever!"

"And now we know what other exciting things were going to happen today!" Leah remarked, and they both laughed.

"Miriam says happy birthday, by the way," Samuel mentioned, his voice sounding a lot more like his own. "She wrote to me the other day asking how you were, so I told her about this weekend and she wanted to make sure I would say this to you."

"She is such a dear!" exclaimed Leah.

"And she was so good to us!" added Rachel. "Please do send her our love. Or give us her contact information and we can write to her ourselves."

"Sure," said Samuel. He sat down next to Rachel on the sofa and, after a momentary hesitation, glancing around the room at her entire family watching, he put his arm around her shoulders. It felt warm and safe and she snuggled into it. *It will be wonderful to spend the rest of my life with Samuel!*

Leah looked over at them with just a momentary twinge. While she was delighted for her sister and very much loved Samuel as a brother after all

227

these years, she had no way of knowing whether this kind of happiness was in store for her.

Just then, their mother came into the living room with a tray. Dishes of frozen yogurt sat on it. "Hold off for a minute, everybody!" she said, setting it down on an end table, and went back into the kitchen. She returned with another tray, on which stood flutes of champagne. "We need to celebrate this engagement!"

"Ima!" exclaimed Rachel, tears in her eyes. "This is the most fantastic day of my whole life!"

Gveret Dina came over and offered her the first flute of champagne, dropping a kiss on the top of her head as she did so. She smiled as Rachel handed the champagne to Samuel and then took one for herself, before distributing the rest to everybody but Eve.

"What do I get? I'm tired of being a baby!" Eve complained.

"Hmmm, there's one more glass on the tray. I wonder what it is?" And Gveret Dina handed it to Eve, who took a sip and shouted out, "Sparkling apple juice! My very favorite special drink!" Everybody laughed as they enjoyed their frozen yogurt and champagne.

The family gradually said their goodbyes and left. Samuel was the last to leave, and Rachel escorted him outside the door. She was rewarded with a squeeze of her hand and another kiss. This could grow on her!

She looked around to see if anybody was in earshot. Then she whispered confidingly into his ear, "Samuel, my necklace is lost!"

He looked at her in horror. "Where, when, how? And how have you gotten through this whole evening acting so normal?"

She pulled back and thought for a moment. "It hasn't been on my mind. The day has been so busy and so full of joy, and of course you were the capstone for that! I discovered it this morning. I took it off at Deborah's when I borrowed her necklace to wear to Solstice Ball, but neither she nor her mother can find it anywhere."

"And yet, look at you. So brave. You got through this entire day without needing it. You've been taking so many huge steps this year, Rachel. Look at all the major decisions you have made!"

She smiled at him. "You know, you're right! If I look at it that way, I have been absolutely fine without it all day. I have proven that I can be apart from Leah when circumstances dictate. I'm even planning to move to Judea and live in a different country! WITH you, of course, or I don't know if I could do it."

When she came back inside, only her parents were still in the living room. "Where are Leah and Jesse, Ima?" she asked.

"They've both gone to their rooms. It's been a long day for you girls!" her mother replied.

Rachel spun around excitedly and then flung herself into an armchair. "And the day is over, but my new life is just about to begin! After all this time, it's almost scary to think that Samuel and I are really going to get married!"

Her parents smiled at her both fondly and wistfully. "I'm still getting used to my little girls being twenty-three and out of school. Soon to be living under a roof that isn't mine," her father said, "and now you're about to be a married woman!"

"You'll have to treat me with more respect now, Abba," Rachel teased.

Gveret Dina rubbed her hands together. "We have a LOT Of planning to do, Rachel!"

Rachel yawned and then rubbed her eyes. "We really do, Ima, but I think I need to get some sleep now." They hugged and kissed one another and she went upstairs, where she found Leah already sound asleep. She sighed luxuriously and then got ready for bed. From long habit, her hand crept under her night frock to touch her necklace, to keep her safe through the night. Then she smiled in the darkness. It was up to her to keep herself safe now. To her and to Samuel. That was what it meant to be grown up.

Chapter 38

Summer faded into fall, graduation came and went, and Leah went away to her drawing workshop. Rachel kept as busy as she could, volunteering at a senior residence, spending time with Deborah or Samuel, planning with her parents (with minimal input from Samuel, who was not terribly concerned about the details of a wedding), or just relaxing with her family. She missed Leah terribly, but at the same time, she was proudly aware that she COULD be away from Leah and not fall apart.

Leah returned before sunset on Sixth Day, bubbling over with all the techniques she had been introduced to, proudly displaying some of the drawings that she had made, which Rachel found highly professional. Leah was now becoming quite anxious over Seth's upcoming visit and had to distract herself from her resulting nerves, which she did by preparing for her internship and practicing some of her newly-acquired drawing skills. "I know he's coming for an art workshop and not just to see me," she kept reminding herself, but it did little to allay her nervousness. "And he'll be tied up that whole week and only here with Samuel at night or for Shabbat. But, but, but …"

The afternoon of Sixth Day arrived, and Rachel asked Leah, "So what's the latest about Seth's visit?"

Leah blushed, then said, "He is arriving in Trabzon on First Day, but he has his workshop all day long and won't be at Samuel's until after dinner each day. But the workshop ends after lunch on Sixth Day, so he'll stay with Samuel's family over Shabbat and First Day, and then he'll go back home on Second Day. Sometimes I hope we'll spend a lot of time together and sometimes I'm terrified to see him at all!"

"Well, if he's staying with Samuel, unless you keep away from me entirely, we're going to be spending some time together for sure!" laughed Rachel.

"And when DO you see Samuel next?" Leah asked.

"He is coming for Shabbat dinner tonight. And then we'll go to his father's service tomorrow morning and back to their house for Shabbat lunch. So it's just a few more hours and I just might be able to wait that long."

Rachel sank onto her bed and looked around their room. She and Leah had spent their whole lives in this room, as little girls in cribs and then small beds, redecorating as their tastes changed over the years. It would be very strange to leave this room forever and go live in a whole new place – where? What would it look like? – as Samuel's wife. Part of her was not completely eager to start that new life and leave this one behind forever. But being with Samuel day and night was a stronger pull than staying in her girlhood room. And then there was Judea, the pinnacle toward which she had been working for as many years as she could remember. She sighed and lay back with her head on her pillow and stared at the ceiling, daydreaming. First the post-graduate course in Jerusalem, which would accommodate Samuel's need to be there while he was being trained at the Temple, and then home somewhere in Judea where she could be digging for the rest of her life.

The time for Seth's visit arrived at last. Leah was nervous and excited, and Rachel had to help her sort through her clothes repeatedly, reassuring her each time that the outfits she had chosen were the prettiest.

On that first evening, Samuel brought Seth over to the twins' house. There was clear discomfort in the air between Leah and Seth at first, as they adjusted to being together in a new place. A place that was home, part of ordinary life for Leah, rather than an idealized pilgrimage site on a special occasion. Soon enough, they began to relax in each other's company, as the initial shyness wore off. They found that they could talk as freely with one another as they had in Jerusalem. Leah winked at Rachel, who smiled at her lovingly. Could it be her turn?

For dinner on Sixth Day, to honor Seth and welcome him to their community, the girls arranged to invite all of their friends. Everybody brought a dish and surrounded him, doing their best to make him feel welcome.

Seth lifted his cup, looking around at all the young people who were gathered there, and called out, "Next year in Jerusalem!"

THE END

Made in the USA
Middletown, DE
06 August 2023

36259582R00136